THE
REARING
FIELD

MAURICE de SOISSONS

WOODTHORPE PUBLISHING
BRANCASTER STAITHE
NORFOLK

© 1995 by Maurice de Soissons

Cover illustration by Annie Soudain © 1995

Published in 1995 by Woodthorpe Publishing, Woodthorpe,
                    Brancaster Staithe, King's Lynn,
                    Norfolk PE31 8BJ

Printed by Witley Press Limited, Hunstanton, Norfolk PE36 6AD

ISBN 0 9520907 1 6

CONTENTS

1. No Other Fool   1

2. Partridge at Risk   13

3. *Guten Appetit*   26

4. History Lesson   37

5. First Blooding   46

6. Just Trespassing   57

7. Holding Game   66

8. One All   76

9. Feat of Arms   87

10. Vermin Control   98

11. A Kind of Waterloo   109

12. Facing Up   120

13. The Real Enemy   133

14. Fog   145

15. Inheritance   157

16. *Wenn du es wüsstest*   168

To Pat
with love and many thanks
for her support, patience,
and forbearance

1. No Other Fool

He was not yet truly familiar with the estate. He knew the position and size of the fields with their unkempt hedges, and the public rights of way, and had already explored the woods and copses, the long windbreaks of Scots pine. He had noted where the old marl and chalk pits lay. He now knew where the pheasant and partridge of the neglected estate were to be found. Perhaps others did, too. He was not sure.

In his position just inside the marl pit he was protected from the wind which came chill out of the north-east. No other fool would be out on such a night. The wind was powerful and steady, not gusty at all. The starlit night was cloudless and the new moon had not yet risen.

Everything that he had been taught, and his experience so far, told him that motorised poachers liked the easier pickings afforded by dense populations of reared birds. Everything inclined him to believe that the locals were gainfully enough employed and too well fed to spend uncomfortable hours away from the television, the pub or their beds.

There remained the eccentric. A rare phenomenon, the Game Conservancy people believed. Certainly rare on the prime Hampshire estate where Tom Gibson had been underkeeper for a year and beat 'keeper for another. But here, further north and east, in countryside more isolated, more deeply rural, did fools exist who poached for the sheer excitement of pitting their wits and woodcraft against the game and the gamekeeper?

Tom Gibson raised himself above the rim of the pit and stared out into the field. The wind tore through the trees above him, through the overgrown thorn hedge which ringed the pit, striking him full in the face. A man's night senses were too easily led astray by wind. A dog's too. He had not brought the dog. Too young and inexperienced. He concentrated on the field. There would be hare in it. Light soil and tussocky grassland. A grass ley left to be invaded by the coarser grasses of the hedgerow. The land would dry out quickly, be warmer than the clay several fields away. This would be where hare would have their forms. And where the poacher would be, if he existed at all, and if the landlord of the Red Lion was to be taken seriously. The drinkers had been unwelcoming, but not as prepared as the publican to challenge and tease the newcomer, to bait him and gauge his reactions. Tom

1

acknowledged that he was an incomer, a southerner whose origins and class appeared to be wrong for his calling. And although for hundreds of years there had been enmity in all poaching villages for the gamekeeper, it seemed unlikely to him to persist into the present day.

The gamekeeper suddenly turned on his back and squirmed down out of the wind. He looked up into the bare branches of the trees that grew in the pit. The fierceness and consistency of the wind produced in them a humming and shrieking without any great tossing movements. He thought about wind and what part it had played in his life. Wind off the Atlantic had so often been an accompaniment to his North Devon childhood, to school holidays, and later on leave. There had been many times when wind had prevented him from jumping, and sometimes when he had jumped it had taken him wildly off-course. And he thought of the wind in that far southern group of islands, 7,000 miles away from this cold, green, winter England.

Abruptly Gibson turned on his front again, put his head above the rim into the winter wind. He smelt nothing, heard nothing except the wind, and realised that he should crawl out and lie in the pasture away from the shrieking trees to be able to hear anything other than the branches humming. He was angry with himself then, that with his experience of soldiering and gamekeepering he should have made such a simple blunder. He decided to rectify his error.

Dressed in old army combat clothes, he crawled across the cold dry grass, avoiding the tussocks. He employed the fieldcraft he had been taught and had taught others. Crawling without a gun cradled in his arm he moved faster. A gun, a gamekeeper's 12-bore in these circumstances, would have been an error, although he had known 'keepers who burdened themselves when out at night and put their consciences and their legality at risk. He reached the middle of the field without encountering anything more than the whistling skeletons of teasels and thistles. No doubt the farm manager, when the new multi-millionaire owner appointed him, would plough the pasture for reseeding, or plant cereals in the spring.

The skyline had changed with the slight rise to the field's centre, and a fall away to the far hedge. This was another neglected thorn hedge grown into stubby trees, with a dead elm or two and live ash and oak at intervals, all now standing up against the night sky, distinguishable by their shapes – elm tall and columnar, ash spreading, and oak heavy-set with twisted branches. There was a gap in the hedge where once there had been a gate. Tom knew that running along the other side of the hedge was a farm track that served fields at the northern end of the farm.

Suddenly he saw a movement in the field away to his left. Whatever it was it hesitated, halted, then came towards him, stopped again. Tom saw the ears of a hare, could see the animal up on its hindquarters to observe something away from him. He tried to keep both hare and gap in view. He thought about oldtime poaching. Gate nets, snares and dogs would be used for hare, a drag net for partridge, and pheasant snared, trapped and shot. The old lady's property which Charles Gailsford had bought consisted of the neglected small park and home farm of 800 acres, with another 1,200 acres let to tenant farmers. She had retained the shooting rights over all, and Tom would eventually have to 'keeper it all.

The hare had settled down. Tom watched it and the gap. What about the locals who had poached in the days of Mrs Pentney's decline? Maybe there had been enough of the older men with long nets to ring the marl and chalk pits and take all the pheasant, and the rabbits on the upgrade from the last attack of myxomatosis. But a long net needed too many men. Probably it had just been snares and gate nets, and out with their guns when the syndicate men who had used the acres for rough shooting had left. The story books told how the 19th century poachers born out of the Hungry Forties had been able to call up hares to within shooting distance. A male call to bring a female and vice versa. What were the calls? Calling vermin by imitating a young rabbit, or bringing a curious crow down to investigate with a 'caw' were normal practice. Tom used the calls himself. But he only quarter believed the hare tale and had been incredulous of several handsome stories his Hampshire tutors had passed on to him. They had had the same folkloric ingredients of soldiers' tales in both barrack room and mess.

The hare moved, came towards him, stopped and hind-quartered. In the gap there was surely some movement. Low down a dark blob had appeared. Another indeterminate shape, taller, appeared beside it. The hare then ran fast obliquely across the field. One moment the low point of darkness shifted into the field. Mixed with the whistling and whining of the wind there came a short, low-pitched sound. Next moment the gap was clear.

Using the wind as a shield against anyone hearing him, Tom Gibson ran to within 10 paces of the gap, dropped to the ground and crawled up to the ditch on the fieldward side. If there had been a dog it would probably sense or see him now. There were too many dogs in the village – labradors by the dozen, spaniels, terriers, greyhounds, and even lurchers. Too many, that was, for a gamekeeper's peace of mind. Tom jumped to his feet and went through the gap swiftly, on to the farm track where he crouched and cast left and right down the hedge. There was no sign of man or dog, and the wind made a nonsense of following any trail, sound or sighting. Using a torch he checked the ground by the gap. If there had been a gate net there would be post holes, perhaps a little fur where a hare was dispatched. He found nothing of that kind. The wind discouraged all effort to read a story from crushed plants, scuffed earth, or footprints on the farm track. He switched off the light, had a moment of doubt and beamed the torchlight on a tuft of grass. Caught in the grass was a short length of newly peeled stick. He put it in his pocket and walked rapidly to his cottage.

The gamekeeper's cottage stood in the centre of the farm, surrounded by woodland of oak, ash and overgrown hazel coppice. There was a small garden, and a big holm oak spread its branches and its shiny evergreen bulk over the roof. The cottage was reached by a rough track over a mile from a tarred road. The isolation pleased its present occupant. Now, as he approached, above the wind he fancied he heard snatches of music. A light shone from the living room window, the curtains undrawn. Beside the holm oak was a white Volkswagen cabriolet 'beetle'. Tom recognised a Mozart flute concerto. He had played it the evening before, and the record must have lain on the turntable. The dog in his iron-grilled kennel yard to the side of the cottage thumped his young body exuberantly against the ironwork, but gave no vocal welcome. The gamekeeper greeted him soothingly.

"On a night like this?"

Tom did not answer. Instead he opened up the stove, riddled the fire, thrust in several logs and increased the draught.

"Do I sound incredulous?" Hilary Aston immediately examined her reaction to this man being out in filthy weather at night because there just might be a poacher out after hare. Tom liked this occasional unsureness in someone who was so dominantly successful in what had

4

until recently been – still was in essence – a man's world.

"Have you eaten?" he asked.

"What had you in mind?"

"Sausages, scrambled eggs, baked beans. Tea."

She was taken aback. "You mean you haven't eaten today?"

Gibson shook his head. "Not really." The mention of food made him immediately and happily hungry. The music filled the room. The only uncomfortable element was the girl.

She rose from the easy chair beside the stove, a supple, quick, decisive girl, now managing and certain of herself.

"I'll cook," she said.

"I can do it." He sounded rough and tried to make amends. "I expect you've had an uptight day." Then he could not resist it. "Punching holes in the inefficient, the inept, the lazy?"

She shook her head as a swimmer does to shake water off the face. "Why do you do it," she said rather than asked. "Because I've used those terms in talking out my problems, there's little need to fling them back at me."

He nodded, blew out his cheeks. "I'm sorry. We'll both cook."

In the kitchen they could hear the wind thrumming in the gable end, shrieking through the holm oak branches. The thick stretch of woodland to the north of the cottage gave forth a deeper roar as if the sea were just beyond it.

Tom watched her as she bent over the stove, shaking the frying pan. When she was not questioning, examining ideas, reporting, fighting the whole male race for her place in the management team, her face was serene, as now. A thin face with prominent cheekbones and a straight nose, a generous mouth, beautiful when she was animated. He was glad she had not cut her brown hair short back and sides with a mop on top as so many did these days.

Tom Gibson had reached that point in a long day when he could barely put two coherent thoughts together. After the meal it would be different. He left her to look after the food while he laid the table in the living room. The act of laying two places jolted him into wondering why she was there. After all they seemed to have snapped at each other before long on the few occasions they had met. She had wanted to know why he was a gamekeeper, why not a solicitor, a doctor, or in a lucrative, testing, enlivening and enthralling business like herself? He had given her no answer. At least she appeared to have abandoned that line of questioning and he was glad. But he could not see any relationship developing. Undoubtedly she was good to look at, and no frailty would be allowed to diminish the workings of that strong body. He liked the look of her, but her way of life was too far from his own. So why had she come? He would not ask her.

At the meal they were silent. Hilary saw that his towering physical need was for food. He ate fast, only touching his mug of tea when the heaped plate was empty. Tackling a much smaller amount of food, she had time to contemplate him. She saw how his eyes were blank while he ate, noticed the wind-reddened face, the blond hair still pressed to his head by the hat he had worn. His hands were large, with strong square fingers. They matched the rest of him, solid and upright, as if he had been a soldier. Despite his size he moved quickly and quietly. She liked his height, for she herself was two inches short of six feet. But was this all that had brought her out on such a night? Was it because he was the only man remotely attractive to her in the village? For the first time she asked herself whether this rather sombre, serious man was only an engaging contrast to the busy, pushing, articulate men she met every working day.

Hilary looked round the living room, at the full bookshelves, the record and cassette player. There was no television set. The furniture was cheap and worn, probably left by the last occupant. But the pictures were his. There were early shooting prints and two watercolours of what could only be a medieval German town. And there were maps of Devonshire. On a side table was a group of Staffordshire figures. Nothing in the room gave any indication of a woman's presence, but everything was tidy and dusted. While she had waited for him to come, having found the door unlocked, she had looked over the books. They made her want to ask more questions, but she had learned her little lesson. She would bide her time. And did she really want to? She decided then that she did.

"When's the first shoot?" she asked.

"In three weeks."

"Will there be anything to shoot? I mean, you've only just come."

"Enough to make a showing for half a dozen drives – pheasant, that is. And despite the lack of stubble there are several good coveys of partridge – red-legged, not the grey."

"I've seen hares."

Tom nodded. "There's plenty about. We should be shooting them now. They fetch twice what they do after the turn of the year."

Tom Gibson had arrived at a difficult time, in late October. Too late to do much except try and keep what pheasant there were on the estate, provide them with food and shelter and guard them against marauders. Once it had been a good sporting estate, set in undulating country with fine southerly slopes. Several generations of the Pentney family had planted small blocks of woodland, spinneys, copses and shelter belts, all with a view to providing warmth and shelter for adult birds and good pheasant release areas. Tramping over the acres Tom had soon become aware of the strategy behind the plantings, and worked out where the drives had been in years gone by. He noted, too, the number of vermin. Small ground predators were abundant – weasels and stoats, and some rats. Squirrels, crows, rooks and magpies had flocked to the overgrown, unkeepered estate. He was surprised they had left as many eggs and chicks as they had, to grow up into the number of adult birds he had found. Vermin control would be a major chore, as would habitat improvement. He would have to rear at least a couple of thousand chicks.

On one of his two interviews with Gailsford, Tom had told him that it would not pay to be overambitious this first year. He had suggested some rough shooting and getting to know the terrain this winter. That had not gone down well. Gailsford was taking lessons in the use of the shotgun at a school in London, and he meant to practise on his own pheasant at a well organised driven shoot. The idea of offering a patrician day's sport to guests brought to his new country house appealed to Charles Gailsford from Hendon. Just as making money from his estate did, too. He had made it plain that a farm manager would soon come. Hedges would come out, others would be cut back to a few feet. Hedgerow trees would disappear. The woodlands would remain, he conceded. But he wanted both an efficient agricultural unit and a prime sporting estate, and he would have them. Tom had had no time to collect his thoughts before the interview was abruptly terminated.

To his surprise, Gibson told the girl sitting by the stove something of his problems. Hilary listened with close attention, seeing the management situation, the clash of interests between farming and gamekeepering. She saw the need for thoughtful, cooperative teamwork, and realised from what Tom had told her of Gailsford that it was unlikely to materialise. Perhaps Tom was not handling Gailsford right. But now was not the moment to suggest it.

"What about poachers?" she asked.

"Ah, poachers. Well –" Tom was now very tired. "I'll clear away first." They did it together, and he told her he had seen a pair of sparrowhawk 'hedging', flying fast down the line of a hedge, from time to time rapidly changing sides.

"What would they have been after?"

"At this time of year – small birds like bramblings, hedge sparrow, maybe fieldfare and redwing. They'll take pigeon – the heavier female will, at any rate."

"Well, they're poachers too, I suppose."

With Hilary's earlier question about poachers unanswered, Gibson was unaware of the faint irony in the girl's voice. But Tom was already thinking about the next day's tasks, the round of feeding sites he had established. After the wind he would need to set out more straw into which the grain would be scattered. At least there would have been plenty of dense cover to shelter the pheasant, crouching facing the wind so that their feathers would not be ruffled.

The washing up finished, they went back to the living room. The wind had died down.

"And the real poachers?" she asked. "The human variety?"

Tom straightened from shutting down the stove. He went to his flak jacket hanging on the door. Out of a pocket he pulled the stick of newly peeled wood. He looked at it carefully, smelled it. Probably hazel.

"They exist," he said. "And I've at least one."

Orion's belt and sworded hip. Tom saw the stars through the branches of an oak. Leaning against the trunk he was warm and relaxed, listening to the night sounds. He was 20 feet inside the 50-acre wood, and had been there an hour. Pheasant were roosting on the wood's edge, for they were birds of the open glades and rides. They liked sun and warmth but needed shelter. All the daylight hours they were on the ground. Now they were up in the low branches. And it was in this woodland edging of hazel and elder under oak and ash that someone had taken pheasant at roost. He was almost sure of it. Most likely shooting with a .410 and a torch. Although the poacher had been meticulous in picking up his cartridges, Tom had found a few stray feathers released in shock as the pellets had struck.

With no wind at all this night, sounds carried. He could distinguish the pigeon clattering from time to time when disturbed, as they forced their way into the sheltering ivy on the dead hedgerow elms that bounded the field beyond the wood. There were fox about, too. He had smelled one at the start of his vigil. And rustlings in the grass and the undergrowth. Stoat? Weasel? A cat gone wild? Feral cats and domestic ones hunting deep in the woods had not been a pest in well 'keepered Hampshire. But up here the situation could be different. He discarded the possibility of a cat being his poacher. It had to be two-legged.

He heard the church clock in the village strike two. The village certainly knew of his arrival after the pub episode. But had the good or the bad news travelled to the surrounding villages, to the RAF station six miles away, that the estate now had an able-bodied young 'keeper? He had a warm feeling for the RAF. He had trusted his life to them so often. He hoped the poacher, if and when he came, would not be an aircraftman out for a night's sport. He recalled stories from his Hampshire tutors of the problems of gamekeepering during the second world war. Gangs of commandos supplementing their diet. Trained in unarmed combat, taught to respond instinctively to attack, and in an altogether definite and uncompromising way. Gamekeepers had been no match for these young soldiers and there had been some ugly incidents.

Tom stiffened. There was a new sound. He breathed deeply, willed himself to pick up not only the large noises of the night but also the undersurface sounds. Below the noise of the pigeon, the movements of roosting birds, the alarm chatter of a blackbird, he heard a hoarse hissing sound. Hawk, owl, snake? Tom remembered that weasels gave out such a noise when mildly alarmed. The hissing sound came closer, followed by a terse, high-pitched bark. Weasels hunting, angry and perhaps scared. They would be after mice and vole at this time of year. He relaxed, secure with his back to the oak. Adams had taught him to lay up and listen. Adams had been very old when Tom had known him. He had begun his career on one of the great sporting estates to have survived almost intact after the first world war. In the depression poaching had been at its height, as it always had been when there was heavy unemployment, when resentment against the people who owned most of the countryside would be at its height. Adams had had plenty of scrapes with poachers, and had managed to eliminate local poachers on every estate he had later head 'keepered. Tom had liked the old

9

man's approach and meant to try it out for himself.

The stars disappeared and a creeping mist that lightened the night but lowered visibility seeped into the wood. He heard less of the pigeons and the roosting birds. Mist and fog put poachers at a disadvantage for they could rarely know a terrain as well as the gamekeeper whose job it was to wander unpredictably everywhere and know his own patch like his own garden. He thought wryly that a poacher out tonight might well know the patch better than he.

When the shot came Gibson did not start, since he had been conditioned for so long to gunfire. But the muffled sound, followed by squawking and noise of birds shifting to other perches, was closer than he expected. The mist must have masked the light of the torch. He carried no weapon but had brought an ash stick that was leaning against the tree trunk. He left it there, dropped to the ground, from where he could see more clearly down the wood. He waited, hearing someone shuffling through the leaves and undergrowth. A pair of legs appeared. A torch flashed into the undergrowth, into the lower branches of trees, catching the mist in its beam. The legs came nearer, were joined to a torso and a head crowned with a cap. One man and no dog. Tom could imagine but not see the gun carried at the ready, the torch attached like a telescope sight. He waited until the figure was level with him, then moved when the poacher moved, stopped when he stopped, until he was behind the man. Tom noted that he was quite small despite bulky clothes and a game bag slung over his shoulder. He closed the gap between them quickly. The man slowly raised his shotgun and beamed the light this way and that into a low-spreading tree where it settled on a roosting cock pheasant.

Tom experienced a sudden wonderment at the night and the mist, and his vigil, and the blessed isolated woodland and its wildlife large and small, including the poacher, and himself rising to his full height. Before the trigger could be pulled he put his arms round the man's chest and squeezed so that the shotgun was involuntarily lowered and fell to the ground where the torch shone across the leafy floor of the wood. The poacher screeched, gave a fearful gasping squeal. Caught in a grip that was as unexpected at it was constricting, he went limp in Tom's arms.

"You're from Glanby."

"That's right."

"How far's that?"

"Four mile."

This man was local, Tom knew immediately.

"What do you do for a living?"

The poacher shivered, lying on his back. "What's it to you? Just take me to the police. Get it over with." He was recovering from the heart-stopping fright he had had.

Tom Gibson loomed over him. The .410 lay several yards away, unloaded, and beside it was the game bag with a hen pheasant in it. The gamekeeper played a small flashlight on him, seeing a wiry, small man with sandy hair and prominent teeth, in his mid-30s.

"How do you earn your living?"

The man shook his head, mute.

"On your answers depend what I do with you," said Tom, seeing puzzlement, then resignation.

"I drive tourist buses, April to October."

"And you poach in the winter."

The poacher licked his lips. "I get some driving, work as a barman. And there's winter chores in the woods – coppicing and the like."

"Married?"

"Divorced," the man answered. "But I still see the kids. Two girls, seven and five." He had begun to understand the drift of the questions. "I pay good maintenance, and regular."

Gibson grunted, and the poacher shivered again.

"What's your name?"

The man hesitated, raised himself on his elbow. Tom saw him glance into the darkness where his gun lay. "I'm Ernie Crawshaw."

"Lie back until I've finished with you." The voice quiet but commanding. "This property is now fully 'keepered, and I've caught you red-handed. But I'm going to let you go. Don't come back. If you do I'll get you again, and I won't be so kind next time."

"And my gun?" Ernie Crawshaw showed relief but no gratitude.

"You'll have it back later. I'll keep the cartridges and the pheasant."

On the way to Crawshaw's van they crossed fields, skirted woods, heard owls, and partridge talking as they clustered in the middle of a meadow. They reached the green lane, the public right of way which cut across a third of the home farm. Tom confirmed his thought that a green lane as broad and well used as this was a huge liability in safeguarding stock.

Suddenly Tom spoke. "It would be a big mistake to think I'm a pushover."

At that Crawshaw became garrulous. He promised he would not come back. Poaching was a mug's game. But he had always poached, and his father and grandfather before him, and further back, he dared say. There was a kind of pride in following their footsteps. And they had only ever taken game for their own use.

For a few minutes Tom fancied that the misty cold night and their escapade wrapped them both in what could almost pass for comradeship. But at the road, where a van was parked, Ernie's attitude changed. He was off the estate a free citizen with county council tarmac under his feet.

"I'll have me gun," he said.

"Not yet. First you'll tell me if this is yours." Tom put the .410 on the ground and his foot on it. He showed Ernie by flashlight the newly peeled stick that lay in his palm.

"No." The once loquacious Ernie was non-committal.

"But you've seen others like it. Maybe on this estate, maybe on another."

"What if I have? It's just a piece of peeled stick."

Tom moved very quickly, stepping backwards, scooping up the gun. "Right, I'll keep this. Away you get."

Crawshaw did not move. "All right. I have seen sticks. Mostly two, crossed, lying in a hare run where a snare's been, or on the edge of a wood or pit, somewhere where there's game been tooken." Ernie paused and Tom waited in silence. Reluctantly the man began again. "On your patch. On others' too."

"What do you think it means?"

"It's a gimmick. Just means 'I've been here and tooken sommat'."

"Who's been here?"

"Ah, that I do not know," said Ernie, the ring of truth in his voice. He took the proffered gun, jumped into his van and was away as soon as the diesel engine came to life.

The quality of the night had changed. Although still long before dawn it was as if the night countryside was aware of approaching light, stopped its activities and quieted, making its plans accordingly. Tom went to his cottage.

2. PARTRIDGE AT RISK

Harsh weather came in December. Only in the corners of fields facing full south and in the day-long sun did the heavy night frosts thaw at all. The conditions brought the pheasant to the feeding areas. Gibson was able to make a more accurate assessment of the numbers, and was pleasantly surprised. When he was not carting feed and straw by Land Rover he was out on foot working out the drives, where he would put the beaters in, where the guns would stand. He was aware that he was treading the same ground, facing the same decisions, as other gamekeepers. He tried to conjure them up in his mind, not so much their looks as their qualities. Self-reliant, liking their own company, first-rate naturalists on a simple practical level, physically enduring, and dedicated and honest. Not that there had not been a minority of 'keepers who had sold game off their estates, turned a blind eye to poaching by accomplices. But in a close-knit countryside with its friendships and feuds, with few outside interests, where most made it their business to know their neighbours' business, they could not have lasted long in their jobs.

For pickers-up he would need reliable men with reliable dogs. Where would he find them, knowing virtually no one in the district as yet? He might try the older schoolchildren in the village as beaters. But they would have to have experienced people with them. Beating was not just a matter of thrashing through the woods making a din. The right level of noise was necessary to encourage the pheasant to keep moving on the ground towards the guns, in groups, well spaced. Noise and agitation at the right moment was vital to make them take wing at the correct place, so that a flow of birds presented themselves in regular waves, not too many at a time, at a good height and flying strongly. All that took skill and discipline.

Since his employer was only interested in pheasant, Tom left the domains of hare and partridge to fend for themselves. The hare could wait. Partridge shooting was altogether more complicated, the driving of them needed experienced beaters, the shooting of them was far more of a feat than that of pheasant.

Then he found stray pheasant feathers in a thickly-tree'd marl pit. He examined the pit minutely, looking for vermin runs. There were not enough feathers for a kill by a fox or a stoat. The floor of the pit was deep in rotting leaves. Small disturbances on the surface indicated a human trespasser. Checking the rim he saw where he himself had entered through a gap in the otherwise continuous thorn hedge which surrounded the pit. This was the only place. Someone else had used it. A tuft of grass had been loosened as if a hand had grabbed it to haul a body up. Below the tuft earth had been scuffed by a boot. And then he found them. Two newly peeled sticks, crossed, lying in a sheltered depression on the slope.

"Surprising to leave his visiting card." Hilary was pleased that Tom had come to her. She liked the way he was serious about his job no matter what it was. But she wished he was not quite so gloomy. Some humour was needed. And surely he could relax sometimes from the rigours of looking after a rich man's game?

"He wants me to find them. It's his challenge. 'Here am I, able to come and go on your patch, and you none the wiser'."

"Why don't you ask around?"

Tom shook his head. "I intend to catch him on the estate. He has to find out that he's not so damned good on the ground. And this one I won't let off." He told her about Ernie Crawshaw.

Hilary was immediately doubtful. "Was that wise?"

"It's worked before." He mentioned the veteran gamekeeper Adams and his poacher-free estates, then suddenly sat bolt upright. "Why did I think the partridge would be safe, that the main worry was the pheasant?"

"They are. That's what your employer is interested in."

"I could be wrong." He thought again, and relaxed. "But no. During the day I'd probably hear anyone after them with a gun, and possibly the same at night. Otherwise it's a net. Those drag nets are too much for one man to handle. That means two men at least." In his mind the poacher with the crossed sticks had become established as one man on his own. One man who knew all the signs that others were about, the movement of birds and animals, the ways of gamekeepers however they tried to vary their routine, to be never in the same place at the same time. But here was he, Tom Gibson, having to be in certain places at the same hour to feed his pheasant. Again, Tom had been out all day and had hardly eaten.

"Come to the pub for some supper," he suggested.

"I'd like to. And we might quiz our landlord about peeled sticks. You'll catch your poacher more easily if you know who he is."

The landlord was cordial almost to the point of obsequiousness. His bar lounge was almost empty, an open coke fire heating the room for nobody much. They ordered bar meals. The limited menu was all deep-frozen and without a spark of originality. Hilary drank a glass of indifferent red wine, Tom a pint of beer pumped from a barrel.

The beer relaxed her gamekeeper, Hilary saw. The face became less closed, the blue eyes less veiled. She noted also how the landlord eyed them with some misgiving.

"Last time I was here," said Tom, "he taunted me. He had the backing of the darts night locals. Maybe he still thinks I'm an easy target. But he's foxed by you."

"Why should that be?" asked Hilary.

"You're the tough, smart type of business person he wants to attract to his pub. He pictures his car park full of management company cars at lunchtime, business parties in the evening."

"He'll have to get a better chef for that to happen," she said. She thought of telling Tom that the landlord was unsure of him because he was a quantity not easily identifiable. That would mean bringing up his background again. She knew that his and her own were much the same. Yet she inspired the landlord with respect and Tom did not. It had to be the job capacity. The village knew by now that she was marketing director of a sizeable firm. Her cottage was listed grade II, built of flint and brick in about 1704. She could afford someone in twice a week to clean, and a pensioner gave her garden the benefit of his wisdom and delight in tidiness. She was the envy of many women and an enigma to many men – a career girl. At 31 she was well organised, successful and commanding.

The meal finished, they moved to the bar. Tom ordered more drinks. "Will you join us?" he asked the landlord.

They established their identities. The landlord with his thick body and well kept brown beard was Roger Hoggett. He had been born and bred in the village, he said, and had travelled in the merchant navy. Hilary half listened as he addressed most of his biographical remarks to her, trying to leave her with the impression that he was a worldly fellow and an experienced womaniser of allure. She thought that Tom's

15

idea of the publican's view of what he wanted for his pub was probably right. However she began to have the definite impression that Hoggett talked to her but was really squaring up to Tom. Whether it was on her account she did not know. Despite the heavy physique, a trifle gone to beer belly, he seemed aware that he could not best Tom. She turned her attention to Tom, at first to break the landlord's gaze then to look at her gamekeeper again very carefully.

Earlier that evening he had seemed a typical worrier about 'his poacher'. Now, in action, he was concentrating, eyes alert in a calm, immobile face. He had a remarkable capacity for stillness. His body relaxed, hands resting on the bar. He looked no longer sombre and withdrawn, but ready and waiting, interested, and as if he might yet have a capacity for laughter and clowning.

"Born and bred here, you'll know everyone round about," Tom said in a mild congratulatory tone which made Hilary smile.

"Pretty well. And if I don't know them, I know about them." Roger Hoggett gave the girl a leery grin, then glanced uncertainly back at Tom.

"I believe it," Tom replied, still admiring, now confidential. "So I'd like your advice."

The publican smirked. "What about?" he asked, forgetting the girl for a moment, a girl he rather fancied.

"There's a man I'd like to identify."

"Describe him."

"He's light on his feet. Knows how to move through countryside at night without raising alarms. An experienced poacher, probably middle-aged. Takes the odd hare and pheasant for the excitement." Tom knew some of this was supposition. "He certainly has a dog, I'd guess a lurcher or greyhound."

"Got an obsession about him, have you?" Roger had caught an edge of intensity that had crept into Tom's voice.

"Not yet. But I might."

The landlord beamed. "There's lurchers and greyhounds in the village. Several owners course them. All above board. Clubs – they hire farms for coursing meetings." He busied himself serving drinks to a couple who had entered. When he came back it was with the air of a man who had given all the information he intended. "There you are – all above board," he said.

Hilary joined in. "We'll talk to the other gamekeepers. They'll know."

Without looking at Hilary beside him, for the first time Tom felt her presence as a comrade, playing the same game and on his side. He acknowledged that this was an unusual feeling for him. His half-sister, older by five years, had somehow never presented him with the idea that she could ever be a comrade. She had resented his mother from the start, and he had grown aware of her antagonism to him from his early days. He had long ago persuaded himself that that had contributed to later episodes at school, at university and in the army.

Hilary gathered up her bag and a cardigan from a stool.

"Well, I could make a guess at your man," Hoggett said.

"Do make a guess," replied Tom unemotionally.

"Go out on the Morton St Giles road. There's a smallholding. Name of Kerr. Major Kerr." He invested the military rank with scorn and disbelief. It was clear he did not like the major at all.

The smallholding lay a mile outside the village. The Gailsford estate surrounded it so it was easy enough for Major Kerr, if he was so minded, to slip out on to the pastures and stubbles, into the woods.

From the road Tom could see a flint-and-brick double-storey house with a steep pantile roof and a massive double chimney in the centre of the ridge. Two barns of the same material were to one side. Between the road and the buildings a track led through two small fields of plough with piles of well rotted manure waiting to be spread. A board at the entrance announced free-range eggs, geese, quail, guineafowl and rabbits for sale. Another, a blackboard, had available vegetables chalked up. House and barns were in good repair. A small square lawn lay to one side of the house with a single wide herbaceous border. A winter jasmine grew beside the front door. Smoke from the chimney rose into the still cold air. Misty sunlight slanted across the south-facing front of the house, picking out the flintwork and the carmine brick. The property had a workaday air, as if the owner and his wife laboured all the hours there were to earn not much of a living by today's standards.

Tom circumnavigated the holding, moving slowly and silently along the thick boundary hedge. There was a bright winter-day quiet about the place. There would be stock to look after, but the ground was too frost-bound to work. At nine o'clock in the morning nothing stirred. He noted kennels with iron grills close to the house but could see no dogs.

17

Several greenhouses lay beside what looked like a walled garden. There were fruit trees, grass for geese and free-range chickens, and a large area enclosed with wire netting. For quail, he thought. He reckoned the holding was about six acres. He was nearly back at the road when a side door in the house opened. He became quite still, peering through the hedge.

A woman came out and began scattering breadcrumbs on the lawn. Tom saw a bustling, energetic middle-aged figure, whose blond-grey hair was set in coils over her ears. He caught his breath. He had not thought of his mother for weeks now, had deliberately put her from his mind while he had a new environment to tame. It was his father who had taught him unawares that singleness of purpose needed complete concentration, dedication. No weakness and no gentleness. He wondered now for the thousandth time how his mother had come to marry the newly widowed foreign soldier in her war-torn defeated country. Coils of blond hair. She had been the Aryan ideal. And now this woman who was pausing to relish the winter sunshine took his breath away. He suddenly wanted to shout out a greeting in German. The woman lifted the latch of the door and, with a last look round, went inside.

Notices in the village shop and post office brought nearly 20 replies from would-be beaters. Some were farmworkers, some 'teenagers, but most were retired people, including an ex-schoolmaster. Tom saw them all either in the village or out at his cottage. The first was an elderly man who had worked on the home farm. He had expressed no feeling of animosity or reserve and had even in a curt way offered some sympathy to Tom having to put on a shoot so few weeks after his arrival and after years of neglect. He had set Tom's mood and, as soon as they found the new gamekeeper relaxed and not unfriendly himself, had been friendly and even jokey themselves. Most of the older men already knew the woods and could tell Tom a thing or two about his predecessors. Jack Turner had lived in the cottage in the woods for 30 years, had been a wizard at drawing birds to his patch and keeping them where he wanted. Then there had been the young fellow from Glanby, who had had a way with training dogs, and taken a girl from the village as his bride. Albert Brown had been killed in the desert battles of North Africa.

Tom sensed in all the older men that he was still on trial. They were prepared to accept him, accent and demeanour and from outside, nonetheless. But he had to do right by them, in running a good shoot and seeing that they had their small perks. By some curious osmosis they sensed the difficulties Tom had had and would have with the owner. They let the gamekeeper know that they knew he was country-bred and that it counted with them. Some had good ideas about driving partridge. And it was this mention that decided Tom to spend that night looking over the pastures and stubble.

It was a Saturday night. Gailsford was up from London with his wife and several house guests. No one had told Tom, and he received no summons. He had refused an invitation to a party with Hilary, telling her when pressed that he would find nothing to say to her managing director and his wife, and other colleagues. He had tried not to sound ungracious but his hostile reaction to such people had been instant. He knew he was echoing his father's thoughts and was aware that his father's views on everything else in life were opposite to his own, save for the care of the land. Hilary had been disappointed, but he had not felt sufficiently involved with her to make the effort. Almost as an afterthought he had made the excuse that he would be out all night and must get some sleep early.

"Can I come?" Hilary was matter-of-fact on the 'phone. The party had broken up early. "I'm glad you haven't left. I can sleep all day tomorrow."

Tom's first reaction was to say no. But he remembered Hilary in the pub, and the feeling that she had been with him. The thought of a companion on his midnight round, someone moving in concert with him, sharing any adventures, had its attractions. But at his prep school he had been taught not to rely on people in this way. He still remembered the boy clearly. In the class above him. They had had such identical interests, building a ganghouse together, roaming on to the downs out of bounds – all kinds of shared country experiences. It had been the first time since his mother died that Tom had known a totally unselfconscious friendship with a human being. Spooner had dropped him after two terms without a word of explanation. His interests had switched to stamp collecting and a boy in his own class.

"All right. But only if you promise to go right away if there's any rough stuff."

"If there is – then I will."

They were padding slowly up the side of a hedge, with a 10-acre pasture stretching off to their right. Tom moved slowly, pleased that Hilary was close behind him, silent and without a single complaint. She was lifting her feet, putting them down quietly. She had night eyes, and she needed them. A depression from the Atlantic had banished the sunlit days and star-filled nights, bringing rain to the west and damp to the east. Heavy low cloud now covered the sky. The air was cold and there was a light breeze from the south-west. Every few paces the gamekeeper stopped and listened.

Ahead lay a field of stubble from a crop of spring barley taken by one of the tenant farmers. Between pasture and stubble was a thick thorn hedge sprung up into trees. Several very old oaks broke the line of the hedge, stubby with branches dying back and rot already in the thick ivy-covered trunks. The trees were much favoured by roosting pigeon.

"Partridge like roosting in the middle of a field. They can see what's coming," he whispered. "Stubble's warm and has food."

"How would a poacher take them?"

"With a drag net, or by firing several charges into the covey."

"Do you think it might be the man with the sticks?"

He shook his head. "Unlikely. I think my poacher's a solitary and takes only for the pot – which you can't do with these methods."

He motioned her to silence and stillness. The light wind brought them sounds of roosting pheasant from the wood across the pasture. The sound he was waiting for did not come. There were no noisy pigeon roosting in those ideal oaks ahead. He put his mouth close to the girl's ear.

"No pigeon ahead. They've been disturbed. There's someone in the field beyond." His night senses were quivering. A group of lapwing – their lazy flight just visible against the cloud – came from the stubble to land in the pasture.

"The lapwing have left, too." He explained that partridge, like pheasant, were always loth to take to their wings. They would sit tight, crouching down, until the very last moment.

Tom led the girl swiftly to the hedge and they slipped through a gap on to the stubble. The stubble rolled away downhill before them. Tom heard what he believed was the swish of a heavy net being pulled along.

"Stay here by the hedge."

"I'd rather come. I won't endanger myself. But I want to be close to you."

"They may be armed."

"No matter."

Tom liked her calm, although she was obviously excited. "Come, then," he said. He set off at a smart walking pace, unlit rubber torch in one hand, a stick in the other.

He slowed his pace. Now he could distinguish a movement, as if the ground was undulating, could make out two moving shadows. The net was wide and the effort to drag it and hold the leading edge well above the ground was evident as they came closer and the shadows developed into straining bodies. He gestured to Hilary to fall back, went to the left of the net, forged ahead until he was level with the first man and about 10 paces away. He launched himself, cannoned into him and sent him sprawling. He flashed his torch down. A young one, this, stunned and shocked. He swung the torch beam across to the other figure. A much older man, muffled against the cold but sweating heavily with the effort of the net. Then the young one was up and running down the slope, straight through the partridge covey that had been their quarry. The birds whirred off into the night.

"You're trespassing on private land with intent to poach," said Tom mildly. "I hope your lad will come back."

"That he will." The older man tried to sound menacing.

They stood a few feet apart. Tom put out the torch. Silence settled round them. A sob came from the darkness.

"Tell him to come back."

"Like hell."

"I want to talk to you both." Tom's soldier's skin, as he always thought of it, told him that Hilary was standing near enough to make the poacher aware of her presence. A tall figure, bulky as Tom was himself. Two big gamekeepers. He also knew that the lad was close.

"Is he your son?"

The old man caught his breath. "Come here, Darren."

Darren was 14 or 15 years old and apprehensive. Tom flashed the torchlight on him briefly, then turned it on the other.

"He must be your grandson."

The poacher nodded. Tom switched off the light. For centuries

21

poachers and gamekeepers had been sworn enemies. But, as with Ernie Crawshaw, he did not feel that these two were alien to him. He could find no animosity in himself and little menace from them now. He allowed the quiet to elongate into a minute. They heard the sounds of their own breathing, drawing the night air into their lungs, and the faint whisperings of the partridge covey settling to earth down the hill.

He asked their names and where they came from. The village was five miles in the opposite direction to Glanby.

"What does your grandson want with knowing how to net partridge at night?" Tom asked. "He should be learning how to take tractors apart, going to agricultural school, using computers."

The old man shifted uneasily. "You the owner?" he asked.

Tom sensed that the poacher was embarrassed at being taken by the man whose partridge he had been about to steal.

"This land is now 'keepered. By me." Tom indicated the lad. "Did he want to come?"

There came no reply. Tom waited. The wind was freshening, presaging sleet then snow as forecast. At last the old man cleared his throat, spat into the darkness.

"Someone's got to know," he said. "You got to pass on ways to the young 'uns." He paused. "He's a good old boy. But he don't care for country things."

As the old man began talking about the need to keep old habits sharpened and in use, Hilary was struck by the ease with which Tom had neutralised any potential confrontation. His voice and his questions had disarmed, taken away apprehension and aggression. She mistrusted the method and the aim, if he was going to treat these two like the first. Here he was dealing with people who were no match for him. How would he react to a rough-tongued, strong-willed adversary, quicker-witted than he?

The old man went on. Hedges were no longer layered but cut with rotary machines mounted on tractors, spewing thorns all over the place. Woodland was no longer coppiced, old pastures were ploughed up. Who could build a rick today, whether of sheaves or hay? Where were the animals in this sterile country of corn, sugar beet and oilseed rape? And where, coming full circle, was autumn stubble to please the partridge?

"So Darren didn't want to come."

"Computers – you said it." The poacher spat again, not nervously but

22

angrily. "Yet he's a good old boy," he repeated.

"Listen," said Tom. "Take the net and go now. Don't ever come back as a poacher on this estate. Tell others that it's 'keepered, that I don't want trouble."

"You should have taken them to the police station, charged them," said Hilary. "Everyone will think you're a soft touch – which I begin to think you are. Sometimes you have to make an example. You let the first man off, you should have clobbered the second."

"Is that a modern management technique?"

Hilary was exasperated. "You weren't taken in by all that guff about the old skills being passed on, were you? He was a con man, and I've seen plenty of them."

She knew immediately that Tom was downcast. From the height of confidence in action, he was edging down into self-doubt.

"He wasn't a wide boy." He tried to rally. "We have them in the countryside, too. They're recognisable, and he wasn't one. I believed what he said. The grandson didn't open his mouth. He was loyal to the old man even though he'd been forced into coming."

"Surmise. Supposition." Hilary had enjoyed the evening until now. But with the turn of the weather and the end of the excitement came the belief that her gamekeeper had mishandled the situation. He needed training like everyone else, not just in the mechanics of his work. He had to handle people as a factory manager or businessman had to. As they walked back in silence to Tom's cottage, with snow and sleet showers bursting in quick succession on the hedges and fields, she asked herself how Tom would handle the poacher who preyed on his mind. The man who peeled short lengths of hazel and left them as a sign of his fleeting, silent and successful presence on another man's land. She did not rate Tom's chances very highly.

The snow stayed only a day. Driving rain from the south-west swept it all melting into the ditches. The day of the first shoot was approaching. Tom tried to talk to Gailsford about the shoot, but he professed no interest in the work of getting it together, repeating that he just wanted a good show. He would be briefed on the day and expect all to go smoothly. Tom might have been flattered that Gailsford had such trust in him. But he felt that he was not so trusted, that he was difficult for the owner to assess. He anticipated trouble if the shoot was not the impossible success the man expected.

Tom contacted two neighbouring gamekeepers. One had a shoot on the same day, the other would pick-up for Tom and bring two others. One more picker-up was needed. On a morning of clear skies and a sunrise of apricot and pale lemon along the rim of the land, the fourth picker-up presented himself.

The gamekeeper was out with his dog. While arranging to have a large proportion of the wild birds on the estate shot in the next two months, he was already ahead with the need for restocking, for rearing 2,000 day-old chicks. Soon after his arrival he had found where the previous occupants of his cottage had had their rearing field. It lay 150 yards south of the cottage in a large glade in the surrounding woodland. It provided shelter from winds from all quarters, was a sun trap, and was close to the cottage for surveillance. In a tangle of weeds and grass he had found broken posts and wire netting, and the rotting remains of wooden housing. Contemplating the place, he thought ahead to the pleasure of watching the chicks grow, to the needs of protecting them from crows and magpies, from the small ground vermin, until they were big enough to transfer to several release pens in sunny woodland spots around the estate.

The year-old black labrador dog he had brought from Hampshire was anxious for Tom to be off on his rounds. Eager and impatient, his eyes roving along the woodland edge where he expected they would go shortly. He was pointing in that direction, stepping from side to side of Tom. Tom checked him quietly, brought him to heel. A movement across the glade drew his attention. He stood still, the gun under his arm, broken. The dog had noted it, too. Man and dog were silent, watching. A fox perhaps, going home to its earth after a night's hunting. They waited a full minute. Nothing stirred. Then the dog growled, a soft warning sound. He looked up at his master, turned his head suddenly to glance behind him, yelped and leaped round to face the man who had appeared on the edge of the glade, only yards away. Tom spun round, forcing himself not to react as he would have done in other times by flinging himself to the ground, his weapon at the ready. As it was, involuntarily he half-raised the shotgun, began to snap it shut, then relaxed shamefacedly.

The man was solid enough. Burly would have been the old adjective to describe such a frame. He was not tall, perhaps five feet 10 inches, with shoulders sloped like a prizefighter's. He had close-cut grey hair and blue-jowled cheeks. A pair of brown eyes regarded man and dog with amusement. He was dressed in shades of green, wore no hat.

"You need a picker-up." The voice was Scottish. "I've a springer bitch. A four-year old, experienced. She's steady on fur, and there'll mebbe be a fair amount of that."

Tom immediately liked the approach. Talk about the dog. After all, the dog was perhaps the major partner in the pick-up team. That argued that the man appreciated real country affairs, understood the gamekeeper's trade. The gamekeeper looked with interest at him. Unsmiling and alert, the amusement had gone from his eyes. Everything about him registered, not hostility exactly, but an independence that was combatative and almost arrogant. Tom wanted to fix the man in his mind – as he was when he had first seen him on spinning round – and had no idea why. He did not answer at once but stared, off-guard.

"That's right. I'd welcome another picker-up," he said at last. The question he might have put remained unasked, and he wondered whether it was because he already knew the answer. He looked at the pockets of the heavy macintosh jacket the man wore. The pockets bulged. But his thought was idiotic. No man would come to a gamekeeper with a snared hare in his pocket, a pheasant knocked on the head with a skilfully thrown stone. Yet the green corduroy trousers were baggy enough to conceal a .410 butt and barrel slid down each leg and tied in place with thongs at the top. The brown eyes were knowing, amused again, as if they read the gamekeeper's thoughts, realising that the custodian of the estate's game would do nothing to confirm his suspicions.

Tom told him where to meet and when. "Do you know the estate? Have you picked up here before?" He had difficulty not sounding inquisitorial.

"I know the lie of the land."

Foolish to think he would have direct answers.

"Thanks for coming over. I'm Tom Gibson."

"See you on Saturday, then," said the Scotsman and turned to leave. Almost as an afterthought he gave his name. "I'm Kerr," he said. "Benjamin Kerr."

3. GUTEN APPETIT

Charles Gailsford was in a foul temper. As one who excelled at adding companies to his conglomerate, he was no longer used to being a duffer. To hit clays on a range after weeks of painful misses was good. But to translate that small ability to the tensions of a shoot with wild pheasant coming over high and fast was quite beyond him that morning. Of his six invited guns three were beginners like himself, the others, experienced, revelling in the 'good show' that the first drive produced.

The weather was perfect for the sport, sun and blue skies this mid-December, crisp enough to need warm clothing but mild enough to have kept the occasional migrating woodcock in the long broad windbreak which Tom had chosen as the first drive. There had been adequate numbers of pheasant, and shrubs grading into taller trees at the flushing point had sent the birds in successive waves up and over the guns to present sporting targets. Three or four woodcock had come out, taking off like jet fighters. All but one had flown clean away.

With every element unknown – beaters, pickers-up, guns – the gamekeeper contrived to be everywhere. He had started the beaters, making sure they tapped tree trunks or boots, without other noise, that their dogs were reasonably controlled and flushed out the bramble and blackthorn thickets properly. He saw that they knew how to press just enough on approaching the flushing area to send a first flight over but not too hard to cause too many to rise at once. Then he circled round to arrive breathless and stand behind the guns. He went to load for Gailsford after checking all the guns, nodding to the gamekeeper and pickers-up, two with golden retrievers, the third with a black labrador. At the end of the line Benjie Kerr stood like a green rock, still and watchful, a liver-and-tan springer bitch beside him.

The last flush of birds came over as the beaters appeared through the trees. Tom was pleased at the way the pickers-up sent off their dogs, guided by whistle and word of mouth. To have competent pickers-up was vital, otherwise wounded birds were left out and runners disappeared.

"Good birds, Charles," said one of the experienced guns to his host.

"Too many got away," added a novice.

"They'll be taken another day. They'll afford someone as good a sport as we had just now." Tom looked with interest at the dapper, small man who had spoken. He was relieved that at least one of the owner's friends was out for the joy and excitement of the whole day without counting heavily on a huge bag.

Gailsford was only partly mollified. "Let's move. Where to now, Gibson?"

The second drive was muffed. The beaters came through the 50-acre wood. Tom knew that birds are best driven out of woodland covering no more than a quarter that acreage. But there were good sunny glades, patches of warm pines, yew and spruce in the predominant oak, ash and sycamore. His predecessors had had release pens in the wood. The undulations of the terrain meant without doubt that they had placed their guns where Tom had put his. But his beaters were too few. Birds turned back, scattered to the sides. The beaters and their dogs became flustered, the birds flopped into the air, already tired from the harassment of being forced through the wood. They came over low and slow, hooting with indignation. They were so low that to fire at them would have put the beaters in danger.

"Let them go, gentlemen, please. Let them go," Tom shouted. He heard the gamekeeper bellowing at a novice gun who loosed a shot at a cock bird that was five yards from him. The pellets had no distance to spread and the bird disintegrated into blood, flesh and feathers, spattering the gun who had brought him down. Tom heard Benjie Kerr's distinctive Scots voice giving a prime piece of advice to a novice gun. "On a driven shoot always shoot at the sky, laddie."

When the beaters appeared, almost reluctantly and with embarrassment, Gailsford spoke up at Gibson, without caring whether his guests heard.

"That was bloody awful. What went wrong, eh? The beaters are no good. You've boobed."

"The beaters are fine. The wood's big and there weren't enough of them. Our tactics were wrong. We'll learn."

Gailsford lowered his voice. "I pay you an experienced gamekeeper's wage. I expect plenty of birds, properly presented. Not this fiasco. And I don't like the way you and these others –" he indicated the pickers-up, "– shout at my guests. My guests are important to me."

"And to me, too." Tom spoke quietly. "We prevented the less experienced of your guests loosing off at birds to the danger of men and dogs. As an experienced 'keeper it's my job to conduct a safe shoot."

Gailsford half-turned away. "Well then, where to now?" he asked sharply.

Tom promised himself a session with the man to try and explain the mechanics of running a shoot. He did not rate his chances of putting across the facts very highly. Good management could take a shoot just so far. There were imponderables – the birds themselves, weather, vermin, men and dogs – which could upset that management. Every shoot needed its share of good luck.

The third drive retrieved the situation. It brought birds from a series of marl pits, through a spinney and into a short windbreak. Here Gailsford downed a high bird, using the swing and stance he had been taught in the shooting school. He was congratulated by the dapper man. A fourth drive was almost as productive. Lunch was taken in the lee of a spinney, on bales set in the sun.

There was then a walk to the other side of the farm for the fifth and sixth drives. At the last one the beaters brought birds gently out of several hedges and tipped them into a small wood of about five acres. Fewer birds came over the guns, but presented themselves well. Gailsford took three birds here, and his novices managed one bird each. The three good shots took six or seven apiece. The station was close to the green lane, and a dealer's truck was already there. Tom busied himself sorting out a brace of good birds for each of the guns, and for the pickers-up. Those badly peppered he set aside for the beaters. The guns were already reminiscing, congratulating, thanking the pickers-up and discussing the merits of their dogs. The dealer went off, none too pleased with his haul. Tom paid the beaters and pickers-up, gave them their birds. By then Gailsford and his guests had gone. So had Benjie Kerr, without his money and birds.

After a hot bath Tom cooked himself a meal, and opened a bottle of supermarket Côtes du Rhône. He had deliberately not 'phoned Hilary, believing that he had had enough of people for one day. By now he had become reconciled to the fact that Gailsford had gone off without a word of thanks to his 'keeper or any of the helpers. The gamekeeper who had acted as a picker-up had generously put it down to ignorance of the form. Tom was less kind. Even a self-made tycoon must realise that a friendly word to pickers-up and beaters was vital. After all, the money was little enough. They had been there for the sport, for the glorious day complete, and that included hobnobbing with the landowner and his guests, as sportsmen to sportsmen, as countrymen who were important to the success of the day.

He finished the wine sitting by the stove, tired, listening to Dvorak's 'cello concerto, letting the music conjure up for him great tracts of sweeping grassland, limitless horizons, blue distant hills. He thought of the United States, of Czechoslovakia, not knowing either country but seeing what the composer might have seen when writing the concerto. When the music had ceased he recalled Devon and other acres, every one of which he knew intimately from his earliest days. By then his mood had changed to one of near-despair. He left the washing up until morning, and went to bed physically and emotionally drained.

On the Sunday morning Tom did the round of the feeding areas and went over the drives again, especially the second where he worked out how to avoid such a mess another time. He noted here and elsewhere that tree canopies would need to be thinned and bushes cut back. He would tackle the farm manager when he came for some labour to help him. A forlorn hope, probably. Gailsford's view of his farming operations to come sounded depressingly maximum-profit-orientated.

By the afternoon the bright weather had gone, clouds built up and a cold north-east wind blew. He took his young dog out for a long training walk. The dog had had no exercise the day before, left in his kennel. They had both enjoyed the afternoon. Always at the back of Tom's mind as he threw the dummy, whistled to bring the dog back to him, whistled for him to quarter a given section of ground, called him to heel and to sit, was the brace of pheasant hanging in his woodshed and Benjie Kerr who had earned the birds the day before. He wanted to know Kerr better, needed to find out definitely that he had no further to look for his poacher of the peeled sticks. The man attracted him, and yet they had spoken no more than a few sentences. He recalled him on the shoot, hardly moving, and aware of all that was going on, where every bird came down and in what likely condition. And there was Mrs Kerr who had reminded him of the half of him which was German. He wanted to talk German again.

Tom recited Heine, Goethe and Schiller on the way back to his cottage, declaiming aloud, forgetting to be vigilant, observant of everything along his path. The unaccustomed noise surprised the dog, and there and then he decided to change the labrador's name. No longer would he be the breeder's Sunstar Bessingham's Forenoon, otherwise Star. From now on he would be Schiller. Tom called him several times by the name, and was surprised and touched by the dog's seeming acceptance of his new identity. Back home he did various household chores as the short winter day faded and a bleak darkness fell. He fed Schiller, washed and changed into corduroy trousers and a tweed jacket, a clean shirt and a pullover but no tie. He decided not to resuscitate the fire in the stove. If the Kerrs were out he would see if Hilary was at home, or have a pub supper.

He would walk. Most days he averaged eight or nine miles, and today he had managed half that number. As he collected the brace from the woodshed he wondered whether the Kerrs hung their birds properly. Too many pheasant these days were eaten unhung or inadequately hung. There were fewer and fewer people prepared to pluck and draw a ripe bird.

The Kerrs' house was dark save for a dim square of pale light from a heavily curtained downstairs room. There was no bell on the front door, only a plain iron knocker. He rapped on the door, noting that there were no radio or tv sounds. He heard footsteps approaching. No bolt was drawn, no key turned in the lock. It was a country home of another era.

Benjie Kerr stood in the doorway. Tom saw again the barrel-like body, the alert, slightly forward-projecting stance.

"Come in, laddie – never mind about the boots." Tom had indicated his footwear. "Just gi' 'em a good wipe." The hallway was flagged in stone. There was a heavy, ornately carved oak chair against the wall, polished until it shone grey-brown. Tom was sure it was a German chair. His hopes, not fully defined until now, rose spectacularly. And he had not been left on the doorstep to hand in his pheasant. There had been no hesitation in the invitation to enter.

"We'll go in the kitchen. It's warm and where the action is, as they say nowadays". He led the way down a short passage, flung open a door and let out such smells of cooking food that Tom almost fainted with the lurch his gastric juices gave. At one end of the kitchen table two places were laid. At the other was an axe lying on a newspaper, a can of oil and a flat grinding stone, where Benjie had evidently been working. His wife stood by the kitchen range. She was of medium height, younger than her husband, perhaps in her late fifties.

"This is Tom Gibson," Kerr said. "He's 'keeper next door."

Mrs Kerr smiled. She had cornflower blue eyes, a face too broad for beauty, but an openness of countenance and a mouth of great voluptuousness. Her hair was blond with grey streaks, and tonight piled on top of her head. She wore a red dress under a large frilly blue apron. When she spoke her voice was a rich mezzo-soprano. Except for the blue eyes and blond hair she resembled his mother only in her nationality. Her English was good but her accent was undoubtedly German.

"You have a difficult job to do, if what I hear is correct."

"What do you hear, Mrs Kerr?"

"Not many birds, and a master who doesn't yet understand the ways of the countryside."

Tom glanced at her husband. In the full light of the kitchen Benjie loomed large and surprisingly benevolent. His eyes twinkled although his face remained impassive.

"That's as maybe, and of no account tonight," he said. "Thank you for the birds."

"Will you eat with us, Mr Gibson?" asked Mrs Kerr.

"Gladly," said Tom, hardly believing his good luck. Already it seemed his defences were crumbling. After all, he suspected Benjie Kerr of being his poacher. Clever, silent, better than he was himself in fieldcraft. If he was the poacher of the peeled sticks then he should get to know his enemy, and what better way than infiltrating his home. Was that fair? But then, if Benjie was the poacher he was also playing the same game. And if he was not then there was no harm at all. He determined to enjoy the evening.

"Sit down, laddie." Kerr pushed forward a chair. His wife laid another place at the table, moving the axe and its paraphernalia to a corner of the room.

"*Aus welchem Gebiet kommen Sie, Frau Kerr?*" asked Tom trying to sound matter of fact but bubbling with excitement.

Silence greeted his question. Then she laughed and clapped her hands. She spoke in German expressing pleasure, asking him question after question, leaving him no time to answer. Where had he learned German? And yes, she came from a village in the Ruhrgebiet, not far from Düsseldorf. She had met Benjie just after the war when he had been her Scottish soldier, billeted in her parents' home. Her father had been manager of a rolling mill in the nearby steelworks. As she continued, releasing a happy flood of language at him, Tom looked at

31

Benjie. The face was still impassive, his eyes fixed on his wife. Tom had no idea whether he understood the rapid German or not. Mrs Kerr had not paused to find out whether Tom himself understood so much. At last, realising perhaps that her outburst might have been misdirected, she asked again where he had learned the language.

"My mother was from Bamberg in Bavaria. I went there every summer with her when I was small. I remember the old city, and the river running through it. And my grandfather's home. He was a doctor and a musician. My grandmother sang beautifully and he accompanied her on the piano. But my mother died when I was 11, and I didn't go to Bamberg again." He was astonished at his own words. Perhaps because they were in German they were able to be said. He did not believe he had ever said those words in English. The desolation of the years after his mother's death, his father's attitude to him and his remarriage, had stopped him from uttering such definite statements. But in German his love for the Bavaria he remembered as his mother's home, and of her people, seemed so easily expressed, and especially to this woman with the blue eyes.

"And your grandparents, your family in Bamberg. You don't visit them?"

"My grandparents are dead. My uncle was killed in the war – or rather he disappeared on the Russian front." Tom paused. "There were cousins, I think, but I don't recall them."

Mrs Kerr could see that he was out of countenance. "You've kept your German up," she said brightly. "You speak more currently than I – living with old Benjie who can only grunt in my language."

Benjie Kerr's eyes opened wide and he grunted in no known tongue. Tom was glad that he understood, but he switched to English.

"Where do you come from in Scotland?" he asked Benjie.

"I'm a Fifer," said Kerr. "I can't really tell you why we settled here."

Mrs Kerr broke in. "Because Irma was in Lincoln when she first came – that's why." She turned to Tom, breaking into German again. "My sister, she married an RAF pilot who became quite high ranking – an air marshal. But they moved away south, and we stayed. Benjie had no training but as a soldier, so what did we do? We put his gratuity into a chicken farm." She gurgled with laughter at the very thought.

"I'll gi' ye my version later," said Benjie in his native tongue. "What about food, Heilke lass?"

Heilke. So that was her name. He liked it, wanted to call her by it immediately, but knew he must bide his time. He washed while the meal was being served up, came back into the kitchen to watch her and look round the room. A heavy German dresser carried a range of blue-and-white china. There were no pictures on the white and uneven walls. This part of the house was possibly early 18th century. Benjie came with a bottle of Bulgarian Cabernet Sauvignon.

The soup was served in lidded earthenware pots. A strong broth with pearl barley and winter vegetables. Tom forced himself to eat spoonful for spoonful with his hostess, listening to her describing visits to her paternal grandparents and their small farm up against the Dutch border near Venlo. How she still remembered their dialect, more like Dutch than German. Tom was aware that her husband was regarding with compassion his valiant efforts not to gobble his soup. His look appeared to say that he knew what it was like to work all day and eat little until that blessed evening meal. The soup was finished.

"Will you have some more soup, Mr Gibson?" she asked.

Tom glanced quickly at Benjie.

"Ask her what's to follow," Benjie advised solemnly.

"You know *Grünkohle?*" she asked.

"A kind of cabbage?" Tom hazarded. "But no, please tell me."

"It is what is called curly kale here or borecole – farmer's cabbage, from the Dutch. We chop it very fine, cook it in boiling salted water, mix it with mashed potato. Then we serve a smoked sausage with it. The rich sausage complements the plain bulk of the potato and *Grünkohle*. It is good for hungry farm men, has been for many a century, I think."

"It sounds wonderful. I'd still like a little more soup."

Mrs Kerr laughed.

"You've given her the greatest pleasure," Benjie said. "She's no' happier than when she's feeding appreciative stomachs."

The sausage was followed by an open apple tart. Gibson talked German one moment, English the next, and could not remember when he had felt so much at ease.

"That was the best meal I've had for many months, Mrs Kerr," said Tom formally when they rose from the table.

"I can tell you that if my grandfather had been here with us, and you a candidate for a job on the farm, he would have given the job to you," she said in German.

"*Aber warum?*" The wine, the steamy kitchen and the good food had made Tom slow.

"Don't you know? When in Germany a farmer wants to hire a man he brings him in for the midday meal, watches closely how fast he eats. The man who takes his food slowly has no chance of that job." She paused. "Although I had my doubts about you with the soup, you removed them by the way you ate the rest of the meal." They all laughed.

Mugs of coffee were carried into the living room. It was plain that Heilke Kerr was of a generation and a background that believed a man should not busy himself with housework, She would wash up by herself. Tom was left alone with Benjie. They sat opposite each other, either side of a fireplace with a simple classical mantel. A log fire was laid and Benjie put a match to it. The sitting room was a lived-in room. A Victorian pedestal sewing box was beside the chair Tom sat in. A bookshelf along one end wall was full. A deep sofa, a standard lamp, a Victorian upholstered chair, chintz-covered armchairs. The paintings were also from the late 19th century, even to an oil of a Highland scene with long-haired cattle drinking from a burn. Three or four small rugs lay on a brown wall-to-wall carpet. There was no sign of television, radio or record player. It was a room that Tom felt happy in, and there was nothing German in it.

"What made you become a lackey to the moneyed classes?" Kerr asked.

Tom closed his eyes momentarily. Everyone wanted to ask him questions. What did it matter to Hilary or Kerr why he had become a gamekeeper? He was a gamekeeper and aimed to be a good one. Maybe this time he would give a piece of an answer.

"I like the life. The isolation. I'm no good for an academic life. I can't understand computers, salesmanship, management by objectives. I don't want to live in a town or work in an office." He stopped.

Benjie Kerr nodded. "But why choose Gailsford – a man who knows nothing of sporting life in the countryside?"

"Because I didn't know. Because I wanted to come north, away from the overfed artificial south."

Such questioning from others, Hilary among them, always turned him morose and uncommunicative. This time, in return, he wanted to ask some questions himself, particularly about newly peeled sticks. This man was an adversary. Now he was angry with himself for having been disarmed by Heilke Kerr, and a little by Benjie, by the wine and

34

food. All right, Benjie only took for the pot, but he poached other men's game on other men's land. It did not matter that the game and the land belonged to such as Gailsford. It would be the same if it were one of the old landed families, or a university college or the British Rail pension fund. He thought of those Devon acres of his childhood and young manhood with longing. *Sehnen und Verlangen.* Longing and desire. He had drunk nearly half a bottle of wine, was tired again, was always tired. He would not go out tonight. Few poachers did just after a shoot. The birds were unsettled.

"What sport do you get, Major Kerr?" he asked, trying to concentrate on the man seated at ease before him by his own fireside. A thoroughly physical man. Canny, very fit, a little paunchy now despite the hard manual work he did. Benjie was observant, well experienced, and to Tom very familiar and of his own kind – a thought he did not then understand.

"I pick-up all over the place, and have my reward with hare shoots and the occasional 'cocks only' drive. Rough shooting, too. And of course there's always the pigeon."

"On my patch in the past?"

"You can see for yourself the neglect. I shoot pigeon on my own land. They come in after the crops in a hard winter."

An indirect answer. Tom said nothing, and Benjie Kerr continued after a pause. "I'm glad you're here. There'll be less vermin. I've had fox after my stock. And crows and magpies over many times. Those rooks of yours will need to be thinned out in May."

"I'll get to it all," Tom Gibson replied. And he thought that he would also get to Benjie Kerr, too. But tonight he had accepted his hospitality.

"You've a fine place here. But it must mean a lot of work."

Benjie agreed. His wife's roots were in small farming. The steelworks had been a hiccup. She was a great help. Then there was Kenny who came and worked with them. Had he not seen the simple-minded young man who lived with his parents in the cottage opposite the Red Lion? When it was a matter of routine that he knew, Kenny was reliable and efficient. Only a sudden change or the need to use his initiative threw him. Yes, the smallholding was hard work. But they had their clientele for the produce and they ate well themselves, almost entirely from their own land.

"You move very silently and quickly," said Tom. "I'm thinking of the other day."

Benjie enjoyed the praise. "I learned where I suspect you did. You'll have been a soldier. You carry yourself like one. And react like one who's not long been out of khaki. I'm thinking of the other day, too."

Tom had to smile despite the memory of his startled reaction. "I've learned mostly as a gamekeeper. It's important to move without disturbing the wildlife – or giving away your whereabouts to anyone unlawfully on your patch." He watched Benjie closely.

"I expect you're good at that. But maybe not quite as good as I am." Benjie was grinning.

"It's an academic argument," Tom replied quickly. "After all, you've no longer any need to move silently through the countryside – not on a smallholding."

Heilke Kerr came into the living room. She gave them more coffee and brought a carton of Belgian chocolates that both men refused. She wanted to know, in German, when Tom was going back to Bamberg. He must find his cousins, reacquaint himself with that ancient city and its sophisticated provincial life. Here of course they led an isolated deprived rural existence. She had liked to go to the theatre in Düsseldorf, and the opera and art galleries. Now she and Irma spent a week in Düsseldorf together, and another week, with six months in between, in London, to fill up with culture for the other 50 weeks of the year. As for Benjie, educated though he was, he was content now to read his books and spend too long working. For what? She wanted to know.

The men let her go on, both of them admiring. Tom had to remind himself that she was an accessory after the crime he was certain Benjie Kerr committed any night of the week in season when there was a light breeze and scattered cloud with no tell-tale moonlight. But he said goodnight warmly, and meant it when he told them it had been the best evening he had spent for years. "Bring your girl next time," said Benjie.

4. HISTORY LESSON

At the second shoot, just before Christmas, Tom omitted the big wood that had proved disastrous, substituting a second wide windbreak of Scots and Corsican pine with elder and hazel edging. The beaters put out flankers to keep the birds contained in the trees. The guns Gailsford had invited were all experienced, and included the dapper man who turned out to be a food manufacturer recently knighted, and a landowner himself over in Northamptonshire. Their influence, their calm appraisal of birds and viable shots affected Gailsford, who had a good day, bringing down five birds, all of them sporting shots. The pickers-up were all gamekeepers or practised local sportsmen. Benjie Kerr was not among them, having pleaded that he was too busy preparing birds for the Christmas trade.

"Would you say a word to the pickers-up and beaters?" Tom asked at the end of the last drive. Flushed with his success and with the plaudits of the other guns still in his ears, Gailsford had been more than ready to praise the 'hired help', leaving behind a mollified gang of local countrymen.

The meteorological office forecast a mild Christmas. Unsure what family Tom had, but suspecting that he was alone, Hilary asked him if he was going home. He was not. So she suggested he came home with her. Her parents lived in Kent. Her younger brother would be there, but her elder sister lived in the United States. She was a businesswoman, too, with a PhD, part academic and part in commerce. She was married to an American lawyer. Both were very high-powered, had no family as yet. Her brother – well, he was a problem. A civil servant in the Ministry of Agriculture, as her father had been. Not motivated, content to rub along. He collected stamps, had his holidays walking the long-distance paths, doing conservation work.

"Sounds a nice gentle person," said Tom.

"That's the trouble. My father was the same – is still, I suppose."

"You mean he didn't progress very far in the civil service, and your brother isn't going to either."

Hilary was in no doubt where Tom's sympathies lay. "The trouble with my parents is that my mother wanted to be a businesswoman. But

37

her upbringing, and my father's hurt pride when she suggested she augment the family income, stopped her from doing very much until she was in her forties, when she opened a dress shop."

"Perhaps easy-going unambitious men are attracted to aspiring, masterful women, especially if they are well-dressed, successful and beautiful," said Tom with a hint of humour which Hilary found disarming, acceptable, even mildly exciting and hopeful. "Benjie Kerr thinks you're my girl," Tom added. "He asked me to bring you to see them."

Hilary forbore to ask him whether he considered she was his girl. She would move at his pace. "So you've met Mr Kerr. And is he your poacher?" she said instead.

Tom remembered his evening with warmth. He could not wait to be back there, for ambivalent reasons. He had been reading German at night before falling into bed, had examined the feasibility of tracing his German cousins. And he had to warn Benjie that he would catch any poacher on his patch, especially a man who left his newly peeled sticks, crossed, where he had taken game. Benjie must be in his mid-60s at least if he had fought in the war and reached the rank of major. Too old to spend cold nights out, no longer swift enough to run away. The fear of being caught must surely be with him now on the escapades. Tom would seek to build on that fear.

"I think he's my poacher," he replied. "I aim to be sure before long."

"Ah, but you like him, don't you? You like all your poachers. They're part of the enduring pageantry of country life as you see it, just as estates and gamekeepers ought to be."

Tom was taken aback. Poachers might be country characters and might have what his father called 'salt'. But they were the sworn enemies of estate owners and their servants. He acknowledged a clash of interest in the far past. Historically there had been times when a rabbit had done an undernourished family a power of good. But today food was plentiful and relatively cheap.

"If he's poaching I'll do all in my power to stop him," he said seriously, then smiled. "But I'm beginning to like him." Hilary found his smile, rarely seen so far, very much to her liking.

"Will you come for Christmas?"

He explained about feeding the pheasant and his dog. For the future he would try and work something out with the friendly gamekeeper. And over the holiday, too, he had to be on the lookout. His gamekeeper friend had telephoned. Word was spreading round the county that a gang with greyhounds and lurchers was after hare – part sport, part business. Hare were fetching good prices. The police had set up a rural crime patrol system. The patrol cars were not on radio standby to deal with any other emergency, and could therefore be brought to a reported poaching foray quite soon. Tom had received a list of van descriptions and their registration numbers. Although there were Boxing Day shoots on several estates, Tom's patch would be quiet and wide open. The Gailsfords would be spending the festivities in the Caribbean.

About then Hilary was hard put to it not to ask why he went on with the farce of looking after a rich man's sport. And for what kind of money? She wanted to say that she had looked over his bookshelves and that they were those of a university-educated man. German poetry, philosophy, and the great novels in the language, and the same in French. And there were books on Cambridge, music, travel, birds and butterflies, and on ecological and landscape subjects. She had noted also the regimental histories of the Devonshire Regiment and the Parachute Regiment. To top it up there were 400 or more paperback classics and novels in English. Did he by any chance have a degree in French and German from Cambridge? She did not ask, but went off to Kent still not having touched him or been touched by him, and yet beginning to think she could, against all the outward odds, be his girl.

Tom thought hard about how to get himself invited to the Kerrs for Christmas Eve dinner, which they would surely have, given Heilke's background. In the end he went round ostensibly to tell Benjie about the hare-poaching gang. He was unprepared for Benjie's reaction. The man was livid that outsiders should be coming to local preserves. He wanted to help, and took down the list of vans and numbers. Tom had no further information. The rumour was that they came from the big town where Hilary worked. The thought that they were townees with no stake in the countryside was even worse. With Benjie choleric, it was Heilke who asked what Tom was doing for Christmas and who invited him immediately to that dinner.

Next day Tom went shopping in the town for presents. Quite soon he found the right present for Benjie – a 1910 second edition of one of the great classics of the shooting world. He then spent a long miserable hour searching for something for Heilke, caught up in the sleazy razzamatazz of Christmas in the stores, looking into small shops selling clothes and perfumes. It was in one of those that he realised he had bought nothing for Hilary. With some distaste he allowed a tired sales girl smelling of half-a-dozen delights herself to dab perfumes on his wrists. He bought the one with the name he liked best – not too tigerish. But there had been nothing he could remotely contemplate giving Heilke. He then wandered by chance into a street of antique shops and found a coloured print dated in the 1850s of the Rhine at Düsseldorf. After that he paused before the window of a wine merchant in which hampers of mixed wines with *foie gras*, Bradenham ham and tinned asparagus were displayed. He always sent something to his father, and to his half-sister and her husband, the once-yearly contact with the only two elements of his family. And they would send him ties and shirts that in his present life he would not wear. Appearances were kept up, but it seemed that his father would never forget and probably never forgive what he believed to be his son's betrayal. Attempts at reconciliation, pleas for understanding, had been rejected. How many generations had been soldiers of substance, rank, courage, often of renown? For generations Gibsons had served in all the major wars and many of the minor skirmishes where first English and then British troops had fought. It had been a point of honour to serve until old age, wounds or death intervened. In the earlier days when promotions were bought there had been a limit to the rank achieved. But promotion by merit and brains had seen Gibsons rising to become colonels and generals. And there had been a steady harvest of awards for bravery and meritorious service. So far a VC had eluded the family. Then it had been up to Tom to follow this line of clever, dedicated and honourable, first-rate soldiers and good sportsmen. A long line with only Tom and his sister's small son to carry it on – so his father had said. Tom sent his father and his sister hampers for Christmas, taking perverse pleasure in the fact that on a gamekeeper's pay the cost of them was extortionate.

Christmas Eve dawned mild and dry after two days of light rain, and by early evening mist lay low in the fields and hedges bordering the green lane as Tom drove his Land Rover to the Kerrs. Swinging off the road on to the track to the farmhouse he noticed that the property was called Shepherd's Pightle. Poacher's Pightle more likely, and tonight – Christmas Eve or no – he would ask pertinent questions of Benjie. All day he had patrolled the pastures, listing places along the hedges, at the borders of woods and windbreaks where he would set tunnel traps for ground vermin. He had made notes for a big plan of the estate, on which he would mark up all the main features, drives, release pens, the rearing field. He might also mark up where he caught poachers, the date, and what they were after.

An outside light was blazing by the front door, lighting up the abundant yellow flowers of the winter jasmine, depressed by the rain and damp. As the door opened to his knock he wondered whether the Kerrs had sons and daughters out in the world, too far away to come and see their parents. Or perhaps, since Benjie was a Scot, they would come flocking from all over Britain for Hogmanay. It was Heilke who stood welcoming in the doorway. Her hair was in coils at her ears. She wore a full-length blue gown, cut square across the bosom, showing the very white tops of her breasts. Tom thought immediately of Hilary, then his mother, and finally, confused, of Heilke herself.

"Am I correctly dressed?" he asked in German.

"Kommen Sie herein. Komm, komm." She slipped suddenly into the familiar form of address, and was herself mildly troubled. With her generation and her *petit bourgeois* background the informal mode of address was reserved for younger relations and close friends most of whom were from schooldays.

He took off his coat to reveal a dark blue suit. "I hope I'm dressed correctly?" he repeated. As one ex-soldier to another, he had thought of looking out a regimental tie. It would have been the first time he had worn one since resigning his commission. He had nearly destroyed them on that occasion, and school and university ties, too. Destroy the past. No, that was impossible, but he could have destroyed such outward signs of the past. He had not had sufficient motive.

"You look beautiful," she exclaimed. *"Sehr schön."* She stayed defiantly in the familiar case, smiling deeply at him, as if deciding for herself on the instant, and seeking now to persuade him, that the Kerr/Gibson relationship was to be of the closest. And of course with Benjie, too. She glanced over her shoulder, then lowered her eyes. She was like his mother. Not as slim, not as pretty – more, not as beautiful, for that his mother had been – but with the same open-hearted warmth of personality, the same innate trust in people, talking a little too much the other night, as his mother might have done, to hide her thoughts and desires until the moment came to release them. His heart went out to

41

Benjie who had kept this warmth and trust alive in her. He would not think again of his father this evening.

"Benjie is out seeing to the animals," she said. And whatever perplexed thoughts there were between them were set aside as she ushered him into the living room. There was a Christmas tree in the corner, a yule log in the hearth, and a thoroughly out-of-date cocktail shaker standing on a side table beaded with moisture beside three slim pale green glasses.

Awkwardly Tom placed his packages under the tree, without looking at the other gifts already there. There were not many, and again he wondered about Kerr offspring. A few moments later Benjie came in. He filled the room, bigger than before, dressed in a Harris tweed suit which set off not only his bulk but the power in his body. With speed and ease he moved across to the little table and the shaker.

"Ye'll take a cocktail, Tom?"

A rum and orange drink, very cold, to contrast with the warmth of the room and the faint scent of ash and birch logs, and the dank mild weather outside. Neither Benjie nor Heilke asked about Tom's family, and he made no mention of theirs. It was an unspoken pact that they should dine together on this family evening as if they were a family. It seemed to Tom quite natural then. The house, the room, and the Kerrs. The smells of cooking leaked under doors and along the passage to compete with the woodsmoke and to win. He found himself in a state of wellbeing bordering on euphoria, listening to Heilke talking about a smallholder's Christmas work. The minutiae of rural life flowed round him. He listened, guessing they rarely found people to talk to about such things. He nodded, laughed, expressed incredulity, mirth and contentment.

After an excellent traditional English Christmas meal, they settled back in the living room. In his chair beside the fire, Benjie immediately raised the subject of the gang that threatened the hare of the county. "There's precedents in history for poaching gangs," he said. "But circumstances were different."

Tom grunted non-committally. Now he wanted to find out more about the Kerrs, talk to Heilke and determine how much she knew about her husband's clandestine activities. History was not the way ahead. But Benjie was on to a subject he relished. Tom relaxed, looking at the woman opposite him, picturing her at his age, at 32 instead of 60 or thereabouts. Heilke was already mending a cushion cover. Always the necessity to have busy hands. His mother had been the same, to the irritation of his father.

"After Waterloo the country was in an economic mess", Benjie lectured. "The year after the battle the government tightened the game laws. Any person found armed at night and trespassing in search of game was liable to a sentence of up to seven years' transportation. The rural population was bitter. The country had just won a war, but ordinary people had gained – what? If they were employed they couldn't earn enough to feed and clothe themselves and their families let alone buy fuel to heat and cook. And if they were unemployed? The poor laws? The workhouse?"

"They were certainly difficult times." Tom spoke mildly. He glanced at Heilke who continued calmly to mend her cushion. She must know the score, that Benjie was a zealot.

And Benjie continued to hold forth. "The landowner resorted to spring guns. No one knows how many poachers died or were maimed. Soon enough the trap guns were turned round and sprung by the gamekeepers. No one knows how many of them died or were maimed. Then the gangs were formed. Safety in numbers. At first they just provided food for their undernourished children. When roughneck elements joined it became more of a business, involving all manner of people. For no one could sell game without a willing dealer. And the dealer had to have a network of people to whom he could then sell, with no questions asked."

"All very different from today's situation," said Tom shortly.

"How so?" Benjie was sharp, enjoying himself. Heilke smiled at both men and continued mending her cushion.

"For the simple reason that there's no starvation. Most people can earn themselves a full belly and much else besides. And the unemployed draw benefits. So anyone who poaches game on land owned by another can't justify his action by pleading dire poverty."

"Unemployment benefit? Have you tried to live on it? Or been self-employed in a recession?"

Tom knew where the argument was leading. He wondered at himself as what Benjie called a lackey of the landowning classes. He thought of himself on those Devon acres that his father still bestrode. His father. He could not keep him out of his thoughts. No doubt he had his own small poaching problems. But the estate was a working farm with rough shooting, two guns and a couple of dogs, taking their sport along the hedgerows, up the edge of the seawind-blasted woodland. His father was a retired soldier with a fine indexed pension, and past the age to be bothered with all the work of the estate. A prime case for bringing in the son to help, one would suppose. Listening to Benjie, he wondered whether his father had remembered him this Christmas. So far there had been nothing. He hoped the hampers had arrived in time.

"Even so," said Tom. "The game belongs to the owner of the land."

"In man-made laws – made by landowners – yes. In nature's law, no."

"Come off it, Benjie." It was the first time he had used his first name. "You don't really believe that claptrap?"

"Claptrap? What is claptrap?" asked Heilke with mock surprise.

"Is it claptrap to say that the wild animals belong to all the indigenous inhabitants of a place, those that spend their lives working the soil, in intimate contact with the sticks and stones of their own countryside?"

"I understand but can't agree," said Tom. "If you acknowledge that the game is free – belongs to no one – and that local people have a right to it for the pot –" Benjie was nodding his head as Tom continued, "– then you must allow anyone to come and take game, no matter for their own consumption or for sale."

"No, no. Never. We who work the land, live the village life and are part of the small community. The game belongs equally to us as to the owner of the land. It is only we who have a right to take for the pot."

Tom shook his head. "It's a minefield," he said. He recounted the story of Ernie Crawshaw, and of the old man and his grandson after partridge. They had been from villages four miles away. Were they local? Benjie twisted in his chair, denying vehemently that those were local. He argued that they had no right on others' territory. And besides, the partridge would have gone for sale, however the old man protested that he had wanted to teach his grandson a country art. As for Ernie Crawshaw, he thought he was out regularly enough to feed a family of 10 with game at every meal.

"I let them go," said Tom.

"Aye, I heard." Tom saw that Benjie was suddenly very tired, physically spent, having made his points but unable to sustain the pace. He had the unworthy thought that Benjie had been out after game on his patch, but recalled the geese, guineafowl and quail they had killed and prepared, the vegetables gathered, washed and trimmed, the deliveries to their markets. They had both evidently worked long hours. But Tom had to explain why he had acted as he had with the poachers.

"I'm a gamekeeper – that's my job and duty. I also have a fellow feeling for the local people, those to whom the spirit and essence of the countryside belong even if they may not happen to own any of it. They're not much considered in high-tech Britain." He paused, directing himself now equally to Heilke as to Benjie. "That's one of the reasons I let them go, and to warn other locals that I'm a force to be reckoned with. I'll catch any local that comes on my patch. Only I won't be so lenient in future. As for gangs out for money –" Tom was alarmed to see Benjie's face. He looked lost and bewildered, incapable, as if Tom had fought and battered him, bested him, and left him without belief in himself. He stopped talking.

"*Na, schluss,*" said Heilke solicitously. "It's time we had our presents."

Benjie rose from his chair, went to the tree and fumbled beneath it. He moved like an old man, far older than Tom could have imagined, remembering him out on the shoot, tough, alert and in total command of himself. He was sorry he had spoken out. He had somehow taken advantage of Benjie, although he could not see how. They gave him a game cookery book and a thick green sweater in pure wool. Heilke was rapturous about the print of Düsseldorf and Benjie demonstrably pleased with his book.

On the doorstep they wished each other a merry Christmas. Tom kissed Heilke three times on alternate cheeks, shook Benjie's hand giving as strong a clasp as his host, who seemed recovered. It was drizzling as Tom drove back to his cottage. He had learned nothing of the Kerr family and supposed that if children had existed they would certainly have been mentioned. But he had found out that Benjie was vulnerable, how and why he did not yet know. And, whether he was a poacher or no, Tom Gibson had been cut himself to see such discomfiture.

5. FIRST BLOODING

Wind had chased away the muggy Christmas damp. The air was crystal-cold, coming across the North Sea from the Arctic, bringing a sky of the palest blue and the sun. There were Boxing Day shoots on all sides. Tom had been asked by the friendly gamekeeper to act as a picker-up. He had hesitated. Schiller, already answering to his new name, would have benefited from the experience. But he had reluctantly declined. The greyhound gang would be looking for an estate where there was no shoot, with a good chance of finding the gamekeeper absent. They might even have local information. The Red Lion landlord's tricky face came immediately to mind, without, as he knew, a shred of evidence. All available men and dogs would be out on Boxing Day.

Tom telephoned the police who told him to contact the rural crime patrol if he should spot a van or see the gang. He was not to tackle them himself. They were rough customers, usually five or six together.

Now he and Schiller were moving slowly and quietly just inside the edge of the big wood. While the wood was large enough to give any poachers after pheasant a big area to work in, it also gave the gamekeeper good cover from which he could observe the central skein of pastures and neglected arable fields at the heart of the farm. He stationed himself at the southern end of the wood. The sound of gunfire had died down. The drive was over and they would be beating the next. For a moment he had a quite sharp desire to be among other people with a common purpose. All together on a cold but bracing Boxing Day, after the excesses of the previous day. He himself had not indulged at all. Christmas Day had been spent by Tom Gibson training his dog, calling in to talk to a newly arrived couple employed at the big house. They were from Lancashire and as temporarily lost as he had been in the strange countryside. He had cooked a meal in the evening, listened to Bach's Christmas Oratorio on Radio 3, and had rolled into bed, knowing with certainty, and acknowledging for the first time, that he was lonely.

Now, waiting in the wood with Schiller, hardly more than a puppy, impatient and questing, pacing round him, he thought about Benjie. He wanted to believe he was wrong about the poaching. Heilke was without doubt confused in his mind with his mother, and yet he remembered his first shocked sight of her mouth, and the pale tops of her breasts.

Schiller growled. He was facing one of the meadows. Tom touched his head and he fell silent. The gamekeeper climbed into a young ash tree. He could see the entire pasture, and over the hedge glimpsed the far side of the next meadow. Beyond was the green lane, screened by a tangle of thorn trees. Nothing moved, the pastures were both empty. He looked down at the dog, looked up again, and the far pasture had two greyhounds in it. A moment later three men broke through the hedge. He noted with relief that they carried no guns, although all held cudgels.

Tom slipped down the tree. Already his soldier's mind was assessing the possibilities consistent with the aim of collecting information. The nearest telephone was in his cottage. He could be there, running, within 15 minutes.

"Schiller," he said, *"sei ruhig, gehorsam und schweigsam* – be calm, obedient and silent." There must be no yelping, no straying from his heels. "Heel now," he said, and ran to the far hedge. Schiller followed at his heels as commanded, and stopped immediately behind him in the shelter of the hedge. Tom was now 300 yards from the green lane. He slipped through the hedge so as to have the poachers and their dogs one and a half fields and two hedges away. Meanwhile the men would have drawn the field he had seen them in. They would be moving in to the next pasture. Would they have left a man with their van? One man he could deal with if need be. Fifty paces from the thick hedge lining the green lane he stopped by a hedgerow ash and put his 12-bore into a recess formed by exposed roots. He wished he had a stick. He moved up towards the green lane, Schiller dutifully at his heels. He thanked Sergeant Siddall at his prep school who had taught him to box, and a public school which had given him opportunity to hone his talents. By the time he had reached the army, boxing was not considered a proper sport any more – the authorities too worried about damage to precious and increasingly scarce fighting material. In a tight situation he would try and remember the unarmed combat he had been taught years before.

By the green lane Tom halted and listened. Schiller was nervous, glancing constantly at his master, the occasional feeble movement of his tail. Tom saw himself at 15 or 16 in the dog, already big and fit but unmuscled mentally. He eased himself part-way through a narrow gap. Up the lane about 300 yards were two vans facing away from him, a white and a dark blue. Halfway through the hedge as he was, he stopped to think. Schiller was pushing against him, wanting to come through. There were two alternatives. He could make a detour to the telephone in his cottage. The rural crime patrol might just be able to come up with the poachers before they left. Or he could saunter up the lane, note the van numbers and anything unusual and walk until he was out of sight. His route to the telephone was then shorter and quicker. There was a strong chance that anyone with the vans would know him for a gamekeeper. He was dressed like one and had a labrador with him.

Tom pushed through the hedge into the lane and the dog followed with a rush. In a moment they were walking together towards the vans, on a public right-of-way, on Boxing Day, a public holiday. The guns on the neighbouring estates were silent now, and Tom knew it was midday. The sportsmen would be huddled convivially round hot food, with the usual friendly banter, becoming more laconic and terse down the social scale. It was midday, when any sane member of the community not on a shoot would be at home in the heart of a family or in the extended family of a pub. Only a benighted gamekeeper would be walking a dog at lunchtime on Boxing Day – a 'keeper with a ridiculous outsized sense of duty. He pushed the thought aside as one Benjie or Hilary might voice.

He could read the number of the white van. He memorised it, moved to the right up against the hedge to give it a wide berth. The blue van was older and he had both the numbers and a clear description of them in his mind. There seemed to be no one around. Suddenly Tom recalled his days as a subaltern, heading his platoon down some nameless Belfast street. Snipers and bombers. Well, his platoon had known the score. All knew that the advantage was always with the other side. He wished he had the wise and battle-hardy Sergeant Penfold with him now. Penfold from his own North Devon countryside. And Private Richards, the Cornishman from Camborne who had strayed into Devon when he enlisted. Those two had stayed in his mind. Richards had been a good soldier and had died without more than a grunt of surprise. Tom remembered his own rage and sorrow. Perhaps that had been when he had finally known that he was not like his father and the long and distinguished line of soldierly Gibsons.

In the green lane, his hands dangling at his sides, his eyes were everywhere as he closed with the vans. The cab of the white one was empty. The back of the blue van was not properly closed. Its cab was also empty. He was almost past it when he heard a clang and thuds of bodies leaping to the ground. He kept walking slowly. Schiller was so close that he butted his muzzle into Tom's leg.

There were three men, and they had a lurcher with them, heavy-jawed and tall, more wolfhound and pastoral dog than greyhound. The men were bearded, two of them heavy-jawed as well, the third a small delicate man in his 30s with dark hair and a pale unattractive face. Tom continued walking slowly. He talked to Schiller under his breath, telling him to run for his life if there was action. The lurcher would gobble him up. Now he was kicking himself for putting the dog at risk.

Then Schiller halted, turned round and growled, a long warning note, trilling in his throat. His hackles rose. Tom came round fast. One of the big men was almost on him, a fist raised.

"I hate gamekeepers," said the man. His beard was black, his accent from Birmingham. "So does my dog." He threw a right, a haymaker. Tom immediately felt safer. He ducked it, jabbed with his right to the face, sent a heavy left to the solar plexis. As the man collapsed he gave him a right hook to the jaw. Schiller and the lurcher were already snarling at each other, making little runs. Tom had a moment to see that the lurcher was afraid, that Schiller was not, before the second big man came at him with the small one close behind. Both had cudgels. He wished he could remember the unarmed combat, but there were no knowledgeable reflexes from brain to body.

Schiller and the lurcher were tumbling out in the middle of the lane. The labrador was fighting like a bull terrier, had clamped his teeth into the lurcher's ear and would not let go. The lurcher was squealing. The big man advanced cautiously, the cudgel out in front of him. He was unsure of himself and glanced momentarily at his mate sprawled in the grass. Tom leapt at the man, grabbing his wrist as he raised the stick. He knee'd him in the groin, flung him groaning aside, and turned in time to receive the force of the small man's cudgel, a blow mistimed that struck him on the side of the head and glanced off his left shoulder. With his right hand he caught his attacker a prime smack on the head which sent him into the hedge. Tom fell to one knee. He was back at school when he had fought the school's captain of boxing, his own weight and a year older. A classical scholar and a fair-minded prefect. It had been his only defeat in the ring and an honourable one that had gained him one friend and some admirers. Schiller brought him back to the present. The lurcher had disappeared, and the labrador paced up and down between the men and Tom. He was the embodiment of cool rage, his teeth bared, his flank streaked with blood. All looked shocked and uncertain.

"Beat it, gamekeeper," said the small man.

"Thank you. Don't come back," Tom managed to say. He walked on up the green lane, the labrador with him turning round and round as if he would dizzy himself, watching the three until a bend in the lane hid them from view.

A patrol car reached the green lane within an hour but found the poachers gone. Tom drove himself to the hospital in the town, but not before he had collected his gun from the hedgerow ash. He needed six stitches in a cut on the side of his head. Schiller was unhurt. The blood on him had been none of his own. Tom saw him in a different light. This floppy puppy of yesterday, inexperienced and indecisive, had turned into a cautiously mature dog. His chest seemed deeper, and muscles that Tom had not noticed before rippled under the black coat.

Although Tom said nothing the word spread that there had been poachers about. The neighbouring gamekeeper rang that evening and discussed across-boundary cooperation. When Hilary came back the following evening there was a message from her cleaning woman to say that Tom had been in a fight with poachers. The Kerrs heard the news from Kenny, the young man who worked for them. Benjie and Hilary arrived at the gamekeeper's cottage within minutes of each other.

Hilary came first. She asked calmly what had happened, and listened to the few clipped sentences Tom allowed her. "The dog was wonderful. A cool fighter, full of courage," he concluded.

Benjie Kerr knocked and entered. Hilary, who had been about to ask whether what Tom was doing was worth this kind of episode, stepped with some dismay back out of the lamplight into the shadows and sat down. Both men were big. They stood in the centre by the worn sofa. The stove bubbled and spat. Benjie dominated the room, shrugging out of heavy clothing, turning briefly to give her a nod.

"I know of you and am glad to meet you," he said to her, then glared at Tom. "What happened?" he asked.

Tom started on the same clipped sentences, but Benjie stopped him.

"All of it," he said, sounding like a senior officer insisting on the full story of a subaltern's night out of puerile pranks. Tom told it all and Benjie listened intently. Hilary watched them, suddenly despairing that she would ever come close to a man like these two – intensely masculine, used to being among men, and about men's work, to the exclusion of women. She saw that Tom needed to tell this elderly Scot why he had acted as he had, risking himself and the dog. He seemed to want reassurance that he had taken the correct action to gain information. And he wanted it from this beetle-browed set-faced man, who the village regarded with respect and some apprehension, and only occasional affection. And there was affection in Tom's voice as he finished his story.

"Did I do right, Major Kerr?" he asked.

Benjie was silent for several moments. He shifted his gaze to the stove. "What rank were you?" he asked.

"Captain, Parachute Regiment, commissioned into the Devon and Dorsets."

"You did well, Captain Gibson. Although your information is inconclusive."

"The small man. The police think they know him."

Benjie nodded. "Perhaps. I wish I'd been there. We could have managed them together. Brought them to the police station in one of their own vans, and their mates after hare none the wiser." Benjie's eyes were shining, his hands and arms making small fighting movements, his head ducking and jinking. Then the light went from his eyes and Hilary saw him slump, shift his weight from one leg to the other as if a hip worried him, as if he felt 40 years older this instant than he had a few seconds before. Tom also noted the change, and was again puzzled by the impression of vulnerability.

Hilary came forward out of the shadows, reasserting herself as a person of substance.

"Mr Kerr, how do you stand – as a countryman – with all these poachers after other people's game?"

Benjie reared up. For the first time Tom saw clearly and definitely that Hilary was intelligent, good-looking and desirable. Very desirable to him. And she had this intriguing potential for companionship.

"I'm flat against poaching for money," Benjie replied.

"And if these poachers were out for the sport?"

Benjie made a derisory noise. "Sport incidentally, maybe. But hare for sale, dozens of them during a day."

51

"And they were outsiders, I suppose?" Hilary asked.

"They certainly weren't any of ours." Benjie paused. "Tom here, he knows my views. We've talked it out. There's all the difference between taking game for the pot and making money out of it. And there's the same difference between people from outside coming on to a patch and the locals. And by locals I mean those who live and work a few miles roundabout."

Tom gave them each a glass of red wine, and wondered whether his guests would find anything else to talk about. There was a small silence as they sat round the stove.

"You both run tough and competitive businesses," said Tom.

"What kind of business are you in?" Benjie asked, interested. "Not receiving stolen game, I'll be bound."

Hilary laughed and relaxed. She told them she was marketing director of a company manufacturing electrical switchgear. Their customers were all over Europe. She was no engineer but had learned enough to talk sensibly. She had a mathematics and physics degree from Oxford and an MBA. She had staff who were electrical engineers. Besides, marketing was her strength, and she supposed that she could market anything given the facts about the product and its likely markets.

Benjie told her about his marketing problems. He had a small, seemingly permanent and faithful clientele which appreciated vegetables and poultry raised without chemical products and inorganic fertilisers. He admitted he was not entirely organic, but he was as near so as made little difference. His smallholding was run like one of the old London market gardens – the vegetables, fruit and livestock in a perpetual cycle of feed and manure. His clients were mostly well-to-do. Many came to him, but he had a round, and some clients in town. His problem was to maintain supplies. He did not mention the long hours and the modest return on labour, but he indicated that he knew something of the rural deprivation of the past, and put up the possibility that there were still families throughout Britain glorying in the unremitting work of animals and fields, independent and proud, who received what any industrial worker would regard as a pittance for their dedicated labour. Most would continue to do the same work, offered a change. What was vital was to be independent, suffer as one might from economic ups and downs. His forebears had known some economic problems. His father had been a miner and his grandfather a smallholder.

Hilary asked questions, her interest in the marketing obvious. Did he perhaps have too many lines? Perhaps he could concentrate on only a few, widen his outlets for these, increase production. How many acres did he have? Well, six acres was large enough for an intensive production unit of some kind, surely?

Benjie thought about it. Intensive was a word which for him implied crowded houses, wormicides, pesticides, hormones and the like. He produced old-fashioned food, and this meant lower yields and lower inputs – all except for labour, that was. There was also an element of great boredom in modern farming systems, with concentration on few crops or on dairying, pigs or poultry, and rarely a mixture. What kind of a working year did this intensification give? In the old days the variety of jobs on a proper mixed farm ensured that no one was bored. It had been the time of the multi-skilled farm worker. Therein lay the key to a contented rural life – a multiplicity of jobs. And he wanted to see more people directly employed in the countryside, and more village people working in rural industries close by, so that the villages were again full of real villagers.

"More people to qualify under your ruling to take game for the pot," said Hilary. "You'd be stumbling over each other out on Gailsford's estate." They all laughed.

Tom allowed himself to be driven to Hilary's cottage. Hilary would cook a convenience-food meal. She ate them most of the time. She gave Tom the orange squash he asked for, set him down in front of the gas fire in her sitting room, and went into the kitchen. He was tired and his shoulder and head ached again. He had had little exercise, kept close to the cottage, taking medicines. He looked round him. Hilary had furnished the room chintzily and comfortably. There were shelves of books on one side of the fireplace and engravings on the walls, of country scenes – moons, poppies, farmgates and lone trees in mist. They gave the impression that they had been bought at the same time from a provincial town's art shop.

On the other side of the fireplace was a music centre. Tom went for the music first. He found a mixture of pop, jazz and light classics. But she did have some Tchaikowsky and Rachmaninoff, and Puccini's La Bohème. Hilary's books showed her interest in physics, but also a taste for biography and history. He found Thomas Pakenham's exposé of the

British handling of the Boer war and took it down, wondering how she could have bought a relatively specialist book. In the flyleaf was a dedication – 'To darling Hilary, with love, Bobby Maxwell-Dalgliesh'. Had he been a soldier, interesting a girl he might marry in the history of his calling? But was Hilary pliable and acquiescent enough to subordinate her own personality and preferences to her husband's? If it were all worth it to provide sound middle-class achievement then she would, he thought. She was strong-minded, and she would be a tireless worker to those ends.

He recalled the first time he had met Hilary. He had just arrived from the south in an unseasonable early October fog. All the way up on the motorway there had been patches, and two small concertina accidents involving several vehicles. In his old Honda Acclaim, since sold, he had hugged the slow lane, marvelling at the idiocy of drivers in lorries and cars, pounding and streaking past him. Much later when he turned off the A road on to a minor one leading into deeper countryside and the village, there had been thick fog lying along the valley bottoms. In one he had found a large 'executive' Vauxhall planted in a ditch with Hilary standing by, angry at herself for missing a bend. There had been no damage to the company car or its driver, and the Honda and a towrope had brought it out. The next Saturday they had met in the village shop, when he had been enigmatic and had made no approach to her. He had declined a cup of coffee, unsure at the time how the different sorts of people in his new life would react to him, and how he would and should to them.

Hilary called him to the dining room, offered him a glass of red wine with the meal, which he declined.

"You read biography mostly, I see," he said.

"And economics. The financial papers are prescribed reading. But I also watch plenty of television. It relaxes me." She seemed intent on emphasising the differences in their interest, eating nervously, drinking a glass of the wine.

"How was your Christmas?" He tried to picture what the holiday might have been like.

"The usual family affair. A neighbourly party or two. A turkey for lunch on Christmas Day. We 'phoned America." She seemed to imitate his own clipped sentences earlier in the evening.

"Was it friendly but dull? Expected? Did you need to think? Were there squabbles? You see –" he spoke without emphasis, "– I don't know what the usual family affair is. The only happy Christmasses I had were with my mother when my father was away. Two of them."

Thinking about one of those Christmasses Tom mentioned La Bohème. He would like to play Hilary's recording one day. The opera had been a favourite of his youth ever since his mother had taken him to it in Bristol during the Christmas holidays. He had fallen deeply in love with a waif-like, dark-haired Mimi and been unable to stifle his tears at Rudolpho's last terrible cry as she had died in his arms. Now here he was with a girl who was no Mimi, no frail maiden to be cossetted and protected. But one who certainly lacked something in her life, as he knew he did himself. They finished the meal talking about opera in general and how so many of the grand operas ended in tragedy.

"Some people guide themselves inevitably towards that kind of an end," Tom said. "I used to think I was one of them. I lost my adored mother early. I was afraid of my father who was indifferent to my mother, and who was glad when she died. My father never showed me the smallest sign of affection, let alone love." He paused. "Sorry to burden you with this. But there's a reason for telling you which I hope you won't spurn."

Previously a little lacklustre and sleepy, Hilary was wide awake. "Go on, I suspect that I shall spurn nothing." She knew now that she had been waiting for this moment. Ever since she had sensed the troubled spirit, seen the books and the music in the gamekeeper's cottage, noted the moments of command and independent mien. From the first she had been intrigued. Now she was much further down the road to wanting to know very much more, and to feel his lips on hers. He was, after all, quite good-looking with his blond hair and blue eyes, and more so now that he had begun to smile and to laugh a little.

He was not smiling at this moment. He was in danger of being earnest. "You've been patient with me. If I read aright, you've put forward the possibility of a closer relationship. You've had to do all the running, and had precious little help or friendliness from me. Well, that wasn't for want of wanting more. I've held back because I believed I didn't bring much joy and light into relationships – that I should better live my life without much human contact."

"Like a tragic hero in an opera?"

Tom smiled. "Well, maybe. Anyway, I'd like to explore that closer relationship. You're stunning to look at and most desirable to me. You're also the right height."

Hilary laughed. "You forgot my mind," she said, and leaned across and kissed him on the mouth, lightly. "You can help me clear away."

Hilary did not ask him what had caused this revelation. She was just glad that it had happened. She took him back to his cottage. He was still evidently in pain from his injuries. They kissed each other more deeply in the car, and she soon disengaged herself. She felt wise enough to walk towards Tom Gibson. The relationship could safely be left to mature at that pace.

6. JUST TRESPASSING

Schiller pointed. Tom was amazed at the dog. He already retrieved in a stumbling, puppyish way, as if it was still a game. He had fought like a bull terrier. And now he froze and pointed at something in the tufty long grass of an ungrazed meadow which was criss-crossed with hare runs. Tom now believed he had been lucky, for Schiller had been the odd puppy in a conforming litter. Not a runt exactly but marked down and therefore much cheaper.

A hare lay in its run caught in a snare, its neck cleanly broken. The snare had been expertly laid, at exactly the right height. A professional poaching job. He called the dog and moved away to the hedge, turned and surveyed the far hedges. He walked away down the hedge as if losing interest in the meadow until he came to a gap through which he pushed himself into the next field. He retraced his steps until he was opposite the dead hare, made sure of a line of sight through the hedge and called Schiller to him. He told him to sit, suggested he emulate him, all eyes and ears, interpreting the sounds roundabout.

It was now half-an-hour after a late December dawn. Pigeon began to be busy, flying off to crops of winter cabbage and kale on neighbouring farms. They were in flights of 40 to 50, and would need hard work on the gamekeeper's part to cut down in numbers. The sky lightened, and from the east and the sea marshes eight miles away came skeins of pink-footed geese. Although they were high in the sky Tom could hear their chatty honking clearly. He waited an hour, having to calm the restive dog. It grew colder and a north-east wind got up. No one came for the hare. There was no one that he or Schiller could detect anywhere within hundreds of yards of them. He pictured Benjie pacing the length of hedgerows, sliding silently into a windbreak, slipping through the 50-acre wood, and coming at last to the series of linked pastures.

What had stopped Benjie collecting his hare? Tom went over the birds and animals he had seen during his vigil. Flights of redwing and fieldfare had been after hawthorn berries in the hedgerow. They had flown out into the pasture, not suddenly but rather as a leisurely change of plan. Brambling had come along the hedge and had been shy but not rushed. Robin and hedge sparrow had taken little notice of him. Field rats out foraging had retreated back the way they had come. Anyone watching intently without being able to see the gamekeeper and his dog would have been clever to have known for certain that danger lurked there. His own green clothes blended well enough, but Schiller's black coat and occasional impatient movements could have proved the hazard. Tom waited another half-an-hour until he could no longer control the dog. He left the hare in its snare and went back to his cottage to leave Schiller. He returned immediately, found the hare and snare gone, and two peeled hazel sticks carefully laid, crossed, where the hare had been. A stone had been placed on them to keep them from blowing away.

On New Year's Eve Tom Gibson drove Hilary up to one of the coastal resorts in her VW beetle. His only transport now was the estate's Land Rover. They dined in a three-star hotel and danced with a crowd of middle-aged and elderly people – quicksteps, foxtrots and waltzes. Neither danced well but both had natural rhythm and, by dint of copying those more expert round them, enjoyed the music and the people they were with. They were beginning to be single-minded about each other's physical presence, to acquire that self-contained inner glow that two people have who are exploring the possibility of falling in love without having yet made the ultimate physical contact. The glow was the elation of anticipation. There was time enough ahead. The new start-afresh year stretched ahead as they joined hands and sang Auld Lang Syne with jovial strangers. They were aware that they were different. Most people around them were nearing the end of their sexual experiences, their active endeavouring lives. Certainly nothing in their future could match the precious moment that comes to two people who acknowledge to themselves separately that they have never been truly in love before, and that this deep, slow and measured movement towards each other must mean the ultimate experience for them. Infatuations followed soon by wary battles and disappointments were forgotten. Dancing close, dancing the old year away and the new year in, their unspoken revelation held them surprised and hardly believing their senses and their good luck.

On the way back to the village they talked round several topics. Hilary expected Tom to speak first. She was old-fashioned enough to believe that was the correct procedure. She was clear-headed enough to know that Tom was not a man to be easily swayed or convinced, not quixotically romantic. He would be slow to kindle and, she hoped, would burn with a steady flame for a lifetime. Amid all the easy sex of the business world and the modern mores of 'shacking up', she had been lost and apprehensive. There had been several who had wanted such a relationship. The only man who had asked her to marry him, a dedicated and worthy young army officer, had woken nothing in her save a desire to flee and a guilty feeling of her own unworthiness. She put aside for the moment this new man's extraordinary means of earning a poor living. She saw confrontation ahead there. After all, there were certain standards to be upheld, that she wanted to uphold.

Tom did not speak, and Hilary relaxed, deeply happy still. At Tom's cottage they kissed in the car and she was deliciously stirred. Tom was responsive but it was he who broke it off.

"I must be up early. New Year's Day. Another holiday when poachers could be out and about." It was only then that he told her about the snared hare and the crossed sticks.

"Confront him," she said.

"I must catch him on the job. I've no proof at all." Then he switched subjects. "I think you and I are an ill-assorted pair, but I've loved every minute of the evening. I hope you've enjoyed it – and thanks for the car."

Hilary was momentarily disappointed at the lack of intimacy. But he seemed only to be formalising their relationship so far. She squeezed his hand. "Less ill-assorted than you may think."

"When shall I see you again?"

"Invite me to dinner next Saturday," she said.

"I have a shoot then. Make it Sunday."

She could not. She was travelling to Germany for a week's work. They agreed to dinner the following Saturday in Tom's cottage.

At the third shoot there were only five guns, and two of the beginners were back, subdued and nervous. Their experiences during the season had chastened them. The Northamptonshire food manufacturer was also there. Tom liked the dapper man, and wondered what he really thought of Gailsford apart from his business acumen. Tom could see no sign that Gailsford, fresh from his Caribbean Christmas, had found any experiences chastening. He had no greetings for the servants of the shoot, and had nothing to say when the first drive produced four flushes of good birds, many of them 'rocketers', most of which flew clear away.

Benjie Kerr was again a picker-up, cocking a questioning eye at Tom at some crass, prickly statement from Gailsford. Tom stood behind the owner as loader and picker-up, with an excited, trembling and unsure Schiller beside him. Bird after bird escaped over Gailsford, and then at the end of the drive he winged a cock. It tumbled out of the sky, picked itself up a few yards behind the guns and ran into a weedy fallow. Tom sent the dog after it, and they turned and watched Schiller flush it out of a thicket of tall thistles, pounce on it and bring it, a heavy bird, changing his grip twice before he presented it to Tom. The gamekeeper sensed that, against all logic, the owner of the land and the man who had brought down the cock expected the dog to have brought it to him.

"Where to, now?" Gailsford snapped.

"It's the wild birds that give the best sport, eh, Charles," said the dapper man, whose bag exceeded those of the other four guns together. "I think you'll be glad some of them got away today. You'll need a good breeding nucleus. Let's hope for a fine warm summer so that they breed well and thrive. I expect Gibson will take care of the vermin."

"We'll rear as well," said Gailsford. "You see to it, Gibson. Next year I want this estate smothered in birds. I want drives to produce five times what we've had today."

"Very good." Tom was taciturn. "We'll do our best."

"You guarantee it, Gibson," said the landowner, meaning every word, but laughing, turning it into a joke as he caught the cynical amused gaze of the dapper man and the stony stare of Benjamin Kerr, leaning insolently on his ash plant.

Gailsford forgot his manners and thanked no one at all for their part in the day's sport. That evening he telephoned Tom to tell him that he did not want 'that old Scots ape' on his land again. And he wanted a final shoot in the last week of January. Tom did not argue then, but the next day he went and saw 'the master' in his study. Mrs Gailsford, small and blond, was in the room and stayed as Tom put his case for leaving the stock, thin as it was, to regenerate. To Gailsford's order for rearing great quantities of birds, he outlined the costs of housing, heating, and buying in day-old chicks.

With ill grace Charles Gailsford conceded that there would be no fourth shoot this year. "But next year I want eight. There are shoots in the south which manage 16 in a season. I'm being reasonable."

Tom did not tell him that the estates where 16 days' shooting were held – and even up to 20 in Hampshire – were bigger by far and had several 'keepers. "We'll try for eight next year," he said, and left, nodding to Mrs Gailsford, who seemed interested in her husband's 'keeper.

Fog and cold descended on the eastern half of Britain. Tom worked with axe, hedging sickle and billhook to recreate sunny yet sheltered release areas in the woods. He took sandwiches and a thermos of tea and was away all day until darkness fell. On the fifth day the fog went, and with scarcely a pause a low front from the north-west brought several inches of snow which curtailed his woodsman's activities. The snow gave him a chance to check on the wildlife of the estate. Ringed as the Gailsford property was by big arable farms, there was little likelihood of deer. He found no track of them. Stoat, weasel and rat were in abundance. He already knew about the crows, magpies and jackdaws, and the rook colony. He found track of several dogs out hunting, most of them large animals. There were hare tracks everywhere in the open country. On land nearest the village a cat had been marauding. Pheasant tracks lay along the edges of woods and plantations, with partridge in the fields themselves, and coot and moorhen near the old marl pits which held water. Several of the pits on lighter soil were infested with rabbits. On his first long foray in the snow he found no tracks of man except his own.

No fresh snow fell. The wind shifted to the east and brought a depth of cold which burnt all the evergreen trees and shrubs in the village gardens. He shopped in the town, determined to make a good meal for Hilary on Saturday. The idea of that evening warmed him throughout his days out in the fog and snow. He hoped there would be no hold-ups for her on her way back from Germany. He was set back by the thought of her in Frankfurt or Essen being fêted by German businessmen, by the twinges of jealousy that came to him often. He went to bed each night tired by 12 or 14 hours on the go.

He rose early on the Saturday. The wind had abated, but the outside thermometer registered minus three degrees Celsius. There was no good reason for him to do a round of the estate. Even gamekeepers had time off. Even poachers did not choose the bleakest of January days to go after something for the pot. But Schiller had had the barest of exercise for a young, fit dog. He took the dog and his 12-bore, thinking of starting his vermin control with the odd crow. The snow had frozen, was crunchy underfoot. The tracks of birds and animals, where the wind had not scuffed them, were clear and crystalline. He made his way on to the green lane, then crossed into the pastures, moving slowly along a hedge where there were several dead elms and stag-headed oaks. The pigeon clattered out of the trees, telling anyone who was interested that some disturbance, going at a certain pace, was travelling along the hedge. He let the birds go. Most of the shots would have been chancy. There would be time enough in the early months of the year to build hides near their roosting places and to organise shoots.

At the end of the hedge he could either go into the 50-acre wood or down a broad windbreak. Tom played a game with himself. Just suppose there was a poacher in the wood. Poachers tended to like woods where there was enough room to manoeuvre. And just suppose that the poacher had noticed the eruption of pigeon from the hedgerow trees, perhaps caught a glimpse of a black-coated dog or a man in green. If the intruder failed to appear in the wood, then he and his dog would have gone down the windbreak. On a hunch – no, it was still just a game – Tom called Schiller softly and loped back along the hedge line but sufficiently far out into dead ground so that no sight of them was possible from the wood. He soon reached the green lane and ran quickly until he was opposite the other end of the big wood. Then he walked across a snow-laden meadow.

A broken-down fence of wooden posts and barbed wire lay at the entrance to the wood. He slipped into the trees with Schiller close behind him. Immediately he found the print of a boot. The edge of the print was sharp, the brittle snow recently crushed. Beyond were more prints and a holly bush where something had brushed against it, exposing the shiny dark leaves. Would Benjie have been so careless? Tom stopped and listened. A faint wind soughed in the canopies of some Scots pines. He heard nothing else. Whatever might have scurried or flown in a recently disturbed winter calm had not yet begun activities again.

Tom hesitated, turned and looked at Schiller, who laid back his ears and gave a cursory thump of his tail before resuming an intense scrutiny of the wood ahead. Skeletal elders, fallen logs, the trunks of oak and ash, and slender saplings of sycamore obscured the view for more than a few yards. Schiller was an embarrassment. He had shown courage and tenacity with the lurcher, and had begun well the long training to be a disciplined and reliable retriever of game. But only begun. Otherwise he was exuberant, flighty, amiable and nowhere set in mature ways. And yet Tom remembered him still and interrogative, showing his master the snared hare. That argued a self-discipline beyond his years. The gamekeeper had no means of detaining the dog, of tying him to a tree. Schiller would howl at such treatment. He had no alternative. Tom leant down and smoothed the dog's head, lifted his ear and spoke quietly.

"Sit, Schiller, sit."

Without looking back he walked very quietly deeper into the wood. He lost the track of boots where there was little snow under dense tree canopies, cast about in vain and decided to continue. He walked so carefully that he did not crack a twig, that his bulk was concealed behind tree trunks. He still did not look round. Schiller seemed to be obeying the last command. The big wood was lozenge-shaped. He was walking the length of it. Nothing stirred as he continued his slow way. Somewhere about the middle, he remembered, there was a planting of yew. That explained the fence, to keep stock away from their poisonous berries. He came to them. There was yew in the woods on the Devon acres, too. He thought how important it was in a winter landscape to have evergreen trees, the yew and pine, the holly and the holm oak.

Just past the yews he froze. Away to his right an animal moved. He waited a minute. Two minutes. The animal yielded first, reassured by the silence, and came across his path 10 yards ahead. A big tabby cat, fur fluffed out against the cold. The gamekeeper waited another minute before moving forward. The wood thinned out, with younger trees and slimmer trunks. Ahead he knew was a bushy glade where a release pen had been. He moved to the left where the tree growth was thicker and would give him more cover. A secretive tree creeper, with its curved beak, ran up a tree trunk ahead. Again Tom stopped and waited. Away in the glade a pair of blackbirds were prospecting for food. They were intent on their own business. He started forward again, hoping they would not take fright. A hedge sparrow flew by, and then blue and great tits. They had accepted him as of no danger to themselves. He went another 100 yards, casting from side to side for boot prints, beginning to believe that his hunch had failed him, when he saw a man's track appear from the right and turn towards the wood's end. Now he was deaf to everything behind him, senses strained to catch the smallest hint of his quarry. He paused every few paces and listened. He heard the church clock strike, and crows cawing away on the wood's edge to his left. He passed a low bank covered with twisted elder and wondered whether it might have had badger setts. Now he could sense the end of the wood. The boot prints continued. He went even slower, checking each tree trunk, every thicket. He also looked up as he approached the wood's end, where open air and sunlight, and lack of competition, had allowed branches to grow out horizontally.

He saw the intruder's boot first, then the edge of a green trench coat. The man was leaning against a beech tree three or four yards in from the wood's edge. Tom laid his 12-bore gently in the snow and moved silently, choosing each step with infinite care. He skirted a tangle of snow-laden brambles, closed with the beech tree. The boot shifted fractionally and the coat moved upwards as if the body inside was affected by cramp. Tom reached out a hand and touched the coat.

"Got you," he said, and stepped back ready for action.

For several seconds Benjie Kerr did not move. Then he sighed, shifted his body round so that he faced the gamekeeper. He lifted his arms, showing that he had no gun, no stick. He looked disappointed, his eyes steadily on Tom. He sighed again and said nothing.

"What are you doing here?" Tom asked irritably, aware that he was losing any ascendancy he might have had a moment ago.

"Just trespassing," replied Benjie. "Out for a stroll away from the crowds."

"What have you done with your gun?"

"I don't have one with me."

"Snares, then. You've snares in your pocket, and a few hazel twigs recently peeled."

Benjie smiled fleetingly.

"The twigs. They are yours, aren't they?" Tom tried to sound aggressive. When Benjie said nothing, Tom roughly told him to turn his pockets out.

Benjie hesitated.

"Look, I don't want to have to take you to the police."

I appreciate that," said Benjie. "But I have no gun, and –." He turned out his pockets methodically. A pruning knife, string, and two handkerchiefs were all he had. He showed Tom that the inside pockets of his trench coat were empty. "I have no snares, no net, no posts, no bag of game, no dog."

"But you're trespassing. You admitted it."

"Out observing nature. Did you know there were badgers in this wood until a few years ago? A visit from the diggers and baiters drove them away."

Tom spoke angrily. "To hell with that. You're on private property without permission."

"I am, I am. And you were good, Tom. You had me fooled. I knew you had your pup with you, saw the pigeon fly out along the hedge. I'd come along the windbreak myself, and thought you'd turn down there. But when pigeon flew in and settled, I had my doubts." Benjie was smiling now. "Your pup should have prevented you from coming at me through the wood. What did you do with him?"

Tom pulled a whistle from his pocket and blew several short blasts.

"You mean he sat for you?" Benjie was admiring. "I'm beginning to think he's no ordinary dog."

Now Tom sighed. The man was incorrigible. He fetched his gun. They heard the sound of Schiller's exuberant passage through the wood, coming fast, not caring about the snow, jumping over logs and bramble patches until he joined the two men. When he saw Benjie he stopped in his tracks. He barely greeted his master, advanced cautiously to sniff at Benjie, resisting his attempt to pat him. Only after Tom had called him to his side and made a fuss of him did the dog, puppy-like, go like a yo-yo between the two men.

Their confrontation ended although unresolved, Benjie and Tom left the wood and walked together to the green lane.

"Stay off my patch, Benjie." Tom spoke mildly. "I don't want to have to book you. But I will if I catch you trespassing again." Then he went on less mildly, an edge of hardness in his voice. "You've been out with a gate net after hare, and you've snared them, too. You've knocked pheasant off their perches, and I don't doubt you've taken partridge, pigeon and rabbit at will. I can't prove it yet. But you know and I know that it's true."

Benjie tipped his hat over his eyes. "Next time I'll creep up on you, Tom. You're good, but I aim to prove I'm better." He walked steadily off down the green lane, and Tom shouted after him.

"It's not a game, you know."

Benjie waved.

7. Holding Game

As soon as Benjie was out of sight, Tom doubled back along the hedge to the 50-acre wood. He picked up Benjie's track in the snow and followed it. He searched for any sign of a hidden gun, game or snares. Old Adams, the gamekeeper in Hampshire, had always reminded Tom that the local poacher was intelligent, silent, and kept his own counsel. He hid his guns and paraphernalia and the game he had taken before going home. No poacher would take his bag direct to his cottage. It was always sensible for a gamekeeper to know where culverts, hollow trees, old badger setts, any old hole in the ground likely to be dry and secluded, were located both on and just off his patch.

Tom found nothing. On the way to his cottage he shot a crow and an incautious magpie. He let a jay go. Jays, said the old hands, were never as black as they were painted. They did not take eggs or young chicks. They warned 'keepers with their chuckling screech when there were interlopers in their woods. He was happy that he had at least begun the big task of vermin control, even if a little early. It was Adams who had warned him that trapping and shooting too early in the season would bring reinfestation from outside. He looked forward to the end of January and the finish of the shooting season for pheasant and partridge. On his way he disturbed several coveys of partridge. The estate was rich in partridge and there had been no shoot to break up the coveys and lessen inbreeding this coming year. He could do little about that until next September. And if Gailsford would not shoot them, he would organise a shoot for the helpers.

The mercury in the outside thermometer stood at minus four degrees Celsius. He fetched more bedding for Schiller, brought logs into the living room, stacked others outside the door. He heated a tin of soup for a late lunch, tried to 'phone Hilary but there was no reply. Normally he would have settled down by the stove, secure in the warmth, read a book and listened to music – German music for preference. He would have been isolated from the world. Before, in Hampshire, that had been enough. Not now.

Long before it was really necessary he began the dinner preparations. He came out of the kitchen, started cleaning the living room, then went searching for a pair of ebony-wood candlesticks. They needed polishing, and he did that, then ran the polish cloth over the battered dining table, and laid two places. About then he wondered at himself. All the time he had busied himself on chores Hilary had been in his mind. Background will assert itself, he thought, as he continued to clear up, hoovering the carpeting. He dusted his Staffordshire pieces. Almost six o'clock. He looked outside to find it was snowing gently again. He prepared Schiller's food and fed him. Then he rang Hilary's number and there was still no reply. He had a bath and changed into a corduroy suit. His father had always insisted on changing for dinner. A black tie affair every night. Standards must be kept up. The effect was vital for morale. He put on a tie, and rang again. This time she answered. She had only just arrived back, had been travelling mightily since early morning. She would be along at eight.

Tom put on one of his happiest records, and Schubert's Trout quintet tinkled and twinkled. What with Hilary almost here, and Benjie and Heilke close, he began to know that he was not quite as alone as he had been in Hampshire. Well, there he had had Adams to talk to, and others, but always about 'keepering matters. He had not found, or had not tried to find anyone to whom he could relate on a more spiritual plane. And even though this included the possibility of sleeping with Hilary, he hoped that spirituality would be part of the act. Body and spirit. He had always hoped, but so far his encounters with women – not very frequent – had been sadly lacking in spirituality. And in Hampshire he had not even tried to find music lovers, people with whom he could have discussed the finer things of life. Why not? He supposed that all his actions or lack of them had been because of low self-esteem, this awareness that he had been unable to sustain the family tradition. But he had been willing to try, and had tried, and had failed for the obvious reason that he was not made of the stern, self-disciplined, practical and perhaps Philistine stuff of the generals and colonels who had preceded him. And now, without training for a civilian life, he had turned to the next best thing to looking after those Devon acres. For that he knew had unconsciously been his ultimate purpose since he had first begun to know them intimately. The elderly agent who had run the estate while his father had been a serving soldier had given him his first .410, and taught him the rudiments of woodcraft and country ways. There had been others who had taken him under their wing, all pleased to teach a youngster who was keen to learn. So he had gone to the nearest craft for which their years of instruction had fitted him.

About seven o'clock he began cooking, and opened a bottle of Crozes Hermitage to go with the meat. He put on a Haydn symphony, and picked up a book of 19th century poaching reminiscences. He read of endless narrow escapes from the law simply because the poacher could run fast. 'If you can't run, don't poach' was the writer's advice. At 7.40 he started cooking the vegetables.

Hilary arrived on time. She wore a green woollen dress, a tourmaline brooch and matching earrings. She had used Tom's Christmas gift of perfume, and she was very tired. She kissed him lightly on the lips and Tom smelled whisky on her breath. She had lost weight in the week she had been away.

"Do you speak German?" he asked as he handed her a glass of Pouilly Fumé. Hilary was taken aback. "Not much. It would be better if I did. And French, Spanish and Italian, I daresay." She realised that she had to get used to the non-greeting from Tom.

"You must have had a rotten journey back."

"A pretty dreadful week. Non-stop travel, business meetings and entertainment."

"But you enjoy it."

Hilary hesitated. Hamburg airport had been snowed in. She had gone by train to Düsseldorf and flown from there. Heathrow had been snowed in and the 'plane had been diverted to the East Midlands airport. Only this fact meant that she was here tonight.

"Yes, I suppose I do. It's adventure of a sort."

"It's great that you've come," said Tom, at last giving her the kind of greeting she might have expected. Now he saw how exhausted she was. Any idea of lovemaking this evening he abandoned. "Let's eat now."

Tom ushered her to the table, lit candles and brought potted shrimps and toast. He saw with pleasure that the efforts he had made were appreciated, that she ate with appetite.

"In contrast I expect you've had a peaceful if strenuous week, eaten well but frugally, slept like a top as my father says."

"You make me feel guilty. As if I've been wasting my time economically."

Hilary sighed. "I didn't mean to imply anything of the sort. I think I've come to accept that we have radically different views of how work should govern our lives."

Tom shook his head. "We both have a protestant-ethic attitude to work."

"Yes," she acknowledged. "The difference lies in the execution."

"How macabre."

They smiled at each other. They heard the licking flames in the stove, its doors open to throw light and warmth into the room. The wind was rising, moaning in the chimney.

"With all the snow," he said, "it's a miracle that you're here. The wind should bring the temperature up, melt the snow." He carved the beef, served the vegetables. He poured the wine, thinking of the cellar in that Devon home, the damp air, the whitewashed brick shelves in alcoves and the wine bottles in serried ranks. His father had a penchant for port, which he did not share. But his grandfather had laid down wines of Bordeaux with either a reckless belief in his own immortality or a thoughtful glance to posterity.

"*Guten Appetit, gnädiges Fräulein.*" They raised their glasses to each other, and ate in silence for a few moments.

Hilary felt better. When she had arrived back home in a taxi, her physical need had been to go straight to bed. A hot bath and a whisky had not changed that. Tom would be there tomorrow. He would understand. But would he? The snow had been light here. He himself was physically enduring. Suddenly she had wanted to see him, with his wind-reddened face and blond hair, with his saturnine, closed expression and the occasional and ever more frequent glow of humour. She had wanted to see him immediately and she had wanted to break down his reserve.

"Do you sometimes wish you could use your language expertise in your work?"

Tom looked over to his bookshelves and back to Hilary. She was beautiful tonight, now that the tiredness had been smoothed away, and her tone had been light, not overly interrogative. For the first time for years he did not resent a question that could open him down the middle like a herring for kippering.

"Benjie Kerr's wife is German. I talk to her. My mother was German. My fair hair and blue eyes are what Hitler wanted in every good German."

He had hoped that the conversation would have been full of dalliance. Instead he found himself telling her about his father and mother and their relationship. He was apologetic. He mentioned nothing of his family background nor his father's position in the army. He only talked about their relationship, and he implied his love for the one and his distaste and fear of the other.

They gradually emptied the bottle of red wine. Hilary declined a second helping of the beef. Tom finished the vegetables. Hilary revealed something more of her parents and their marriage. Their children had soon realised where the power and the push lay, and where gentle, cultivated thoughts were to be had. In most ways it had been a good marriage. They were still together and remarkably happy deep down, although there were, she supposed, surface irritations and the occasional silly appeal to their offspring to note how one or the other of them was reacting to some trivial provocation inspired by the other. The home was still there. Well, home in the abstract sense that they had moved from the house their children had known all their lives. But the furniture, pictures, bric-à-brac, the cutlery and plates, were in the new house as old friends and reminders of their real home.

They finished the wine, talking round subjects that people raise when they are thinking seriously and thoughtfully of steady relationships.

Now Hilary was exhausted. The effect of the food and wine had passed the period of stimulation. She was drowsy. They stood up from the table.

"No washing up tonight. You must be dead-beat. I'll follow you home." He fetched her coat, and she put it on by the stove.

Tom took a deep breath. "All day I've thought about you, and about tonight – perhaps all night," he said. "In a certain way – I –."

"I know." Hilary interrupted him. "I too – when I wasn't utterly frustrated by my journeyings."

"We seem to be moving in a direction," he said. "I want us both to want and be happy about that."

She kissed him. "I am happy about it. But I need to know a lot about someone with whom I'm about to enter such a relationship. More than I know at present."

"There's not so much more to know. I'm a simple fellow who's found his level of skill and interest."

She shook her head, smiling at him. "I think you underestimate yourself. But I'm not going to argue tonight."

"When will we meet?" he asked, then kissed her before she could answer, and was astounded and excited by the strength of her body in his arms, and the warmth and sweetness of her mouth and breath. She would cook dinner for him the following Saturday, she said.

Outside, flurries of snow appeared on the wind but the gusts were clearing the lain snow, piling it in small drifts against tree boles and bushes, along banks and the sides of the cottage and its outbuildings. The temperature had risen. It was a wild winter night with its own beauty.

He followed her in the Land Rover to her cottage, saw her safely indoors and came back to the woods. The wind had risen further and the snow trapped by the evergreen leaves of the holm oak was cascading down. He took Schiller for a brief run. He and an unproved puppy had come north from Hampshire. Were both of them about to flower in this countryside near the North Sea? He fondled the dog, felt again the newly perceived muscles, remembered his steadfastness against the lurcher and the poachers. Had his master acquitted himself as well? So far, not badly, he thought. But he knew that his flowering, if it came, would be through Hilary, through Benjie and Heilke, the first people that he had contemplated loving since the age of 11.

As he sharpened his billhook Tom remembered Benjie's axe on the kitchen table the first evening he had been there. The billhook was a Devon one, given him by the widow of a labourer who had worked on the Gibson estate for 40 years. It had been his wish, the widow had said. Tom now knew that the gift had been an acknowledgement of their mutual deep attachment to the same few miles around. As he honed the cutting edge he recalled the man with his sweat-stained trilby, waistcoat with the gunmetal watch at the end of a heavy cheap chain, the canvas gaiters and dubbined boots, the collarless shirt. Tom Hawker had been his name. He finished sharpening the tool, thinking now of Benjie. He knew that Benjie would take game only in season. He would respect the eight months of grace when the exhausted birds could regroup, breed, and grow their young to provide for the coming shooting season. The Scots ex-major would poach only for his own pot, so he was in most ways the least of Tom's worries about poachers, but in one way the largest. For Tom felt, as a gamekeeper, that he must stop all poachers regardless of their background, whether taking game for their own use or for sale, whether local men or from outside. Benjie could prove the most difficult of all, and Tom rejected any idea of recourse to the law, to the prowling police cars. Whatever was between Benjie and himself was between them alone.

The south-west wind blew warmer and the snow melted. Tom went to clear the bushes that had sprung up in the long-abandoned rearing field. He continued the work begun earlier on the release areas, lopping bushes so that they would thicken up below, cutting overhanging branches. Sun was as important as shelter from chilling winds. He continued feeding his depleted wild stock. Even with raising 2,000 chicks there might not be enough for the eight shoots he had agreed with Gailsford. He would introduce him to the partridge, and he hoped the man would continue his shooting lessons.

Hilary spent two days in her office, then unexpectedly took the place of her managing director at a business conference in London. Tom felt unease again at Hilary being in such potential wolf territory. He was working on the release area in the big wood, keeping his mind off Hilary in London and trying not to think too much of Saturday evening and dinner with her in her cottage. Schiller was restive, raising his head and wrinkling his nose in the direction of the green lane.

After a while Tom heard the sound of shouting. He distinguished his own name. He found a Mercedes with two men, both consciously dressed in the height of country fashion. They were from the East of England land agency, and would be bringing the neglected home farm into profitable agricultural shape. The older man was affable. The younger was colder, clearly wanting to establish a master/servant relationship.

Tom spent the day with them, took them all over the 800 acres and told them his requirements to hold game – strips of maize, sunflower, canary grass and kale close to the release areas. There were several ponds that needed digging out, one of them big enough to bring duck. There was woodland work to be done, far more than he could manage by himself. While the older man, the partner in the firm as he discovered, listened to him, Tom knew the younger one was estimating field sizes, scuffing the earth, noting clay, loam and sand. Hedges would come out, trees come down. At least they would have to leave the established woodland, the spinneys and windbreaks, and the 40 or 50 pits dotting the fields.

They gave him a sandwich in a pub away from the village, brought him back and continued their tour until the light went. Tom realised at the end of it that the older man had just been polite, listening to his gamekeepering requirements. The young man was the key, and Tom saw that despite growing European surpluses of cereals, sugarbeet and oilseed rape he was looking at the home farm in these terms. The sort of property on which he could win his agency spurs. He would no doubt have quite recently left university. He would be studying for his chartered surveyor's qualification. He had a sharp manner and Tom's hopes of feedstrips and cooperation faded.

"We'll have bulldozers and tractors in shortly," said the director. "We'll let you know in advance."

Without doubt the agency was not thinking of working the property as a total and enduring producer of crops, animals, game and wildlife, and giving a living to the motley of country people that the old farms had provided. They had probably misrepresented the gamekeeping needs to Gailsford, and the disruption to the game of all the work planned, when giving him an assessment of the income an efficiently farmed arable unit could produce. He wondered why Gailsford believed in them, and saw that it was because they were confident, had statistics on their tongues, and an evident 'track record' in the estates they already managed. He did not doubt that these were run for top agricultural profit, with the desultory shooting let to town syndicates who did not know what a real shoot was. He thought back with some longing to the rich man's Hampshire estate on which he had spent two years of his life. Twelve to 16 shoots in a season over 3,000 acres of mixed farms. A pedigree Jersey herd, a Hereford-Friesian beef herd. Sheep on the uplands, and a vineyard on a sunny, chalky slope. Money pumped in to generate more money, but also love and care lavished on the countryside and thought given to gainful employment of people. Despite his city fortune that he must have built up with great skill, Gailsford seemed to have no feel for the countryside. Tom wrote him a report on the game-holding requirements.

More snow came, and Tom abandoned the work in the big wood. He set up a workbench in his living room and made up wooden frames for tunnel traps. He already had a budget agreed for the rearing and release pens, and confirmed orders for housing, netting, poles and rearing and feeding equipment.

In London the snow came and went quite soon, leaving piles of grey slush, so Hilary said on the telephone. Her cleaning lady was down with 'flu. Would Tom please get the key from her and check that all was well with her cottage? Tom did as he was asked. Downstairs all was in order, the boiler heating the house sufficiently. He checked the radiators. Upstairs there were three bedrooms and a bathroom. It was obvious which bedroom was the main one. He began with the others. One was full of suitcases and 'attic' contents. The second was the spare room with two beds. It had cream-painted furniture, chintzy flowered curtains and matching bedspreads. There were Redouté prints of roses on the walls. He hesitated before the door of the third bedroom. He had not yet reached that stage of intimacy, not yet been invited. He understood so well the laws of territory from his studies of birds and animals. They applied with as much sensitivity to humans. But she had asked him to check all the radiators and windows, and he would go in and look only at these things.

He opened the door and could smell Hilary in the room. There was a wide single bed, and no matching bedroom suite here. A burr walnut Victorian chest-of-drawers, a Georgian dressing table on slender legs, opened out with the mirror up. Tom checked the windows and radiators, and his interest overrode his scruples. The pictures on the walls had not been bought in a gallery as those elsewhere in the cottage. There was an oil painting of a pretty Victorian cottage scene with a bonneted girl standing by a garden gate, a look of sweet expectation on her innocent, guileless face. Then his eye was caught by three portraits in crayon. A young boy and two girls. Hilary's brother was about 11, good-looking with mid-brown hair, rather anonymous and withdrawn, his blue eyes staring as if at a distant view. Hilary's sister had reddish hair and hot brown eyes. The eldest, she was already sexually aware, questing and peremptory. Hilary's eyes were blue in the picture, and she had cascades of brown hair. He remembered her eyes as grey and was surprised at his lack of close observation. She must have been 13 or 14 and she had the same freshness, innocence and expectation as the Victorian miss in the cottage garden. Without further searching he left the cottage.

That evening Tom rang his gamekeeper friend to ask whether he contemplated a fox shoot and just to talk gamekeepering. He was told by the man's wife that he was out on his patch, and would be for most of the night. And for the next few nights until the end of the season. Immediately Tom knew that he should be out, too. For those poachers who abided by closed seasons the last few days represented the final chance to bag a brace of pheasant. He had Benjie firmly in his mind's eye.

Tom slept in the armchair beside the stove for three hours and went out at one o'clock in the morning. He walked all over his patch. The

74

countryside was quiet, muffled in snow. He heard tawny owls calling from the big wood, and all his game birds roosting, sheltering, keeping warm. The sky was overcast but the light reflected off the snow lit his way. He found nothing and no one. The only man-made sounds were the occasional car in the distance and the hours struck by the church clock. He would come out again on Friday night. But on Saturday night Mr Charles Gailsford's pheasant – what was left of them – would have to take their chance.

8. ONE ALL

One side of Benjie Kerr's big barn was organised and neat. There were stacks of hay and straw bales, bags of livestock feed, of blood/fish/bone fertiliser, wire fencing and posts, automatic feeders, waterers and troughs. The other side was his workshop. Some of it was neat, too. A big bench with vices, and shelves above with ranks of tins – screws, nails, hooks – all labelled. There were boxes of spare parts and a tool board with the outline of each tool painted on to the wood. Alongside the workshop corner a grey Ferguson tractor from the immediate post-war years separated the workshop from the junk corner. There, piled up, were rolls of old linoleum, canvas tarpaulins, hessian sacks, two bicycles, a rotovator, old boots, tools that Tom hardly recognised, and box after box of odds and ends.

Tom eyed the piles with astonishment.

"My father was a miner when you could be out of work at the end of the week. He had a fine allotment, rabbits and chickens, and a share in a pig. He made sure we wouldn't starve, although there was just the three o' us." Benjie sounded aggressive.

"So he was a collector of anything that might one day come in handy – to mend, build, contain, keep something going," said Tom. "I can understand that."

"You can?"

"I had friends in Devon who were like-minded. Hoarding was natural when hard times could be round the corner."

"It's no different today," replied Benjie.

Again Tom wondered at the long hours that Benjie and Heilke must put in. He had been out on his rounds, had found himself close to Shepherd's Pightle at about 11 and seen Benjie busy washing down housing and equipment used by the poultry that had gone into the Christmas trade. He had helped for an hour before more snow had sent them into the barn for shelter.

"While we're here, will you gi' me a hand moving the sawbench out. I've a load of logs coming." He indicated a cast-iron stand that stood by the barn door. Beside it was a belt and a round sawblade.

Tom took the edge of the sawbench and tested the weight. "We move it little by little, I suppose." He glanced at Benjie and surprised a look on his face. Sadness? Disgust? He saw Benjie's big frame made bulkier still by a dark blue donkey jacket. "You mean, you normally move this by yourself?"

Benjie groaned. "Growing old is hell," he said savagely. "Let's get to it."

Together they moved the sawbench out into the yard where Benjie covered it with a tarpaulin. From its weight and shape Tom knew that he could not have moved it by himself.

Heilke came from pulling leeks at the other end of the steading. She kissed Tom, disappeared into the house to summon them within minutes to lunch. She took Tom over entirely, speaking only in German, asking him to bring Hilary to dinner on Saturday week, telling him that the trip – the usual jaunt she and her sister had each year in London – was postponed for the time being. Her sister was not well. Some stomach trouble. They would go in March when she would be better and the weather kinder. Once again Tom relaxed and let his mother's language wash over him. She was so like his mother in her warmth and sparkle. More talkative perhaps, less spiritual. Tom saw Benjie's eyes fixed on his wife. He looked pleased, as if he had not seen this Heilke for some time.

For the first time Tom saw Hilary harassed. He had come at eight as bidden. She had firmly shut the kitchen door, given him a glass of chilled white wine. Although she had greeted him warmly she had immediately become abstracted, glancing angrily at the closed kitchen door.

"It smells good," Tom said tentatively.

"I don't know why," she answered. "Well, we'll see, won't we?"

"May I ask –"

"No, you mayn't."

"All right. I saw the Kerrs yesterday. They've asked us both to dinner next Saturday. I hope you can come." He was about to say that Heilke was a wonderful cook, and did not. He found himself enjoying Hilary's evident discomfiture with what lay behind the kitchen door.

"I can come," she said. "And now I have to leave you. I bought some cassettes this morning. All Beethoven's piano concertos." She disappeared into the kitchen, shutting the door.

Tom put on the Emperor concerto, listening to Beethoven's enormous self-confidence and *élan*, the musical breadth and subtlety of his writing. He listened remembering years before in Devon hearing on parched earth – it must have been 1976 – the first thunderstorm of a drought summer, and translated the vigour of the thunder and the sound of rain on the fields round the house into the Emperor, totally familiar, much loved, and easing and welcoming.

"Oh, no."

He heard the cry of anguish during a soft passage in the music. He opened the kitchen door. There was a smell of something 'caught'. There was steam, and every available working surface used.

She turned and looked at him. "Help," she said.

He kissed her, realising that he had not noticed until now the black-and-white dress she wore beneath an apron, nor the silver earrings. He kissed her again, took off his coat in the heat of the kitchen, and they salvaged the meal together.

They were both nervous. Hilary removed her earrings and laid them with exaggerated care side by side on her dressing table. They had kissed and kissed downstairs, and on the way upstairs, without a word being spoken. She had taken him by the hand and had led him into her bedroom. But once inside with the door closed, in her sanctum with its single bed and its family furniture and pictures, its keepsakes of her childhood and youth, she experienced a moment's heartache but had no doubt at all. Shakily she unbuttoned her dress, took it off and placed it as deliberately over the back of a chair. She had wanted this with all her strength and had prepared for it. She removed her petticoat but still did not look across the room at him. Her eye caught the Victorian painting of a girl in the cottage garden with her look of animated expectancy and her innocence. Slowly Hilary turned to search for Tom somewhere in the gloom by the door. He was looking at the painting as well. He had removed his tie and trousers, stood still and silent. She saw that he was unsure, his blond hair falling over his forehead, the muscles of his upper arms and his wide shoulders plainly outlined by the shirt he wore.

"I'm not like the girl in the painting," she said.

He shook his head. "All forgotten. For me too. This is the first time with love, with meaning."

"I'm glad. For me, too."

He advanced slowly undoing his shirt. Together they fumbled with the bedcover, with the blankets and sheet.

"We'll get better at this," she said.

Half-an-hour later he repeated the phrase with emphasis, and she kissed him once more, calmly at last. They lay side by side. The village street was silent. The pub had closed and the last cars gone. Tom had not thought this far. Should he get up and go to his cottage, or stay and sleep beside her? He remembered again the end of the 1976 drought. He touched her as if thanking her for an end to another drought. She stirred, almost asleep, and he put his arms round her, held her close to him, his head buried in her hair, until his arm went to sleep under her body. He gently disengaged himself, falling asleep, half waking during the night with her warmth beside him and the scent of her perfume and her body in his nostrils.

He woke before her, at his usual early hour, turned and watched her sleeping, reckoned it was the most calmly happy moment of his life since the age of 11.

Back in his cottage by mid-morning, Tom exercised the dog, had him picking up a dummy, answering to whistles and words of command. Then he cleaned his cottage, riddled the stove and brought in more logs. He ate bread and cheese for lunch and slept in the armchair beside the stove. By five o'clock he wanted to go and see Hilary. He resisted the temptation. Instead he 'phoned her and talked for half an hour. There was a concert in the town on Tuesday evening. Would she come? Yes, yes. And afterwards? Tuesday was February 1, the first day of the closed season. At 10 that night he made amends for his neglect of his patch and went out and about, through the woods, creeping along hedges, down windbreaks of Scots pine. The snow still lay and the temperatures hovered just above freezing. He went without Schiller, but he missed the dog's companionship and his sharp senses. He smelt a fox in a spinney and promised himself to check for prints in daylight. He heard all the now familiar sounds of the estate in dead of winter and at night. The snow lightened the darkness and his night eyes were at their best.

All day on Monday he worked on the rearing field buildings, just delivered. The sun shone and the temperature rose to send melting snow from the surrounding trees thumping on to the ground. He took an hour off to check the spinney with Schiller, and found track of two foxes. Back at the rearing field as the afternoon advanced he thought more and more of Hilary, accused himself of becoming obsessed with the sexual act, reminded himself that she had a mind which as yet he knew little about, that she in her turn had so little knowledge of him and his thoughts. He went over Saturday night again and again in his mind, reassuring himself that the experience had been as rich and fulfilling for her as for him.

He 'phoned her that evening to finalise arrangements for Tuesday. He rambled on about his day and hers, and told her that he would be out most of the night. And by one o'clock of a cold morning, with the remaining snow crisp and frosted, he was defending Charles Gailsford's game from the last onslaught of the season by local poachers.

Pheasant would be the target, therefore he patrolled the woodland edges, warm spinneys with conifers, the old marl pits. The sky cleared to reveal a three-quarters-full moon riding high. The effect of the bright light on the snow was to trick him into believing he could see almost as far as in sunlight. No poacher would surely be out on such a night, even if it were the last of the season. But soon the cloud came back to obscure the moon. He reached the big wood again, propped himself up against the smooth bole of a beech tree on the edge, and listened. The church clock struck four. Although it would be several hours before dawn the quality of the night had changed, the hunters had hunted and were gone to rest, the hunted breathed more easily, searching for food or in their nests, burrows and holes in trees. He pictured Hilary asleep with her precious possessions round her, curled up on her side against the cold. Without him to warm her. Tomorrow he could begin to relax a little. Tomorrow he would work again on the rearing field buildings. Tomorrow he would see Hilary at the concert in town and he would later make love to her, this time with more confidence.

There was a sound out in the meadow, as if an object had landed in the grass. He strained his eyes to catch a movement. He wondered how many hare the poachers and their greyhounds had taken. A further sound that he could not identify came from along the wood edge to the right, a swishing noise that lasted only for seconds. A few moments later birds shifted on their roosting branches, and he loosened up. The night was almost over and all good poachers were snug in bed. Even Benjie Kerr who was no doubt in bed with his wife. Tom thought about Heilke and found that, after Saturday night, he had Heilke more in perspective as a woman twice his age, someone else's wife, and someone he respected and liked – no longer a confused sex symbol for him.

Tom shifted his weight from one foot to the other. He was stiffening up, beginning to fight sleep, cramp and the cold. When the church clock struck the half hour he would go home to bed. The night was darkening. His head dropped. He shook himself awake, but could not stay still and fight his need for sleep. His head fell forward again.

"This time I've got you, gamekeeper," said a Scots voice in his ear.

Instinct catapulted Tom sideways to place the beech trunk between him and the voice.

Benjie began laughing, and after a moment Tom joined in the mirth, came forward, and they slapped each other on the back, shouted at the silent wood and pastures, disturbing their rightful inhabitants.

"One all," said Benjie when he could draw breath. "And you fell for the stone thrown into the meadow. It started you probing and then relaxed your concentration." Benjie was thoroughly pleased with himself.

"I will repay," said Tom. "If you come on my patch don't ever relax. Keep an eye ahead, on your flanks, and especially behind you. One day or night I shall be there."

"Bullshit, Captain Gibson."

"I'll prove it's not, Major Kerr."

They walked home together in silence. By tacit agreement they moved as soldiers do through hostile territory, hugging the shadows, covering each other when there was a gap in the hedge. Benjie walked with a spring in his step, in command of himself and whatever the night could throw at him. They were two of a kind, Tom recognised. He knew what Benjie would do at each small obstacle to their concerted return to Shepherd's Pightle, and equally Benjie must know what he would do. And all without practice. Although it was in the infantryman's rulebook there was an added dimension, as if they were – in Hilary's terminology – programmed together. Programmed. With Hilary too, he hoped.

When they reached Benjie's gate they halted, at ease.

"You've got permission from now to be on the estate, Benjie. Take what you want."

Benjie was silent, immediately crumpled, and Tom cursed inwardly. He had meant to take away his motive for poaching on Gailsford's land, so that their friendship would not be at risk. He saw immediately that he did not yet understand fully why Benjie poached.

"I'm sorry, Benjie. I withdraw permission."

Benjie touched his arm in the dark. "Have you ever seen a man with Parkinson's disease? Who's had a stroke?"

"But you're fit."

"Aye. For the moment. I exercise."

"But you can take exercise without poaching."

Benjie was hushed for a moment. "Aye, I could. But it's the excitement, the adrenaline in the blood. Especially when I'm up against someone like you."

Tom's relief was immense. "But you don't need to poach. Like tonight – you were only out to get your own back. We could –"

"That would be playing at it."

"You mean you'll continue to poach – on my patch."

"Don't take it personally."

"I have to."

They fell silent.

At last Tom spoke. "Look, go to bed. We'll talk about it on Saturday. It's the end of the season. We can both relax."

Benjie started down the track towards his house. "On Saturday, then," he said over his shoulder. "But there's always the hare," he added loudly when he was some distance away.

In the first days of February the weather turned mild and the snow began to melt. Tom shot several crows and another magpie. He had used his shotgun very little since he had come to Gailsford's estate and was anxious to make sure that he still had his eye in. He worked on the rearing field, on the housing and the netted runs, going over the supplies and equipment that had been ordered. Old Adams, the gamekeeper in Hampshire, had regaled him with tales of trapping wild hen pheasant and bringing them in to a rearing field to lay, sit and hatch their broods in relative peace and absolute safety. Clutches of wild eggs which had been abandoned had been put under broody hens in individual coops. That was when there were broody hens, in the days of bantams, of Rhode Island Reds, Plymouth Rock, Light Sussex and Black Australop. When breeds were hardy, laid fewer eggs than the modern hybrids, and went broody.

On the Friday, about half an hour before the sun went, he settled himself in a hastily contrived hide in one of the long windbreaks. He was close to old oaks in a nearby hedge that were constantly used for roosting by pigeon. He fetched home eight, six of them young birds, and hung them in his woodshed. All Saturday, as the snow melted finally and he worked on the rearing field, he pictured again the housing complete with infra-red lamps, feeders and waterers, where the chicks would stay for up to a week depending on the weather. The wire-netted runs were carefully contrived to give sun, shade and shelter. 'Get them on to mother earth as soon as ever you can,' Adams had advised Tom. 'That's where they take strength for the release pens.' The release pens would be the natural habitat but still protected, where they would gradually acclimatise and plump up on pellets, and later cracked wheat and increasing amounts of natural food. And with luck and reasonable weather be quit of the need for protection and be ready to face the guns of Charles Gailsford and his guests in November. When the shooting season opened on October 1 reared birds were often not ready to provide any sport at all. Tom would have to explain all this. He would work through Mrs Gailsford. He had had no reply to his report on the shoot's needs from the agricultural standpoint.

That Saturday, Tom walked through misty rain into the village to Hilary's cottage. They drove to Shepherd's Pightle in the VW.

"*Es nieselt, Tom, komm schnell herein.*" Heilke stood in the doorway dressed in German folk attire, a white blouse embroidered with flowers, a pleated skirt.

She kissed Tom once on each cheek, turned to Hilary, paused with her hands on the younger woman's arms. She looked a trifle theatrically into her eyes then kissed her in the same manner. "Welcome, welcome," she said, and laughed at her acting, half asking for approval, half deprecating her forwardness.

Her husband was scrubbed, shaved, and dressed in a green Harris tweed jacket and green corduroy trousers. Before the meal they talked in English. Heilke had difficulty restraining herself. She interlarded her English with German words, then a phrase or two. Mostly she addressed Tom and he would not break the general conversation. They talked about family, Hilary's family, giving a little of their own background. Heilke soon discovered that her young guest spoke no

German. She seemed pleased at that. As Tom listened to the women he watched Benjie nodding indulgently. He saw that he was physically very tired, wanting his food, sipping a Scotch and water. Tom hardly touched the sherry beside him. He too had had a long day. He hoped they would both wake up when the food came. He could smell it infiltrating from the kitchen along the passage. Heilke was intent on impressing Hilary – and not favourably. She seemed to want to make certain that Hilary knew she was a woman to be reckoned with. She did not look at Tom but the inference was clear that she held a place in Tom's affections and had been there before Hilary.

Tom finally decided to break the general conversation between only two of the four, and struck up some talk with the somnolent one. He asked which of the old breeds of chicken Benjie had kept and whether he had any now, and were they ever broody? The answer was that Benjie had all old breeds and there were broodies. If Tom was to find abandoned nests of pheasant and partridge would Benjie lend him broodies? Of course. Tom was aware that Hilary was monosyllabic in her conversation with Heilke. Ignoring the scents from the kitchen the hostess stayed in the living room, animated and enquiring, play-acting.

The situation at last became apparent to Benjie. "Heilke, lass, food," he said.

"Are we ready?" Heilke asked brightly.

"We are. We all are. In fact Tom and I are starving."

The quality of the food and wine should have lifted the evening on to a high plane of maximum enjoyment, sharpening wit, sensibilities and conversational abilities. But Benjie was weary, trying to respond and failing. Heilke wanted to talk German and Tom would not follow her, instead leading the conversation round to Hilary and her recent visit to Germany. The humour, the bubbling happiness, the ease of himself in this house with its two inhabitants, had gone this evening. Now he was alert and troubled, watching Hilary, checking Heilke. Benjie was nearly out for the count, Heilke was glowing and Hilary retreating. Tom saw Heilke's heightened colour, the sparkling eye, a woman looking years younger than she was. He knew the evening would end in defeat. He had had such hopes that the two women who engaged all his attention would enjoy each other's company, would have found affection and accord.

84

Tom tried to coax Hilary out of the shadow. She seemed wilfully to stay closed up. She would not look at him. Only Heilke would do that, blue eyes bursting with merriment and triumph. Benjie was asleep at the table. Tom ignored Heilke, concentrated his mind and his eyes on Hilary. At last she lifted her eyes, glanced at Heilke and then at Tom, and was held by his gaze. Heilke talked on about the plays, the exhibitions of painting and ceramics they would go to when her sister was well again. Had Hilary seen any plays lately? Hilary smiled at Tom, at his intense, eager appeal. She nodded slightly to him.

"I was in Düsseldorf a fortnight ago, Mrs Kerr. I saw Rigoletto at the new opera house."

"Please, please. I am Heilke. Heilke. Did you enjoy my home town? Well, not exactly my home town, but –"

They woke Benjie and took him to the living room where the fire had reduced itself to embers. There was a debate between host and hostess about rebuilding it.

Tom did not say that the evening was over. "You need to get to bed, Benjie" he said instead. "I too."

"May we help with the washing up?" Hilary said sweetly and deliberately to a Heilke who was beginning to realise that her triumph had been short-lived.

"But never – thank you," she answered vehemently, and broke into her mother tongue, asking Tom when he would come again, putting her hand on his arm, saying in a rush that she had need of advice from him on many matters. When would he come?

Tom spoke in German very briefly. He would come and see them soon. Then in his father's language he told them what a fine evening it had been. Benjie, on his feet but swaying with fatigue, was evidently aware that all was not right but could not begin to redress a situation that he only dimly perceived.

"She's in love with you."

The misty rain had ceased and the night was muggy. Hilary drove fast with the driver's window wound down. "I don't really understand your relationship with them. Benjie – well, he's your poaching friend. I can see his attraction for you, I suppose. Countrymen, soldiers together. But she – what sort of game was she playing? She's old enough to be your mother."

85

Tom stayed silent. It was a new idea for him. He recalled his first visit and his muddled thoughts. Attracted physically, then the switch to equating Heilke with his mother. They would be the same age, had the same build, the same eyes and blond hair.

Hilary parked her VW abruptly beside her large company car in the garage behind her cottage.

"It's more likely I'm the son she never had," he said at last. "That would explain her possessiveness. And it's obvious to her that I'm in love with you."

Hilary considered. As he made a move to take her in his arms, she gestured him back. "I didn't enjoy the evening at all. All right, you did come to my rescue. I know that. But she went on and on."

"She did. And I was powerless to stop her then. But we'll find a way." He paused. "Did you hear when I said that I was in love with you?"

"So you should be," she replied and allowed him closer. After an interval she asked, "Shall we go indoors?"

"Good idea. The partridge will be pairing soon," said Tom. "It's lovely to see them chasing each other, rushing neck and neck for a few yards, then back again. And they talk to each other non-stop."

They went into the cottage.

"I'm sorry I misbehaved tonight. I should have seen what she was about, should have coped with her." She paused. "But I'm in love, too, you know."

Tom kissed her.

"Are partridge monogamous?" Hilary asked after a little while.

"They certainly are," he replied cheerfully. "And great companions – mates in all senses."

9. FEAT OF ARMS

February was no fill-dyke. The weather turned dry with an occasional advance spring day that set the birds singing in the woods and along the shelterbelts. Tom finished the woodman's work on his four release pens to bring more light and warmth. He sent a message to Gailsford asking whether he would participate in a hare shoot. The estate owner declined but asked for a couple of hare to be taken to the big house for freezing.

Tom rallied his pickers-up and beaters, and several village people. He also gave Benjie an invitation, knowing that Gailsford would be away. They drove the home farm in four long drives, a line of 20 guns spread out across the fields. Benjie had brought the unarmed Kenny, the retarded lad who worked with him. The atmosphere was relaxed but purposeful, everyone played his allotted part in the sport without anxiety. It was as if the fields this indeterminate bunch of villagers bestrode, the hedges they pushed through, the hare they shot, did not belong to Charles Gailsford Esquire. Maybe only for the day while their feet trod it, their guns cracked, in a very important sense the land was theirs. Tom put the thought from him. This was Benjie infiltrating ideas into his head.

Halfway through the shoot they arrived in the green lane, where wives and other village people gathered. Sandwich boxes and thermos flasks were produced, hare pulled thankfully from game bags and brought to Tom's Land Rover. Tom accepted sandwiches and an apple and began organising the next drive. There were around 40 people milling about. He saw Roger Hoggett, the Red Lion's landlord, village people he knew by sight, and a couple of unidentified men. This prompted him to get one of the sightseeing villagers to guard the Land Rover, on promise of a hare.

"Ready for the next drive?" Tom called out. He began ushering the guns through a gate into the first field, and as he did so saw a small man with a wispy beard. He cast round for Benjie. "The little man – one of the hare poachers from town," he said, indicating the direction with his head. Benjie moved away.

Soon the line of guns was spread out and ready to start. Tom hesitated, went back to the gate, then to the line again, to stand by Kenny who was a little uneasy without Benjie. Tom told him Benjie would be back shortly. Kenny was reassured, as if knowing that the gamekeeper and the 'boss' were close.

"What's to do, gamekeeper? Not finished your tea, then?"

For answer Tom used a parade ground voice. "Spread out, spread out. Every man 20 yards from his neighbour."

"We're country bumpkins not soldiers, Tom."

The laughter made Tom grin. This was a lightly worn camaraderie that he understood, so much less intense and demanding than that from which he had been excluded, or excluded himself, at school, at university and in the army.

He stood out in front. "Let's inspect you, then. No tea stains down the front. No squashed sandwiches up the barrels." Suddenly Benjie was back. "Let's go." The line started forward with a cheer. Tom, Benjie and Kenny walked close together at first.

"He joined a bigger man, bearded. There was a van. A Mercedes, colour beige, registered last year." Benjie gave the number. 'They scarpered.'

"Did you see Hoggett with them or near them?"

Benjie shook his head.

Tom thanked him. It was good to be out with Benjie, shoulder to shoulder as it were. The first hare of the new sweep leapt away in front of the guns.

As the sun went down into a bank of yellow and orange cloud, each man claimed one hare and went home in the dusk. Tom took the two for Gailsford directly to the big house, added another for the Lancashire couple. He delivered the remainder to butchers in the town.

Tom then went to the police station and talked to the duty inspector about the two men and the Mercedes van. He heard more about the poaching gang. They had none of them been caught as yet. They were well informed, went after anything that would find a market. Deer, pheasant, partridge, hare. Last year poults had been taken from release pens and rearing fields were not safe. The police were gradually building up a dossier, and if their information was correct, the gang used the motorways to take their stolen produce far away.

Tom expressed surprise that the types he had described might be members of such a gang. They seemed not very well disciplined, opportunist rather than organised, and thugs.

"Don't underestimate them. There's brains and organisational ability somewhere, and a network of informers," the inspector said. "And don't forget that they market the stuff, the hardest thing to do without trace. If they were as you suggest, we'd have caught them by now."

"Marketing is all," Tom said to Hilary. "You're in the right place." He told her about the gang who used the motorway to shift their stolen goods. "Success is being able to sell whatever you produce."

They were in town, at a restaurant that Hilary wanted to check out for a company dinner. It purported to be a French restaurant. The menus were in French with English in smaller type. There was a fixed price menu of three courses for a reasonable sum and only a handful of *à la carte* dishes.

"It looks as if it's all from fresh produce – what's available today," said Tom. "We should introduce them to the Kerrs."

A waitress dressed in black with white at the collar and wrists came to take their order. She was from France, and Tom spoke to her in French. Moulins in the Bourbonnais was her home town, and the chef also came from there. They were brother and sister. Altogether there were four of them from France. She complimented him on his French, and he explained that he had spent six months at the university in Lyon. He ordered the menu for them. The food was delicious, *nouvelle cuisine* as to colour contrasts and display, but substantial enough. At the end of the meal the chef appeared and made directly for their table. Did monsieur know a restaurant in Lyon where he had worked – not the greatest but meriting one star in the Guide Michelin? Tom explained that as a university student he had had no money for such places, and went on to describe some of the student restaurants he had frequented. They reminisced about a great city from quite different viewpoints.

Hilary was enchanted. She had never seen Tom so animated, so sure of himself.

"You should be using your languages," she said.

Tom laughed. "I can only talk about simple things – the everyday life of ordinary people."

"Vocabularies can be acquired, no doubt," she countered, and wished she had not spoken for his face closed up.

"I only know about the countryside. Not much chance of using German and French talking to poachers and gamekeepers, and rich City gentlemen from Hendon." He paused and his tone lightened. "Of course the majority of my partridge are what are known as 'Frenchmen'." He shook his head, good spirits found again. "You're not suggesting that I change my way of earning my living, are you?"

She shook her head, changed the subject. It was too early to begin working on what she now thought of as her plans for the future.

Next morning, without prior warning, two bulldozers arrived on the home farm, followed by the young land agent, Doddington-Smith, in a Range Rover. The machines laid about a hedge separating two smallish pastures. The hedge was a thick one and paired partridge were already along it choosing nesting sites. Tom again demanded a map of the hedges that would come out. He was about to start his vermin control. Doddington-Smith was vague and hostile.

"You wrote to Mr Gailsford," he said aggressively.

"I did, and have had no reply."

"He passed your report to me."

"And?"

" I shall take out as many hedges as are necessary for the efficient use of machinery and the profitable running of the farm."

"He wants a profitable shoot. Plenty of good birds."

"Pheasant, not partridge," replied the land agent. "He only cares about pheasant. And you'll be rearing them."

Tom tried to be diplomatic. "A well run estate has to take into account the wild stock. They provide the best sporting birds." As he spoke Tom knew that it was useless to appeal to the man. "At least let me have a plan immediately, so I know where your machines will be working."

Doddington-Smith took that as signifying victory. "I have an office in the big house. See me there tomorrow at nine a.m. Be punctual, please." He went off to shout at one of his bulldozer drivers. Tom watched him go, praying that the heavens would open up and bog down the machines. They did not. He wondered how old Adams would have handled such a situation. He had probably never met the like. He had been gamekeeper on estates where their owners had wisely left operations to carefully chosen professionals – farm managers, foresters and gamekeepers – who had, give or take an altercation or two, worked to produce a fair balance of crops, livestock, timber and game from the land. Tom supposed that it was a matter of the Hampshire landowners being rich enough not to need practices for maximum profit. But Gailsford also did not depend on the harvest of his acres for a living. He had not answered his report, written in careful detail. Stony ground. Gailsford was stony ground, and so was Doddington-Smith. Hilary would talk about giving the bosses what they wanted if it was reasonable. And she would think good flushes of reared birds a reasonable request. As for the hedges, despite growing European Community surpluses, she would have understood the need to maximise production by making fields larger. Meanwhile he would go and see Benjie and Heilke. At some stage he had to talk to Heilke about Hilary. He still had not figured out how and in what terms.

They were expecting him. They had heard the bulldozers and Benjie had been to have a look.

"Inevitable," he said, when he had heard Tom's story.

"Depends how far they go," said Tom.

"Aye," Benjie acknowledged. "And I'll wager they'll take out too much to leave us with a good-looking, game-rich countryside."

"Us?" queried Tom.

"Us," repeated Benjie with emphasis. "Us because of all the arguments you've heard before. The ownership of land does not confer the right to pillage it without thought for the other people who have undeniable ancient customary rights to that stretch o' countryside – although less immediately possessive, I concede."

Tom sighed. "Benjie, you weary me. We're in a modern world where money means everything. Perhaps it always did, only those without it in the past had more reason for taking the law into their own hands."

"Ha, you've come to believe that, have you?" Benjie was pleased. "What's different today?"

It was then that Tom noticed the whisky bottle and glass. Benjie was grinning at him in a manner he had not seen before.

"Listen," said Tom, "the landowners have the responsibility to make a piece of land productive, not only for themselves but for their dependents of all kinds – family, farm workers, foresters, even gamekeepers –"

"And local men who poach," shouted Benjie triumphantly and drained what looked like neat whisky in his glass.

"All right, all right. But the ultimate responsibility for the wellbeing of the land lies with the owner. He's the man who has to keep faith with the past, the present and the future.'

Benjie was silent for a moment, looking at Tom with a quizzical, comic expression. "It's good to believe in ideals," he said solemnly. "I did for a while. Even today I still find myself harking back to them."

Tom pursued his line of thought. "And is Gailsford understanding enough to take that ultimate responsibility? I doubt it. He's put the estate in the hands of a young man with a cold eye and his way to make in a competitive world."

The Scot nodded. "The signs are not good. You'll find out tomorrow. And now, Tom, while we're waiting for Heilke to give us our food, I've a little experiment which I want you to help with."

He took Tom into a lean-to room on the north side that he had not seen before. It was Benjie's office, a tidy desk against one wall with shelves of files and a large filing cabinet. In the centre of the room was a plain deal table with two hard beechwood chairs, one on either side of it. A hank of rope lay on the table.

"You're taller, Tom," said Benjie mysteriously. "But I'm a heavier build. Bigger shoulders. More muscle in the arms."

Tom eyed Benjie doubtfully, and the small glass of neat whisky he now proffered him. He refused the drink, watched Benjie pour himself more whisky and toss it back. Enlightenment came to him. "You don't want to try that old trial-of-strength game with the clasped hands and elbows on the table?"

Benjie snorted. "Not that. In my prime no one could beat me at it. But that's become tedious. Now this –" he indicated the table and the rope "– this I read about somewhere. It was a contest when men were men. The table width is between us. We're tied to the table legs. We'll just be able to reach each other."

"What purpose did it serve?" Tom asked flatly.

"Och, weel, you're no goin' tae question the game?" Benjie asked, aggrieved, his Scots voice more pronounced.

"Why, Benjie ?" Tom watched him closely, not understanding.

Benjie busied himself cutting four lengths off the hank of rope.

"It was a way the men hereabouts settled their differences," he said at last. "They slugged each other until one gave in."

"With bare knuckles."

"Aye, aye," replied Benjie absent-mindedly, sitting down and beginning to tie his left leg to a table leg.

"What's the difference we have to settle?" Tom asked, scarcely believing the scene before him. "If I beat you, you'll never poach again?"

Benjie banged his head on the table edge as he rose to his feet. "I'll poach till I die," he roared angrily, rubbing his head.

Tom burst out laughing. "Come on, Benjie. It must have been a brutish way of settling a score."

"You public school men prefer a little gentle fisticuffs behind the squash courts, eh?" said Benjie.

Tom recoiled. "I never said that, nor thought it. I don't have the kind of quarrel with you that warrants either. For heaven's sake, I'd have thought our friendship would transcend petty differences in our upbringing."

Benjie pushed two pieces of rope across the table. "Sit down," he said, "and lash your legs to the table."

Tom sat down involuntarily. "I'm half your age, Benjie. I'm a boxer."

As well as he could with his head under the table, Benjie snorted in derision. He rose, pulled the chair under him close to the table. "The book didn't say whether to sit or stand. We'll try both."

Tom wished Heilke would come in, would announce that the meal was ready. How many neat whiskies had Benjie had? What was he trying to prove to himself? His manhood? Ah, now he understood. Benjie wanted to show that he was still the man he had been 40 years ago. The fear of growing old, not being able to shift the sawbench by himself, not being able still to outpace, outsmart any gamekeeper that he pitted himself against.

"Tak' off your coat," rasped Benjie. He himself wore a heavy brown sweater. Tom did as he was told.

"Look, you are still as virile and strong as me," he said. "And you have the advantage of much greater experience –"

"Bullshit, Captain Gibson," said Benjie. "You're scared. You're afraid. That's the trouble with you, Captain Gibson."

Tom Gibson saw again his father's icy eyes when he said that he wanted to resign his commission. That four tours in Northern Ireland had shown him what the Falklands had not, that he was no soldier, that he was a small man of peaceful ways, that he wanted to work the land, grow crops and animals. If there was a just war – all right. But he questioned now whether any wars were justified. Well, yes, perhaps some wars in the past had been seen at the time to be just. Yes, yes, he

93

understood what his father was saying. He was sorry to be found wanting, sad not to be like the other Gibsons, to be with them all the way in their long years of service to the crown. Yes, he saw that other Gibsons had had misgivings and had hidden them and done their duty, and no, he did not see it as mindless subservience to a caste. He did understand, and for all the years of his soldiering had hidden his misgivings and done his duty. And yes, Northern Ireland would come round again, and he would not be there with his battalion, his brother officers, his men. Speaking softly as befitted his rank and prestige, but cuttingly, his father had told him that he had never thought he would see a Gibson scared, afraid, and allowing emotion to dictate his behaviour. Not scared, not afraid, Father, apprehensive, worried, yes, but not afraid. Not in Ireland, not in the Falklands, not in Hong Kong, nor in Belize, not in the air nor plummeting down. Didn't he understand? He had had enough, done his duty to the crown. He wanted another, gentler life – music, growing things, Devon in all seasons. His father had shaken his head vehemently at that, and spoken briefly again before striding from the room.

Tom lashed his legs to the table's. If this crazy old man wanted to prove himself as young enough to withstand the shock, this young man was willing to show him that he was no coward. They were both mad, and Heilke would not come to release them from their madness. He stood up, pushed the chair away so that it fell with a clatter.

"Stand up," he snapped. "Or I'll hit you sitting down."

Aggravated, Benjie shouted out. "We should have tried the chairs first."

"Get up. You don't call me scared, afraid. Get up or I'll hit you now."

Slowly Benjie rose, his eyes on Tom's, a grin beginning on his face. Tom hardly saw the left jab that Benjie threw at him even before he was fully upright. It grazed his cheek, and he blocked the straight right that followed it. They stood, legs uncomfortably apart, testing the difficulties of balance. Benjie still grinned, his eyes wary.

Almost in a leisurely way Tom feinted with his left, aiming for the geographical centre of the brown sweater before him, withdrew rapidly and sent his right towards Benjie's jaw. Ducking as quickly, Benjie collected the blow on the side of the head. Tom felt his fingers crack and he gasped with pain. Benjie growled, shook himself, and the table, which was too light for the game, jumped up and down. Tom did not let him rest. He leaned forward and hit Benjie twice very fast on his nose with his left fist, blows without weight but uncomfortable. Benjie reared backwards, shifting the table and upsetting Tom's balance, then sent a right swing curving upwards towards Tom's ear, who swayed back, saw that Benjie was now off balance, teetering forward across the table. Tom pushed out an exploratory left that Benjie tried to block, leaving his chin exposed. Very carefully Tom aimed a controlled blow, a hard but not too hard right hook, at the point of Benjie's jaw. With his left hand he caught at his sweater, stopping him from catapulting back, breaking his legs or his back – he didn't know which – and lowered him on to the table.

"You did well, Benjie – fought like a good 'un. You throw punches with remarkable speed." Tom went on and on. They were untied, sitting opposite each other on the beechwood chairs. Benjie was unsure of himself, remembering little of the fight, accepting Tom's word that they had slugged it out until a lucky blow had put him out for the count. And they had bruises and cut knuckles to prove it.

Benjie was pleased with himself and needed no more whisky. Tom thought what a frightful prankster Benjie must have been in the mess. He remembered some mess nights of his own when the subalterns had been joined by the captains and majors in similar stupid escapades, trying to perpetuate their days of youth, virility and irresponsibility. Yet he thought that perhaps it was right to keep going as the years gripped you.

Heilke came in from the kitchen, unaware of what had been going on. She looked sharply at Benjie, then at Tom.

"What have you two been up to?" She smelt the whisky on her husband, was disapproving, saw the blood and was immediately solicitous, saying that she would bathe his head and Tom's cheek. But Benjie gently told her to desist. They were both fine. They had participated in a little experiment, a feat of arms, in which they had both acquitted themselves well. They would wash themselves and be ready for food. Heilke went to the kitchen chuckling at the games the men got up to.

At the meal Heilke asked Tom about his work, talked about Hilary with faint praise and said she was after all a city girl, whereas he, Tom, was wedded to the countryside. Tom told them about the night of the partridge poachers, and illustrated how interested Hilary was in country matters. He saw that Heilke was still jealous of her. After the fight this evening he had resolved to take a step back from the Kerrs. But the ease and happiness with which he sat in their home, the realisation that he was beginning to understand them both, changed his mind.

With Benjie somnolent, Tom broke into German. He told Heilke how much he loved coming to their house, how like his mother she was, in looks and spirit. Gay, determined, but a happier person – and a better cook. His mother had been forcedly gay through the difficulties, at least with him. She had not had many friends in England, being essentially shy and speaking an English that did not go far beyond everyday matters. In all that Heilke was not to be compared. And she had a loving and understanding husband. Tom saw Heilke raise an eyebrow at that, then nod indulgently at Benjie. Tom then wanted Heilke, because of their shared German background, to help him with a difficult time in his life, as his mother would have done. Heilke had read him aright in his love of the country. Hilary now, she was a town girl as Heilke had sensibly noticed. But really there need be no barriers between town and country people. It was the inner way of life that was important. Did she not think so?

Benjie was asleep at the table. Heilke's German became more rapid still. Sometimes Benjie became depressed at old age creeping up, and then drank too much. But it happened so rarely that it did not matter. He always woke happy, she said.

"He'll wake happy tomorrow," Tom assured her. He would say no more about Hilary tonight. Little by little he would bring them round to each other. He kissed Heilke on both cheeks, made his excuses and left.

Doddington-Smith was 24 years old and puzzled by Tom. He had no idea how to handle him. He resolved to be cool and factual. Once show an older, public-school-educated gamekeeper that you had a soft, unprotected belly – a lack of knowledge and experience – and discipline would be finished. Business was business, manager and underling.

"Mr Gailsford has appointed me estate manager. In future you'll report to me. I've seen all your accounts and everything is in order."

"Thank you. Have you thought any more about crop strips, about help with some of the forestry to get the woods in better shape for game?"

There was no possibility of any secondary estate jobs until the pioneering work of bringing back a derelict farm had been achieved. While seeming not to care about the gamekeeper's problems, Doddington-Smith held out the politician's promise of a better future and agreed to try and limit disturbance of the crucial nesting areas.

That afternoon Tom found snowdrops in the ruins of the garden round his cottage. In the next days aconites appeared and later a small clump of scyllas. Daffodils showed above ground, and quite suddenly the year turned the corner. He could see, all over his patch of adopted countryside, trees and plants preparing seriously for spring. The wild pears showed themselves in the hedgerows, and wild plums. He worked for 12 hours a day, on the rearing field and on the release pens. He set 10, 20, 30 tunnel traps, and began catching rats, including several sows full of babies, then a stoat, and another, and a couple of weasels. He remembered how the ground vermin contrived to have their young early so that there would be plenty of feed such as gamebird eggs and young chicks at the time their litters had a maximum need for food. He tried to shoot magpies but they were too wary, and he resolved to set up cage traps for them and for crows. He cast a reconnoitring eye over the rookery. He exercised Schiller, kept up the training games.

He began to feel some confidence again, and took Hilary to dine at the French restaurant, then on to a repertory performance of Ibsen's The Doll's House, and they enjoyed the tough beginnings of the liberation of women from men's domestic tyranny. They made love and began quite seriously and without qualms or jealousies to be more deeply in love.

10. VERMIN CONTROL

Hilary came early to spend the Saturday with him. He took her first to the rearing field. Then they went out along hedges checking tunnel traps. She walked seven or eight miles, mostly in a cold drizzle, spoilt Schiller, ate bread and cheese back in Tom's cottage, and came out again to help him work on one of the release pens and talk about her family.

The Astons came from Somerset. They had been yeoman farmers until the 1850s when an enterprising son had developed a boot-making business in Bristol and made enough money to buy a good town house and enter the society of other prosperous merchants. Her mother's family were from Yorkshire. Her father teased her mother about inheriting her hard business sense from her northern ancestors.

Tom was silent about his own antecedents. But he told her about the habit of hedgehogs to attack the nests of sitting gamebirds, to chew up the eggs and strew the remains round the nest. One could usually tell which predator had robbed a nest. A fox would kill the sitting bird and eat the eggs whole. Stoats hid the eggs a few yards away for later consumption, while a crow would eat the eggs about the same distance away from the nest. On the other hand, magpies usually took the eggs to their nest and dropped the shells at the foot of the tree.

Before dark there were other tunnel traps to check. Painstakingly Tom reset them and scuffed the earth at each entrance. "An animal is attracted to fresh earth," he explained, putting a couple of sticks to prevent a curious pheasant from getting too close. At one point Schiller went off into a dense thicket at the edge of a spinney. Tom followed where he led and found a concealed small warren that had evidently been abandoned by rabbits. Remains of food were scattered under brambles and elder. Tom called Schiller off and had Hilary keep him 20 yards back. He stood off a few paces, still and waiting, for several minutes. Then he imitated a young rabbit's squeak, again and again at short intervals. At last he was rewarded. A bitch stoat popped her head out of a hole, paused, crept fully out into the light. Tom shot her.

"We'll pick up the litter soon enough. See, she's feeding." He turned her body over with his boot.

"All this for Mr Gailsford's pheasants?" Hilary said involuntarily.

"We have to keep a balance." Tom replied shortly, then felt as if some explanation was needed. "It doesn't matter that I think my employer isn't much of a countryman. In an artificial countryside we have to give our game and the songbirds a fair chance. There are predators we rightly can't touch – birds of prey, owls. So we cull the others – the fox, the corvines, and all these small ground vermin."

Hilary nodded dejectedly. "Anyway," she said, "my parents want to meet you, Tom. Can you get away for a weekend?"

"You see I can't. By law I must check each trap every day, for obvious reasons."

Long after dark, when the drizzle had been succeeded by squally rain showers, they reached his cottage. Tom fed Schiller, and they began cooking a meal. "Couldn't your parents come up here for a weekend? I'd like to meet them very much," Tom said.

"I'll ask, although my father's waiting for a hip operation and doesn't travel gladly at present." She paused, watching Tom's profile as he stood over the stove. "What about your father – will he come and visit you?" She saw the bleak expression.

"I sent him a hamper for Christmas, and one to my half-sister and her husband. My sister replied, sent me a book. My father did nothing."

"Why not, Tom? What is there between you?"

Watching the cooking food, Tom told her about the long line of Gibsons and of how he had failed to measure up. He did not recount in full his last interview with his father. He missed out his father's cold statement of his son's cowardice.

"What was so special about your father's career? Did he fail to do something that he hoped you would achieve?" Hilary asked, happy that Tom seemed at last to be talking again.

"I hadn't looked at it precisely in those terms." He thought for a moment. "His first marriage was into an old army family. Just right. She died of pneumonia at the end of the war. They had one daughter. He married my mother for love, maybe, but really infatuation, soon lost. I think he broke my mother's heart showing her what a mistake it was. But he rectified all with my step-mother, back to the good army family." He paused. "Well, she was all right. But as straight up and down the parade ground as he is. She died two years ago in a car crash in a Devon lane."

"And he didn't get a VC," said Hilary, recalling an earlier few terse sentences from Tom. "He had hopes of you."

"I didn't have a big war as he did. Well, the Falklands. A VC was won by the Parachute Regiment. Not by me."

They sat down beside the stove to eat, both ravenous after so long in the open air. Hilary knew there was more to come from Tom, and she wanted it this evening. Perhaps the washing-up would provide the confessional, when all would be revealed and equilibrium restored. With her own completely civilian background she was straining to understand aspirations and codes of behaviour of which she had no experience. Her father was a gentle non-combatant by nature who had nevertheless braved some horrific times on Arctic convoys.

"Is he in good health – your father?" Hilary asked.

"He has heart trouble. So far the doctors have kept him going well enough."

Despite Hilary's probings, Tom said nothing more about his family that evening. He searched for a cassette and they washed up listening to Mozart's concerto in F for two pianos, written when the creditors were baying at his door. When it was finished Tom exploded mildly at a musical public in Vienna that could have let such a precious benefactor of their lives live in such worry and anxiety about money.

"Maybe it was the spur – he wrote and wrote searching for money-making works," Hilary said.

"But that doesn't explain why his music, in spite of money and family troubles, is eternally joyful, deep, loving, and so sane. It reminds us that our petty lives and problems are as nothing to the glorious march of civilised people."

Hilary was nonplussed. "I must listen more," she said. "But I do remember someone at university repeating Richard Strauss, who said he had lived a lifetime of gratitude to Mozart."

At that Tom kissed her. "Stay the night. Tomorrow's Sunday."

Sunday for the gamekeeper began at 5.30 a.m. He and Schiller went out to look along the next hedges to be bulldozed out. He noted nests of partridge and one or two of pheasant, which he would try and save. Hilary had bacon and sausages ready for his breakfast when he returned. By 9.30 they were back at work on one of the release pens. After lunch he left her reading a Sunday paper beside the stove, went out and checked his traps.

In the late afternoon he took Hilary pigeon shooting. She carried with trepidation a 16-bore that had been his at the age of 14. She had never used a gun in her life. He dressed her in an oiled jacket of dirty hue and blackened her face with burnt cork. He told her about the depredations of crops by pigeon. No matter how hard the shooters tried they had not done more than dent their numbers. For a proper war there would need to be men to destroy the nests for a number of years. But the countryside was ever less well 'keepered, the clearance societies had folded, rabbiters grown too old, molecatchers died. She protested not at all at her camouflage, and they went out to hide in thickets close to the edge of a small wood with oaks and good roosting places. When the time came for her to fire her gun at pigeon flying into roost, she actually hit and killed two of them outright. They came back to the cottage with nine birds, and Tom showed her how to pluck and draw them. It had been a companionable weekend.

On Monday the bulldozers began in earnest to change the landscape of the home farm, ripping out hedges. The dead elms and the living ash were uprooted, chain saws were brought in. Only the younger oaks were left, many of them to be isolated in bigger fields. Tom collected up pheasant and partridge eggs and took them to Benjie, who unearthed from the back of his barn a stack of single coops. Together he and Tom searched out the broody possibilities among his Rhode Island Red and bantam hens.

All week the bulldozers and the chainsaws sounded. The noise coupled with the smoke from burning tree trash disorientated all the wild life in a corridor 300 yards on either side of the hedges grubbed out. The contractor brought in huge tractors with five-furrow reversible ploughs to turn the long-disused pastures and fallow under. In a hurry, Doddington-Smith followed the ploughs too soon with soil-breaking implements, heavy harrows, to try and produce enough of a tilth to sow late spring varieties of barley.

As the countryside swung inexorably, and on some days happily, into an English spring, Tom was busy for 14 hours a day. He now had 80 traps out, and he did the final preparations of the rearing field.

In a lull before the pheasant chicks arrived, Tom was invited over by his gamekeeper neighbour for a fox shoot. There were eight guns, all locals and countrymen. Benjie was there and they walked the woods together, starting early in the morning before first light. Three fox were shot, two vixens in cub and a dog fox with a scarred pad. The following week the gamekeeper brought his rods over and, with Benjie, he and Tom went to poke out the grey squirrel dreys in the 50-acre wood on Gailsford's estate. They chose a wet and windy day when there would be sure to be occupants in the leafless bundles of twigs set high in the taller trees. Benjie and either Tom or the gamekeeper – whoever was not doing the poking – were stationed on either side of the tree armed with .22 rifles. Tom and the gamekeeper had to acknowledge that Benjie beat them for sharpshooting, unerringly picking off any squirrels that came out on to the branches or trunks. Any that came to the ground were quickly dispatched by the gamekeeper's two smooth-haired fox terriers.

April had had good days, when the countryside had declared itself, identifying its maples and sycamores, the old coppice of hazel and ash, and spindle trees and wayfarers on the chalkier land. Bluebells and wood anemones showed themselves. But in May the weather deteriorated and temperatures dropped, with cold grey days. On a day in mid-May a thousand day-old chicks were delivered, with the same number 10 days later. Tom's life then revolved round the rearing field. As the chicks grew into poults, Tom cosseted them as much as he dared, trying to acclimatise them to the rougher life they would experience in the release pens within seven weeks of their arrival.

He heard from the police about poaching gangs. Poults fetched a reasonable price on the market. He developed the habit of checking the environs of the rearing field a dozen times in each 24 hours, searching for any sign of two- or four-legged predators. But the danger period would come when the poults went out to the release pens far from the gamekeeper's cottage.

One weekend Charles Gailsford came to his Georgian country house, his wife and himself splendidly sunburnt. Energetically, he castigated the Lancashire couple struggling to manage a large house and bring back long-neglected gardens with a limited budget. After a good Saturday lunch he turned his attention to Doddington-Smith. Gailsford did not consider the weather enough of an excuse for not having sown the target acreage to spring barley. He demanded 20 acres of potatoes and wanted to see sheep on his reseeded pastures in the autumn. By then, too, there had to be oilseed rape and autumn-sown wheat and barley. And what about his sugarbeet quota? He wanted them all, fast.

On Sunday Gailsford came to his gamekeeper's cottage driving a new Range Rover, with his wife beside him. For once the sun was shining, hot on the face, strong enough to brown the English skins of Tom and Hilary who were on the rearing field when Gailsford came unannounced but expected after a call from Doddington-Smith. The farm agent had been almost friendly and Tom had soon understood that he had had a rough time. Tom expected the same.

Gailsford gave Hilary a terse greeting, his wife stared at her, nodded slightly and fixed her attention on Tom. The gamekeeper took them round the rearing field, saying the minimum about the operation, saying nothing of the clutches of wild pheasant and partridge chicks with hens on the smallholding of 'that old Scots ape'. He made no excuses of poor weather to account for the fact that the poults were not as advanced as they normally would be, reckoning rightly that Gailsford would know no better.

"What happens next?"

"Four release pens." He explained where they were, soon losing the attention of them both. Hilary watched and listened as he launched into those curt sentences he seemed to be fond of. How many of each type of vermin disposed of, an estimate of the wild broods safely into the poult stage, a suggestion of an early partridge shoot which would give good sport. Tom then made what Hilary afterwards told him was a deliberate mistake.

"Have you kept up your shooting practice?"

"Why do you ask?" Gailsford was instantly aggressive.

"You made good progress last season," answered his gamekeeper mildly. "It would be a pity to fall back without summer practice."

Gailsford was silent, displeased.

"Makes good sense to me," said his wife, smiling at Tom. Abruptly she stopped smiling, turned to Hilary. "Who are you exactly?"

"Exactly, I'm Hilary Aston – a friend of Mr Gibson's."

"Lovely, lovely," she replied, as displeased as her husband now. Gailsford cut in. "Show me a tunnel trap and one of the release pens."

They all went out in the Range Rover, Gailsford taking it at jaw-breaking and spring-busting speeds over bulldozed hedge land on the way. He had little to say at the pen for there was little for an unknowing eye to see. By the time they reached the tunnel traps both Gailsfords had had enough. There was nothing in any of them since Tom had cleared them early that morning. They barely listened as he told them he had disposed of 11 rats, two stoats and a weasel that day. He explained that he was keeping accurate records which could form a basis for tactics in the future.

"There's a lot to be taken on trust." Gailsford snapped suddenly. "I don't want any excuses from you, Gibson, as I've had from others. The weather, the predators, too much work for one man, all that crap. I want a brilliant pheasant shooting season. I'm paying for it and I will have it. Right?"

Hilary watched Tom open his mouth then shut it with a snap. "I'll do my best, of that you can be sure."

Gailsford turned on his heel and climbed into the Range Rover with his wife. There was no invitation to ride back with them. The vehicle set off in the wrong direction, riding over a field of young barley.

"You did wonderfully, Tom. I would probably have blown my top."

"I had hoped to work through Mrs G," he said.

"She lost interest in you when she discovered me," said Hilary.

Tom looked at her quizzically. It was, he admitted to himself, a new and not unpleasant revelation, if it were true, that women of various ilk found him not unattractive. He was perceptive enough to thank Hilary for it. He kissed her there by the hedge and its tunnel traps.

"If they're sensible they'll be back in a few minutes. The rains have made a mess of the latest hedge removal. There's no way out unless they ram their way through an overgrown thorn hedge."

"I'm amazed at your forbearance. All those hours of work and effort for that man. Just exactly how much does he pay you?"

Tom did not enlighten her. On the way back he told Hilary how a hen partridge when laying her clutch gradually covers the eggs over with leaves. "Then she goes off and feeds while the cock guards the nest. Then she begins the incubation."

"And they're monogamous, you said?"

Tom nodded. "Unlike the pheasant. A cock could have four or five hens in his harem. That's why there are cocks-only shoots, so as to stop too many cocks chasing too few hens.'

After that episode with Gailsford Tom decided to live from week to week, doing his short-term best for the coming season, but not looking to the long-term work that any gamekeeper secure and contented in his post would have in mind. He decided to leave the rooks proliferating in

104

one of the spinneys, but the hard-pressed Doddington-Smith came to the cottage one evening to ask when the rook shoot would take place. The rooks were all over his newly seeded fields.

Tom offered the land agent a glass of white wine. He could see clearly, now that he was at one remove from caring a great deal about the estate, his visitor's problems. He felt as he had done in the army as an operationally experienced and hardened officer with his captaincy, when one-pippers turned up in Northern Ireland. Subalterns just out of Sandhurst and the six months shaking-down period in Belize – a little jungle exercise and how to deal with the men. He gave him a second glass of wine and listened. He was surprised and happy at himself. He was coming back to his earlier self but with added experience, soon perhaps with poise. Three years after the interview with his father. And it was due to Hilary and the Kerrs. They drank more wine and Tom heard how Gailsford had bogged down his Range Rover that Sunday afternoon and had had to be towed out by a tractor. He offered diffident advice about telling Gailsford the minimum, doing the best he could, and staying calm. And they would have the rook shoot the first dry early evening. Doddington-Smith called Tom by his Christian name. "I'm Richard," he said. They finished the wine.

"He has gone on his delivery round, Tom." Heilke Kerr was busy feeding the livestock. Tom had brought her half a dozen pigeon. He stayed to help her with the work.

"Will the sun ever shine again?" she asked. "Lucky some of our land is light. We can work that quite soon in a dry spell. But the clay land, it is waterlogged." She talked about Benjie, and how in the past few months he had become less stressed, much happier. He had taken Hilary's advice and cut down the variety of vegetables and stock. Would Tom please try and persuade Benjie to buy a modern vehicle that would not always be breaking down? They could afford it without difficulty. But he was so fond of his Morris Traveller.

Tom tried to raise the subject of Hilary. At mention of her name, he saw Heilke closing up. "She and I find we have much in common," he began hesitantly, wondering suddenly whether that were really true. They seemed to have been marking time of late, he working long hours alone, she in conferences, meetings, and travelling. But, watching Heilke, he saw at last clearly why he wanted her on his side. He could see his mother in the drawing room in Devon, arms akimbo as Heilke had her arms now, looking into his heart. What had been the episode? He could not now remember the details, but recalled that his mother had had only a few months to live. Now, today, there was no doubt of Heilke's good health as she stood sturdy and ruddy-cheeked before him.

"I love Hilary," he said. "One day I hope to marry her. I want you, please, Heilke, to be with me, to take her to yourself, too."

He was unprepared for the reaction. Very quietly, charged with emotion, Heilke began to cry, the tears starting from her eyes and lying almost joyfully on her cheeks. "I will love her, too, Tom. Oh, I will, I will." She kissed Tom on both cheeks. "We will love her, Benjie and me."

Tom left quickly, alarmed and unsure of the reaction. He took Schiller and they walked a dozen miles. He found Hilary at his cottage when he returned at seven that evening with a couple of rabbits.

"Are they safe to eat?" Hilary was evidently tired.

"I'll know in the morning." He explained that a healthy rabbit obeyed the laws of *rigor mortis*, while one with myxomatosis – without evident physical sign of it, of course – remained flaccid.

Hilary advanced on him and kissed him deeply, wanting to feel his arms round her. She held the kiss, until he broke away, laughing.

"I need reassurance," she said. "Don't laugh. I'm serious."

"Light the stove," he said, throwing her a box of matches. "I'll make a cup of tea – there's nothing alcoholic left."

He made the tea, brought it in two mugs. Hilary was dejected, unsure of herself. He vowed to reassure her immediately, wished to have her here in his cottage, listening to music in the sitting room, reading opposite him, in his kitchen, in his bed. He wanted her out with him in the May countryside, in January's ice and snow. Dancing close to him, driving with him. Everywhere, all the time. And surely he had spoken the truth to Heilke, his mother figure, when he had said that he wanted to marry her?

"Do I need to reassure you?" he asked. "I love you every way there is."

Hilary nodded. "Perhaps, yes. I think you do at the moment. But our lives are abrasive, rubbing up sparks. Parallel but not converging, not merging."

"Go on," Tom felt cold, clutching the mug of hot tea.

"I'm beginning to lose contact with the details of my job," she said, keeping her voice quiet with an effort. "My colleagues have noticed."

"They're teasing you? After all, even marketing directors are entitled to a life outside the office."

Hilary was silent for a few moments, then rose and came close to Tom where he stood by the stove. "They're not teasing me. One is happy because he wants my job. The others – I think they can see that I'm miserable. And I am when I'm not with you." She paused. "And now I'm being miserable here, too."

"What can I do?" Tom gulped the hot tea, spluttered.

"How can we co-exist?" she asked. "You leading an isolated life in the woods, me travelling all over Europe, attending sales conferences, meeting clients." She put her hands on his shoulders. What she saw in his face did not ease her mind. "My rational self tells me I think of you for an absolutely absurd amount of time. But I need to be with you. You would probably have me to live with you here, and I would have to give up my job for that to satisfy me."

"You could find a less demanding job. Less travel," said Tom, attempting a cheerful tone. He knew the question she would ask next.

"How much do you earn, Tom? Could we both live on it?"

"Gamekeepers do – and raise families," he replied defensively.

"But not to have good food, music, plays, holidays abroad – a cultivated life."

"Not to have expensive cars, send children to private schools," he said. "But a cultivated life – books, music, an inner civilisation of the mind – well, that's possible. I think I demonstrate the feasibility of it."

Hilary shook her head. "Who can you talk to about your civilised ideas? Benjie and Heilke? Me? The village pub-goers?"

Tom smiled uncertainly. "I've only just begun to return to some form of spiritual equilibrium. I tried to explain – about my father and his rigid attitudes. And my failure – my failing the family ghosts."

"But is this the way to regain your position in the world?" She saw she had made a tactical error. "Tom, my darling Tom –" She was beautiful now. "What I mean, for you to regain your confidence in yourself, your self-esteem, is by showing all those people out there that you can succeed in a career other than soldiering."

"Gamekeepering," he said shortly, and did not smile.

"But it doesn't give us enough scope to bring our lives together," she wailed, at last breaking her calm.

He moved away from her, went to stand by his bookshelves, took down a book and turned its pages. "This is Schiller," he said. "You really think that I can utilise my knowledge of his works to earn a better living than I do looking after Gailsford's pheasant?"

Hilary sighed. "Germany is the motor economy of the European Community, France the old civilised nation beginning at last to find her economic feet. There's the single market ahead in 1992." Deliberately she did not follow him across the room. "You know, Tom, we have talents that could complement each other. If we worked at it we could be an unbeatable team."

At last Tom grinned. He came quickly across the room and gathered Hilary into his arms. "I understand what you are saying, and I will think long and hard about it."

Hilary kissed him long and hard.

11. A Kind of Waterloo

"Poachers took 500 duckling from that farm beyond Glanby," said Benjie. "Sitting targets all out in a great field." There had been two unaccustomed fine days in the progression of a cold, wet English spring and early summer. Tom and Benjie were out looking over the rookery.

"Surely they had some means of protection?" Tom asked.

"What could they have? Microwave alarm fields? Closed circuit television? Intruder alarms?"

"Some sort of guard?"

Benjie shrugged. "Night surveillance over a field that large – must be 20 acres – would put the price of duck beyond what even the affluent of the south-east would care to afford."

The police had warned all stock owners to be on the alert. In this case the farmer had been decoyed to the other end of his farm by a burst tractor tyre, and the police to a Forestry Commission woodland across the county.

"What can you do, Benjie? I'll keep an eye on Shepherd's Pightle when I'm out at night."

"Come by if you will, and thanks," said Benjie. "But I've thick hawthorn hedges. Only six acres to guard and I'm on the spot. And plenty of geese around."

In default of elms, the rookery had re-established itself in beech trees. It was a strong colony, left in peace for years.

"They're as bad as crows and magpies," said Benjie. "Egg thieves."

Tom nodded. "Our land agent wants to come and help shoot them up. They're after his newly sown crops."

"Do you care?" asked Benjie.

Tom had to acknowledge that he cared less than he should for the farming operations, given the lack of cooperation so far. And yet, if he believed in a fully integrated and productive countryside, with a balance of all the good things the earth could produce and sustain then he must work with the land agent. And now there were signs that cooperation might be forthcoming.

The young fledgling rooks were just about to try their wings, coming out along the branches. If the weather was dry that evening – and the forecast was for more rain spreading from the north-west the next day – they should come back with their guns.

The sun was already casting shadows when they arrived at the rookery. The quality of light and the clarity of distances were more akin to a September than a mid-May evening. The young rooks were on the branches, and adult rooks fluttered everywhere. A light breeze from the south rustled the fresh young green leaves of the beeches. Tom and Benjie carried .22 rifles. Richard Doddington-Smith had a 12-bore, as did the retired schoolmaster who looked after the beaters on a shoot. Schiller and Benjie's springer Sally had been joined by Benjie's lurcher. Tom had not seen the dog before. He was a greyhound/wolfhound cross, with the aloof unemotional demeanour of a greyhound. In a puppyish way Schiller danced round him and was given no encouragement at all. Tom was pleased to find that Doddington-Smith was subdued, waiting to be told what to do.

"The riflemen will go for the branchers," said the gamekeeper. "Richard, you and Mr Manners will pick off the fledglings that launch themselves. If you take a few of the adults, so much the better. The colony's too strong by half."

He placed the guns with the sun behind them. "It'll be difficult shooting – almost vertical. Take your time."

As the guns began firing, Tom stepped back to mark the effect. He saw that Benjie was shooting calmly and with extraordinary accuracy. He began firing himself, trying to match Benjie's skill. The two shotguns opened up from time to time. The colony was in upheaval. Tom thought about the number of pheasant and partridge eggs which would be saved next year, the number of wheat and barley seeds left to grow and ripen into grain. He had a vision of gamekeepers and farm labourers of the past gathering up the small black-feathered bodies and taking them home for the pot. Rook pie. He supposed they ate only the breasts. But then in hungry, poverty-stricken days everything had gone into the stewpot. Pigeon, rook, thrush and blackbird. He thought about Jack Turner, the 'keeper who had lived in his cottage, and Albert Brown who had gone to the war and not returned. And there would have been numbers of 'keepers before them. They would have taken the rooks home to their wives. He thought of Hilary in the cottage kitchen, in his apron.

The rook shoot was over. The guns gathered up their bag.

"It's hardly sport," said Richard, a little pale.

"Not much," Tom conceded. "But there are still plenty up there. We've just evened the odds."

They walked home with the westering sun a golden ball sinking into a cloudless horizon. There was a comradeship within the small group that they all felt, talking quietly, congratulating each other on their marksmanship, calling the dogs to heel. Doddington-Smith was grateful to Tom. Perhaps it was not too late for maize strips for the gamebirds.

Tom went off to dispose of the carcases. He dug a hole out among the tangled red- and blackcurrant bushes where there had once been a productive fruit and vegetable patch, and buried them. If he was here next year he would bring the patch back into production. Once he had had a small vegetable garden in Devon. He had grown radishes at first, then become more ambitious. His father had come back from an overseas posting and had promptly taken away his enthusiasm with a cutting remark about only labourers concerning themselves with such tasks. The essence of command was to get other people to do that kind of thing for one. Tom Hawker, now, he had grown all kinds of vegetables, and kept hutches of rabbits and a few hens, and had fattened a pair of cockerels for Christmas. Tom went indoors to prepare Schiller's food, cook his own meal, and listen to Elgar's Symphony No. 1, which always made him think of English countryside, as if he were floating high on thermals with a buzzard's eye view. This time he saw North Devon winter woods and fields, streams, hills, and solitary trees in green meadows. He thought of Tom Hawker again, remembered the closeness of his cottage, for men who spent their lives out of doors seldom opened windows. For a moment he was Tom Hawker, felt the cosiness and safety of the cottage, the ache of tired limbs. There was a plate of piled food, a pipe of tobacco, and the prospect of Saturday evening in the pub, among his own people and talking the north Devon dialect. Tom Gibson was glad that he had the billhook.

After the few days of sun the weather turned wet once more and continued dank and grey-clouded into June. The poults did badly on the rearing field and prospects were poor for them when they would be put out into the release pens. The chicks hatched under broodies at

Shepherd's Pightle were doing much better, in small groups with fussy, protective mothers. Out along the hedges and on the edges of the dripping woods the wild broods did not fare well. With the rearing field work and vermin control, and his insistence on maximum protection for his charges, the gamekeeper was working a 14-hour day again. He reached home too tired to cook, subsisting on bread and cheese, cold baked beans. He became thin, the taciturn look that Hilary had thought she had banished came back. He was gentle with her and thoughtful, but abstracted, his mind always out somewhere on the estate, willing the sun to come back, the poults to feather up quicker. After all, he had promised Gailsford eight days of shooting, and a good show of birds.

Hilary came and cooked for him at weekends, made a casserole dish on the Sunday which he could heat up on his return. She hesitated to take advantage of him when his responsibilities seemed to weigh so heavily on him. But her own work was suffering. Although they made love regularly and both were happy and satisfied, she was no nearer bringing him to consider their future together. He spoke not at all about his family. Instead he told her about stoats, how they selected their quarry, be it a hare or rabbit, and followed it until it began to weaken and go round in ever-decreasing circles. Gamekeepers believed it was not lack of strength but loss of stamina. After all, a hare could run itself out of trouble. The stoat just kept on until its quarry submitted to it in sheer paralysing terror.

One Sunday evening Hilary at last tackled him. "Why don't you tell me more about your family? I understand about the Gibson line. But I can't see that once you've chosen to renounce its influence and make another life, your defection should haunt you so."

"I am reconciled," he said. "Of course I am." He sounded unsure.

"Then let's discuss our future. I must earn five or six times what you do. All right, I know money isn't the be-all. But it's bloody important."

Reluctantly at first, then in a rush he told her what he earned. "I get more in kind," he said, knowing that the items added up to little in real terms. "The cottage is free, and my electricity is paid."

Hilary changed tack. "I don't have any prospects – from my parents, I mean. Well, nothing much. They own their own house. They have savings in equities, a building society. But there are three of us, and anyway my mother's very fit and will long outlast my father."

Tom nodded. "I understand," he said. "Look, I must check the rearing field and give Schiller a run." He paused, kept his thoughts only on his few possessions here in his cottage. "I don't have any prospects. None at all. Really, it's best that way."

"And our future together?"

He had been shrugging into a raincoat by the door. He came back to Hilary and took her in his arms. They were so well matched in height, he thought, looking into eyes that were grey-blue, more blue than grey this night since she wore a blue cardigan. Matched in many ways. He wished he could give her the assurances she wanted, tell her that he would come out into her world, tell her about Devonshire in detail. But he was not yet reconciled to the rift with his father, not yet ready to give pledges again that he was not certain he could keep. He told her he loved her, and would come to terms with his love and the compromises and new duties that his love dictated and conferred. But he could not now. "Meanwhile," he said, "be patient and keep faith in me, and with me."

"Patient for how long?" Hilary was dry-eyed, but knew that if he did not go immediately she would make a fool of herself.

Tom thought of the Kerrs and his growing sense of kinship with them. Heilke's sweetly theatrical gestures, Benjie's fear of growing old, and whisky-laden breath from across the table when he had deliberately knocked him out. He thought of Benjie's barn with its hoarded treasures, of the peace inside a building that dated from the early 18th century. How many men had worked in that barn, stuffed it with sheaves of corn, flailed the grain out in hours of patient slogging work, kept livestock there, slept in it, made love to girls in the hayloft? Were these his people? Had Tom Hawker's billhook cut through the line of Devon squires, severed it clean, freed him to find another family? His mind continually shied away from living in a town, working in an office. He could take the countryside pressures – the needs of his gamebirds, the rearing field, the release pens and the shoots. But not the pressures to make sales, mount marketing campaigns, persuade people to buy, to worry about servicing and maintenance, to control a task force. Yet was it all so different from his training as an army officer? He was still confused, still seeing his father's white nostrils, hearing the cold, biting voice.

"I'm close to some kind of decision," he said at last, standing by the door again, the latch raised.

He went out, and Hilary began softly to cry, feeling the tension leave her.

113

By mid-July all the pheasant poults were out in the release pens. Benjie and the retired schoolmaster had helped Tom catch them on the rearing field, and with the clipping of their beaks and of one wing, so that they would neither harass each other nor fly out of the pens for about three weeks until the feathers had grown again.

He concentrated his vermin-catching activities in the areas immediately round the release pens. Each pen had anti-predator grids and entrances, mostly against fox. Here the poults would gradually become acclimatised to the wild, would eventually fly out of the open-topped area of each pen for the day, and return to the security of the pen at night, where water was available, if not some food. That would depend on the weather, and Tom knew that he might have to feed extensively if the dull weather and rain continued and limited the amount of natural food available. As to human intruders – he strung black cotton across paths towards the pens, where there was little light in the woods.

The police circulated all gamekeepers to say that there had been instances elsewhere in the county of poults being taken.

"Prices of shot birds will be high," Benjie predicted. "Landowners will do all they can to make sure they've a good stock of birds on their land."

"But not to buy poults without knowing where they're from," answered Tom dismissively.

"Some landowners are capable of cheating and conniving."

Tom would not believe it, but laid out more black cotton and took to patrolling his release pens every few hours night and day.

One evening towards the end of July the gamekeeper returned to his cottage tired out. For once it was warm. Only let the sun through and the countryside smiled and sang. The wind was from the south. He had gone out dressed for the cold and wet, and had discarded garments here and there as he worked. Schiller had caught a mole moving incautiously above ground. Yellow-hammers in the hedges had intrigued Tom, and he had seen a barn owl steadily beating up the hedgerows in the half hour at twilight, a great white bird, beautiful in its isolation and dedication to the hunt. As for himself and food, he already believed himself too exhausted to bother about it.

He found Hilary there. A subdued, thoughtful Hilary with an

omelette pan at the ready and all the ingredients of a Spanish omelette laid out to be cooked. Tom prepared the dog's food. Schiller was a great companion, he told Hilary as he washed, while the scents of cooking food began to revive him. Again there was no drink in the house. It was days, if not weeks, since he had been to a shop. He came into the kitchen and saw the food in the pan.

"I didn't know I had all these ingredients."

"You didn't. I discovered only a tin of tuna fish and some baked beans," she replied. "Eat first," she added. "Then we'll talk."

Obediently he did as he was told. He ate in silence, trying not to wolf the food, pausing now and again to look round the living room, avoiding Hilary's eyes as she sat opposite him.

"You're not eating," he said at last, ashamed that he had not noticed before.

"I had my supper long ago. I've been browsing in your bookshelves, reading about the battle of Waterloo."

"A cold and wet summer then, too."

She nodded and told him about the battle. He ate and listened, seeing for the first time that she had also lost weight.

She finished her tale. "Drink your tea," she said. "And now, my darling Tom. We have a problem to face. We have come in some manner to a kind of personal Waterloo."

"Go on," he said, gulping hot tea, certain that he would not be able to give her what she wanted – a conventional husband of her class. He listened to her now, loving her and keeping his distance, wanting to be what she wanted him to be, and unable to see the way forward. She said that she wanted to be with him always, she wanted his children, she came of a family that married late and stayed together. They were 'marriage for lifers' believing in all those supposedly old-fashioned virtues of faithfulness and duty, in a family system that supported all its members. She guessed there were similarities in his background. Could they not bring the common traits in their backgrounds together? He had told her so little about himself. She had tried not to be inquisitive. But if two people loved each other there should be no holding back. They should be entirely open with each other.

"I couldn't work in an office," he said when she fell silent.

"Well, there are other possibilities – other than what you do at present." She had wanted to use the phrase 'menial work' and, watching Tom's eyes avoiding hers, she discarded it. Being forthright

115

and blunt was one of the weapons she employed from time to time in her staff relations. Being understanding and roundabout, and letting the other person come to a realisation by him- or herself was another. She used the latter ploy now, with trepidation. In the office she used it with cool forethought. Now it was with an intellect dangerously overruled by the heart.

"Maybe," he mumbled. "Maybe. I must think about it when I'm not so damn tired."

Hilary conceded her defeat in this skirmish. She rose quickly from her chair, making a decision now in the way she was well known in her company for making them. Research done, all circumstances weighed and taken into account, personalities assessed, and then the decision, enunciated with force and a certain attractive diffidence which softened the words without diminishing their strength.

"I have to go to the United States. We're expanding there. And I shall visit my sister." She found relief in the statement. The pressure had been on from her managing director to go, and she had resisted it. She knew that she had begun to acquire a black mark or two on her record. Now she could recuperate, give of her all to the company again, at least across the Atlantic. And she had to hope that distance and time would change circumstances for the better when she came back to England. She would be away a month.

They made love that night. Both holding back at first, almost apologetically, until their enthusiasm for each other's bodies overcame the slight coldness that their talk had engendered. At four in the morning Tom went out to check the release pens. The brief period of sun and high pressure had been swept on into the North Sea. Rain had spread from the south-west.

"You're lavishing overly much love on these birds," said Benjie. "And it was the same in the Hungry Forties. If that love had been directed to the young men of the cottages–"

"– they wouldn't have poached." Tom finished the sentence for him. "And listen, I've been reading about those times. By the 1860s there were better cottages, more allotments, improved schools. And still there was poaching. One night with no attempt at concealment nine men with guns attacked a gamekeeper's house. Not so far from here, Benjie. The 'keeper and his wife and children were lucky to escape with their lives."

They were at one of the release pens. The poults were stunted, wet and miserable, not taking their food with enthusiasm.

"In 1855," said Benjie, counter-attacking, "a policeman stopped a labourer with a few 'neeps to feed his family. He got two weeks in prison, and because his family had no means of support they were put in the workhouse. Under a new poor law, relief could only be given to those in the workhouse. Women and children were separated there."

Tom sighed. "Don't tell me things aren't different now."

"Only in degree. The rich still get richer, and the poor put up wi' the leavings."

They argued all the way back to Shepherd's Pightle, and arrived at their destination agreeing that a policy of three or four acres and a cow for everyone, or its equivalent in a town property, would help but not solve many of mankind's problems. Schiller and the springer Sally were playful together all the way home, Sally fleeing gleefully to the protection of the aloof stalking lurcher, named Khan after an Afghan wolfhound ancestor. At least the conversation made Tom forget that Hilary was in Colorado Springs, staying at some wonderful hotel up against the rampart of the Rockies, where there was no rain and she ate tender beef by the pound. A month. And there were still 17 days to go. He had already written seven letters to her at her sister's address, feeling foolish at the ridiculous image he must be creating for the red-haired, hot-eyed sister. Nowadays people 'phoned, especially in the States where calls were cheap. He was the static one, and he had no idea of her itinerary or telephone numbers. She would surely call him. He had waited in vain, blaming his erratic hours and the time difference.

Heilke had bidden him to come and eat with them every evening if he wanted. She had been alarmed at his thin appearance and his inward-turning eye. Tom took to eating virtually nothing on the days when he knew he would be having one of her meals. He walked everywhere, taking Schiller with him. They covered a dozen miles a day. He perfected ways of surveying the countryside from a distance, using trees, hills and slopes, moving silently and unseen round the estate. At night he slept deeply and dreamlessly, but only for two or four hours, before doing the rounds of his release pens. He then slept for another four hours. Although he knew that he had to vary his visiting times, he found that his working day and night fell too often into a pattern.

The Kerrs only asked after Hilary in a gentle, unprobing way and Tom gave them each time the same answer – that she was having a good time, had sent him several postcards. But he knew they saw he was disorientated by her absence. He tried to be objective and believed that he was not jealous of whatever she might be doing in America. She came from faithful stock. She loved him. Although the thought of her physical being, her verve and enthusiasm in lovemaking, was often recalled, it was the lesser known, the bigger part of Hilary, her total worth, that he tabulated with greater and greater insight. All the while he did his best to protect and bring on Charles Gailsford's pheasant despite deluge and cold, wind, drizzle, numbing rain from the north-west, and a day when it felt as if the skies would suddenly mantle the drenched countryside with snow.

There came a moment when he wanted to talk to someone. Heilke was solicitous and sweet. He hoped that she was reconciled to Hilary. She seemed to be. Her conversation, always in German, ranged over the news from Germany, the films, plays, operas and spectacles of all sorts that she loved and missed, read about in Benjie's Guardian, but never saw on television for Benjie would not have a set. He was, she said, a founder-member of the post-television society, although he had never been part of any TV society anyway.

That evening Tom listened, relaxed for once, in the steamy kitchen with good food inside him. He was glad that Heilke was there if he needed her. Yet he knew that if he wanted to talk anything out it would be to Benjie to whom he would turn.

"Roger Hoggett," said Tom to Benjie. "The publican. Have you known him long?"

"He's local. Knew him when he was a schoolboy. Not above a little poaching. He's sly, as you've found out."

"He and the bearded thin man were close together, the day of the hare shoot. I've nothing to go on but a hunch. Do you fancy a pint of his beer?"

Benjie looked across at Heilke, who nodded, pleased that her men were taking a simple pleasure together.

They went in Benjie's Morris Traveller, rattling, a hesitant engine, and lights that left something to be desired. The MOT was in December, and Benjie acknowledged that someone would have to work on the car before then.

The pub was crowded. There were few locals there, mostly summer tourists, and the landlord was busy.

They drank together in friendly silence, then talked about the smallholding. At last Benjie spoke. "What's bitin' ye, Tom?"

"Clash of views on how to live a life, and earn a living," said Tom.

"Have you told her everything – about yoursel'?"

Tom nearly said there was nothing more to tell. And there was not, he believed. "She knows about the Gibsons and about me and my small problem of identity and self-confidence."

"She sets conditions?"

Tom smiled. "Indirectly." The noise in the pub was loud. A group of young tourists were drinking too much and laughing too loudly.

"You want her – to marry her?"

"Yes, I do – I really do."

Benjie looked quizzically at Tom. "A hare when it knows it's outpaced will head for rough territory and begin dodging," he said.

"I'm not dodging –" Tom began, indignantly.

"But you are like a hare, laddie. You've got no sanctuary, have you? Not in Devon, not here. You've only your speed and stamina to save you – if you want to save yourself."

"What are you saying?"

"Compromise. She's a fine lass. You've got to work at the game. All good relationships need thought and care."

Benjie dropped him at the entrance to the track to his cottage. That night Tom slept the whole night through, the first time for 10 days. Just before he woke he dreamed that he was a hare making for broken country on one of the old tussocky pastures, with Benjie, Khan, Schiller and the springer Sally all barking and baying after him.

119

12. Facing Up

As he approached the release pen in the big wood he found the black cotton across the path broken. There were no noises of recognition to his whistle, instead the silence of devastation. Tom halted at the edge of the clearing. He waited still and silent. Schiller imitated his master, moved no muscle, his head pushed forward and up, watching the carefully contrived citadel of posts and wire. Now some posts lay flattened, the wire netting hummocked over the ground where 500 pheasant poults had had their being. Tom went forward slowly, his 12-bore shut, the safety catch off, noting on the wet ground the print of a track shoe here, of a studded boot beyond. They had netted them, he thought, brought them down from their low roosts in the bushes within the pen, herded them quietly into a corner and taken a net to them. Poorly grown as they were, the poults were still potentially high-flying birds on some estate in November – the first time any right-minded shoot owner would try and take birds reared in such a season. In such a year a brace of young birds could fetch up to £6 in feather. But the worth of the birds on a dinner table was little to that of their value to an owner with business interests, with important guests to fête. He squatted down in the middle of his release pen, smelled the birds and their droppings, and Schiller put his wet nose against his hand.

The other three release pens were untouched. He came back to the big wood and began methodically searching for clues. There must have been five men, and no dogs. He cast further afield, backtracking the way the poachers had come to the release pen. They had left a different way. Tracks led him to the green lane – boot marks, crushed grass and weeds where nets had been half carried, half-dragged. He thought about Roger Hoggett. In the Red Lion last night, he and Benjie had spent about an hour and a half. They had had two pints of bitter each. Hoggett knew Benjie well enough and did not like him. Tom Gibson he knew hardly at all. Both had been dressed in their working clothes. Both would have presented Hoggett with the decided impression that they were physically very tired, finished for the night. Supposing Hoggett had made a telephone call?

Tom went back to his cottage and telephoned the police and Richard Doddington-Smith. The first were business-like and would come and check the pen. The second was sympathetic. Richard would report it to Gailsford but would like a note from Tom.

"I slept all night. The first time for 10 nights," Tom told him.

Tom wrote the report, setting out the facts without comment. He did not seek to excuse himself. He explained about the poor growth of the pheasant poults due to wet weather conditions. He said he had raised another 200 chicks from abandoned wild eggs set under broody hens, without explaining where. He felt better when it was written, and thought of writing again to Hilary in America, telling her about the release pens and his suspicions of the Red Lion's landlord. But he did not, realising she would be back before the letter arrived. In her month away he had received five postcards, open for all to read. Friendly little messages, written carefully.

His own letters had not exactly been love letters. Yet he had made plain in an understated way that he thought of her night and day, wanted her beside him in a hundred small commonplace incidents and times, wanted her to talk to, to make love to. He knew that he had said nothing about a change of career, nothing about his prospects. But even so he thought the postcards carried altogether too far a feigned indifference in the expectation of bringing him to heel. He would rib her about it when she came back. In three days' time. He had crossed off the days on a calendar, the date of her return ringed in red. He would take the calendar down, put it away before Hilary came to his cottage.

Hilary was slim and sun-tanned, wearing expensive casual American clothes. She was poised and non-committal as she greeted Tom in her living room. He knew immediately that her business trip had been a success. She had presents for him, a snakeskin belt and a bottle of bourbon whisky. Tom's heart sank watching her act like any tourist generously squandering travel moneys and too much time on presents for 'the folks back home'. She seemed unaware of the impression she was creating. He had come determined to talk out their problems, to tell her he would not be staying beyond the end of the shooting season with Gailsford, that he was open to suggestions for using his languages. He said nothing of this, smarting under the kisses on both cheeks she had given him as he entered.

"Has something happened to change our relationship?"

Hilary was cool, poured him a glass of red Burgundy. He sighed and he drank. The wine was beautiful, full-bodied.

"I think it has, Tom. Not anything that happened in America, I promise you. Just a more careful appraisal of what I was – what we were about to commit."

"The heart ruling the head," he said.

"Yes. All my training is the other way round. Yours should be, too. The army, I mean."

Tom looked into the deep red wine in his glass. So that was his trouble. Always heart over head. He must ring his father and tell him he had found out the difference between them. He took no pleasure in the prospect. Did the man really believe so blindly in the Gibson mystique that he could not find it in his head, let alone his heart, to understand his son?

Watching Hilary, he fancied he saw that beneath the calm she was nervous, and he had the impression that she was acting a pre-arranged part. Was this a part she really thought necessary? If so, he was about to come to heel. He opened his mouth to say that he would move into her world, when the telephone rang. Hilary answered it, looked puzzled for a moment. "You want Tom Gibson, I think," she said, then covered the speaker. "It's the man at the hall, Gailsford's factotum. A message for you to ring your sister urgently."

His sister met him at the station and they drove up through north Devon lanes to his birthplace. She was kind and a little distant. This younger half-brother was an enigma to her. Her views on life and duty were explicit and rigid. She and Tom had never exchanged confidences, never been close. She told him that their father had died peacefully, had been out with the dogs, had a good lunch, watched his grand-daughters play tennis, had enjoyed his whisky and soda, and had died in his dressing room changing for dinner.

Was that a good way for a soldier and a countryman to go, Tom wanted to ask but did not. He could better have fallen stricken into one of his own hedges on the estate – a hedge tended for 40 years by Tom Hawker. Unaware of these unconventional thoughts, Mary Barkworthy recounted the doings of her children, and especially of Richard, aged five. Roddy, her husband, was at the house now. He was enjoying retirement at 48, was mixed up in so many village and county organisations. Tom pictured his well-off polo-playing brother-in-law, retired gunner lieutenant-colonel. The Barkworthys lived two villages away in a William and Mary house behind a high rose-red brick wall, with stabling, paddocks, large gardens. A pair of daughters and a son who, if all went aright, and they did not fall foul of subversive influences, were destined to perpetuate the Barkworthy place in the upper-middle class, duty to sovereign and country in return for a healthy slice of the plum pudding of England. Well, he, Tom Gibson had been part of all that himself. Still was, perhaps.

He began shifting in his seat as they came to his native heath. He saw trees he knew, and banks, and clumps of woodland. A row of cottages out in full countryside were quite as he remembered them. He was tingling, twisting, peering through the windows, to left, to right, forwards, trying not to miss the landmarks of his earlier life as they registered themselves on his brain moments before his eyes saw them. Village lads out on a spree had taken this gate off its hinges. He had gone after tadpoles in that pond. Over by this spinney he had shot his first rabbit. They would be skirting the village in a few moments and he would see Tom Hawker's cottage. A line of flowers up to the door, with vegetables in ranks everywhere else in the small garden. And here it was, on the corner of the lane which led to the lime tree avenue and the drive up to the house.

"Father must have sold it," he blurted out.

"Sold what, Thomas?"

"The cottage on the corner." The old casement windows had been replaced with diamond leaded lights. The door was now a neo-Georgian panelled affair too grand for the cottage. There was an outside lamp and fancy ironwork. Gone were the vegetables and the pathway of flowers. Lawns and a shrubbery had taken their place.

Apparently his father had sold all the cottages of the estate that had been in the village. There had no longer been any need for them, and with the influx of Londoners seeking weekend cottages it had been a profitable occasion. Tom did not ask his sister if she thought it had been a good move. She was – had always been – so practical and sensible. There would still be properties with land for such as they. Although some places would be sold on, gentrified, suburbanised, they would still have their land, could still, as some wag had once said of the landowning classes, dig their ha-has deeper to keep out the vulgar who invaded the countryside, and keep out the vulgar who had always lived in the countryside, too.

The house was exactly as he had it in his mind's eye so often, a symmetrical Georgian house relying for decoration on its proportions and the colours of its red-brick walls and stone quoins, its top balustrade with a low roof of Cornish slate just showing through. The portico with its two pairs of Ionic columns had recently been repainted. Tom recalled in every detail the south-west front that he had not yet seen, with its flagged terrace, the cedar of Lebanon off to the south-east, and to the west some distance away a pair of tulip trees planted by the first Gibson in the 1820s.

"You're in your own room, Thomas," his sister had said after he had greeted Roddy and his nieces and nephew. He had found a kind of decent-hearted embarrassment in Roddy that he had never seen before. "Then perhaps you'd like to see him."

His room was unchanged, with its windows facing the unseen but always felt sea, several miles away. Now there was no great wind to rattle the sashes as there had been so often. Late summer in Devon was providing a fine day, still and full of sun. He made his way to his father's bedroom.

General Sir Richard Gibson was laid out on the bed. On his side table were the insignia of a Knight Grand Cross of the Bath, a Commander of the British Empire, together with his other decorations and medals. His son touched the Distinguished Service Order, the campaign medals from the second world war, the general service medal with several clasps, and the Croix de Guerre of France. Now they would join the array of decorations and medals in the big oval display cabinets in the drawing room below. Every honour for every masterly Gibson was there. Tom knew them all by heart, what they were and who they had belonged to. Knowing the medals and their histories had been part of the Gibson indoctrination.

Reluctantly Tom looked at his father's white marbled face with its faint bluish tinge, the closed eyes. He felt no sadness, only a regret that they had had so little in common, so little other than acerbic conversations down the years culminating in the awful interview three years before. On reflection after that day, his father had seemed to him to have been childish, over-simple in his beliefs of family behaviour, and had acted as no highly experienced general officer should have done. Had he not known of the frailty, stupidity and small-mindedness of men and women? Equally, had he not seen that so many people do their duty in ways which did not attract the medals and decorations, and that their contribution to the commonweal was important too?

Watching his father's unmoving mask, the strong features as formidable in death as in life, he knew that the family solicitor would confirm what his father had said to him three years ago. He sat for half an hour in the still room. The window was closed and the air smelt of soap and ether. He tried with concentration to remember his father in some little affectionate fatherly moment. His father was so seldom in his memories, and then only as a lurking worry that he might come or a blessed relief that he was away. He remembered how much happier in a sad way his mother had been when he was absent, how she had always begun to look younger and expectant, and happy in a frenetic, merry way when he was due, and each time had become fretful and miserable so soon after his arrival. At last he did recall one moment of near-friendliness. It was long after his mother had died. His father and stepmother had come to Wellington when he had been captain of shooting. The school had won the public schools cup. Tom's own score had been in the middle range, but he had worked hard to support and encourage his team. And his father had noticed, putting a hand for a moment on his son's arm.

The memory was not enough, Tom thought, to make him feel remotely sorry that his father had died. And at that dire thought, and his own isolation from his loved surroundings, he left the room.

Mary Barkworthy found Tom stalking round the gardens. "Father would have liked us to dine tonight as usual," she said. "I've had your dinner jacket pressed. Shirt, tie, cufflinks – all organised." She paused. "You left them all here, you know."

They ate that evening in the dining room with portraits of past Gibsons looking down from every side. All the men of paint were in uniform, some with battle backgrounds. The ladies were in their finery or sitting out under the cedar with children and dogs. The evening passed off less unhappily than Tom anticipated. Roddy and he told stories of their soldiering days. The housekeeper did her best with the food, the sort of meal that had been served to Gibsons here for

125

generations. They drank one of Tom's grandfather's clarets. They drank to the general lying upstairs – Roddy's toast. Tom proposed a toast to the grandfather who had laid down the wine.

"That's flippant, Thomas," said Mary.

"I intended only respect," he said, "and gratitude."

As a daughter of the house, Mary in turn asked them to raise their glasses to the Gibson line.

"You mean there will always be Gibsons here, to continue what we are doing tonight?" asked Tom, with a momentary spark of hope.

His sister and brother-in-law were immediately embarrassed, and Tom fixed his eyes on the portrait opposite him. His great-grandfather, major-general, inspector-general of cavalry in India. Tom thought that he had been odd in one sense, a cavalryman among infantrymen, in a family that had given its sons otherwise unswervingly to the 11th Regiment of Foot, the 11th North Devonshire Regiment, the Devonshire Regiment, and finally the Devon and Dorsets since 1958.

Roddy and he drank port together, laid down by Tom's father, after Mary had withdrawn. Now the conversation was desultory until Tom asked about Roddy's family background. His brother-in-law dwelt happily on the soldiers from which he had sprung, mentioning only in passing that his father and grandfather had been wealthy Church of England rectors of a village just across the Somerset border for a total of 51 years between them, hunting and shooting, and living in an enormous well founded rectory. He listened to his brother-in-law's good opinion of his impeccable West Country and English background. It was surely unsullied by any wayward foreign blood, and German blood to boot.

They sang Hymn 477, 'The day Thou gavest, Lord, is ended'. The vicar spoke of the general's place as squire of the village and the good work he had done over the globe and here in the heartland of Devon. That he had suffered the grievous loss of three beloved wives, and fortified by his faith had continued to lead a campaigning fruitful life on his own acres. The vicar mentioned his orders and decorations, his bravery, and his appointments within the county as a deputy lieutenant, high sheriff, and chairman of the Red Cross. They sang Psalm 23, and followed it with Hym 676, 'Who would true valour see'. The funeral was for family and close friends, for retainers and villagers, and the church was full. There would be a memorial service in Exeter cathedral. They buried him in the Gibson plot contained within trimmed yew hedges. The mourners crowded in to commit the general's body to the earth beside his first wife, and with the other two on either side a little spaced. Tom stood by the simple flat gravestone beneath which lay Siegrid Anna von Weissenbach.

After the interment Tom talked to every one of the estate people, most of whom he had known all his life. They were warm towards him, happy to see him back. Although none said so in so many words, it was plain that they expected him back for good. The cattle had done well and the market for breeding stock was buoyant. An early hay crop had beaten the rain and was green and scented in the barn. The arable crops, well, next year would be better. And meanwhile there were enough pheasant for some good rough shooting.

Some of the mourners came to lunch and Tom was affable to them all, asking about their lives since he had left, evading questions on his own doings. He did no more than shake hands with Mr Rowlands, the family solicitor, with his silver hair and kindly, abstracted air.

The library was on the north-west corner of the house, a square room which emphasised the height of the ceiling. Books filled mahogany shelves on all the walls.

They sat at the round estate table in the middle of the room – Mr Rowlands, Mary and Roddy, and Tom. There were bequests to old retainers and the church, with an addition of moneys to a Gibson trust for the disadvantaged of the parish. Tom kept his eyes on Mr Rowlands, and knew finally that his father had told Mary and her husband the contents of his will. He knew that the last words his father had said as he strode from this very room three years before, were embodied in the document the solicitor held in his hands.

Mr Rowlands ceased talking. He was not relishing his task, but had to continue. The estate – the house, park and farms – was left to Richard Yeo Gibson Barkworthy, to be held in trust for him by his parents Mary and Roderick Barkworthy, until he reached the age of 25. Until then his parents would have certain interest from the estate, which was entailed and must be held intact. Richard was asked to change his surname to Gibson when he assumed ownership of the property, but this was not insisted upon.

Mr Rowlands continued in his dry voice that Thomas Richard Yeo Gibson had known since a certain date why he had been excluded from inheriting the estate, for opinions and beliefs, and above all conduct unacceptable in an heir to the Gibson line. His father bequeathed him his guns and rods, and a dozen shooting and fishing books. He was also to have shares in a number of companies, named, free of inheritance tax. Other shares, and working capital for the farms, went to Mary and Roddy. The sale of the redundant cottages provided a major part of the estimated tax to be paid. Certain ornamentation – statuary, pictures and jewelry – had been earmarked to provide the rest.

They all shook hands with the solicitor. Tom fancied he received a particularly sympathetic handshake.

Tom kissed his sister, shook Roddy's hand. "I wish you all luck," he said. It was now a relief to know the worst and to be able to look at new plans. At least his father might be proud of him for not showing much emotion, for being the good loser that he wondered if previous Gibsons had always managed to be. A thought came to him.

"What's to stop Richard deciding against the profession of arms, or resigning his commission and becoming a piano tuner?"

Mary's face paled. She looked, thought Tom, so like their father. Unswerving and implacable.

"Only us," she said. "He's down for Wellington. He'll go into the Devon and Dorsets."

Tom nodded, thinking that his own medals, the general service medal with Northern Ireland clasp and the South Atlantic medal with rosette, would never find their way into the showcases in the drawing room.

He picked a posy of flowers from the garden and laid it on his mother's grave. Deliberately he did not look across to the heaped earth smothered in wreaths where they had laid his father in the morning. He tried to think about his mother, but the fields and woods beyond the yew hedge filled his mind. He walked into the early evening fields, still full of sun with lengthening shadows. Snatches of Finzi's *Dies Natalis* came to him, a tenor voice singing Thomas Traherne's words of a child's wonder at the natural world. He recalled all kinds of incidents and little adventures, moving slowly and quietly through the woods, noting birds, the signs of animals, going up to a bank with beech trees where badgers still had their setts. There it was isolated and peaceful and he could look back and down to see the house with the westering sun full on it. He walked on over the hill to further woods and fields, always remembering. This was his native place, and he would probably never come back to it.

As he came to the gate that led from the pastures into the garden, it occurred to him that his father's will had freed him from his gamekeepering straitjacket. Hilary was right. He should use his languages. Between them they might be able to set up a business, dedicate themselves to making money. Enough money so that they could buy a place, an estate, up by the North Sea. A sharp break with Devon and the south-west, a welcome to the robust north-east. He had no idea how much they would have to have in order to buy an estate. He would find out, set to. He was still only 33, and he had Hilary. Then, remembering the ambiguity of his last meeting with her, he was in a fever to get back.

In the stone-flagged hall of the house that might have been his for a space he kissed his nieces, shook hands with Richard, an undemonstrative, stolid little boy. Then he bent down and hugged him. He hoped the pressures that would be brought to bear on him would not prove intolerable. Roddy drove him to the station.

Everyone knew that the gamekeeper's father had died, had been a general and warranted obituaries in all the serious newspapers. The weather produced rain and cold for his arrival back. Hilary was travelling on business in eastern Europe. Tom checked the estate with Richard Doddington-Smith, who had looked after the release pens. He went to Shepherd's Pightle to collect Schiller, found Benjie and Heilke with Kenny, all working among the long beds of vegetables, boxing young carrots and turnips, lettuces and endives. After supper Benjie would drive them to town in his old Traveller. Tom helped and they worked largely in silence until Heilke went into the house to prepare a meal, Kenny left for home, and Benjie and Tom loaded the boxes into the station wagon.

"Have you thought of buying a new van?" Tom asked, remembering his promise to Heilke. "This one's nearing the end of its life. Could cost you much more than it's worth."

"I've thought of it," Benjie replied. "Heilke been talking?"

Tom lied obliquely. "I thought when you drove me to the Red Lion that you needed something more reliable."

"She's an old friend."

"You could keep her – just for local trips. Do her up when you have time."

Benjie barked out a laugh. "She'd just stay in the barn. To be found by my heirs and assigns." The mention of heirs made Tom wince, and he was angry with himself for having shown any reaction. They went into the kitchen.

"We saw the obituaries," said Benjie. "A brave soldier."

Sipping a glass of Trockenwein from the Ruwer, Tom told them everything, about his father and mother, the family estate, the grand quarrel in the library, the inability of his father to see his point of view. "There was nothing for it but to get out – to drop out, maybe," he concluded. "And I had my come-uppance when all he had said three years ago was confirmed by our solicitor."

"Could you fight the will – in the courts?" asked Benjie.

Tom shook his head. "In the eyes of the world my father was in his right mind. He had his reasons, his attitudes. Maybe the establishment of old England would agree with him." He stopped talking for a moment to look at Benjie sitting opposite him with a concerned, sad expression, and at Heilke at her stove, agitated and flushed. "I have neither the will nor the money to go down that road."

"*Zum Essen, meine Herren.*" Heilke kissed Tom as she brought him his plate of food. "We will think of something," she said cryptically.

Tom threw himself into the work of the estate. He whistled up his bedraggled, undersized reared poults and assessed how many he had. It seemed that at least 10 per cent had fallen to predators, wandered off or died of cold. He spread straw in wider swathes and continued feeding pellets.

Hilary came back from Czechoslovakia and Poland. She was bright and almost garrulous, and avoided giving Tom an opportunity of talking seriously. She had read the obituaries. She was sorry his father had died, and did not ask anything about the Devon acres that she now knew existed. They had met in the town at the French restaurant. Her attitude stopped Tom in his tracks, uncertain, immediately lacking confidence. She pleaded exhaustion when they reached her cottage, kissed him lightly at the door. Tom did not force the issue.

As he went to his cottage in the woods two voices spoke to him. The first was small and hesitant, telling him she could not change so quickly, she came from faithful stock. When he felt more confident he must win her back with steady heart. A louder, more strident, voice told him that she did not want him any more, that he was disinherited, that he was a gamekeeper and could not keep her in the manner to which she aspired. The small voice came back, a little stronger, telling him he would not always be a gamekeeper, that he would go out into the business world, might even become a tycoon, that he needed her to effect such a change, and for all kinds of other reasons, too. The loud voice drowned the small voice, recalling the failures in his life, telling him that he should be accustomed to failure and that this was just another one.

The loud voice won. With sadness he found himself becoming once more taciturn and introspective. He lost himself in the work. He knew Hilary was travelling again. Kenny lived close to her cottage and kept him informed. The bad weather continued. A rotten summer was often followed by a fine autumn. Not so far this year, it seemed.

At last Heilke and Benjie together accosted Tom. First Heilke told Tom that her sister had cancer of the stomach and she would go to see her the next week. She reflected that a pope had said something like 'God has given us life and we might as well enjoy it'. Her sister had not enjoyed her life, she did not think. Not nearly as much as she and Benjie had, despite some obvious lacks. Tom should be making the very best of his youth and strength. It was not the bad summer and the troubles it caused with his pheasant. It was not the loss of his inheritance, she did not think. It could only be to do with Hilary.

After the reconnaissance by the light armour, the tanks were brought up. Benjie began an interrogation, rumbling, keeping his voice down with difficulty. It seemed to Tom quite natural that they should ask him these questions, with diffidence, affection and concern. He was grateful and relieved that he could at last talk. He told them how Hilary had appeared to turn away from him, seemed to have second thoughts. He had been too indecisive, bowled over by it all and had not forced a showdown. Perhaps he had been afraid of what the answer would be. He had retreated, he knew, absurdly hurt by her withdrawal from their close loving relationship. He had not forced the issue, he repeated again. He had been prepared to tell her that he wanted to enter her world of commerce, use his languages.

All talk had been in English. Now Heilke switched to her mother tongue. "She's asking you to fight for her. She's not sure of your love

131

for her. She wants to be sure that you will not swing back into self-pity – yes, self-pity – as soon as you come up against a big obstacle. I don't know what went on in your life before, and it is anyway all past. The present and future are what matter."

Heilke paused, and Tom found Benjie nodding approval. With a part of his mind he knew that Benjie had understood all that his wife had said. Not just the gist of it. He thought about Benjie and his potential, from a Fife coalmining background. Had he squandered some bright future back in his own countryside, in Edinburgh, even in London? Had he been fulfilled as a smallholder? Well, he had his mate, his boon companion. No matter what he had done or might have done, she had been and would have been at his side. It was the stuff of a Hollywood weepy, and also the stuff of an intensely private, sane and sensible life. His father and mother had not had it. Perhaps Mary and Roddy did, although the tenets of their life together would not be his. Where had he gone wrong with Hilary? He began to see at last. He would talk it out with Schiller on the way home. No, he would not stay for supper. he had arrangements to make. He kissed Heilke and shook hands with Benjie, a clasp more than a formal handshake.

"No depression. No self-pity," he said. "I understand".

13. THE REAL ENEMY

Hilary agreed to come with Tom on his rounds, and would stay for Sunday night supper. Tom believed the best way to talk was out of doors. He would draw confidence from the surroundings which he now knew so well, from the work he had done. He might even feel that other men had taken other maids out into these gently undulating acres, to listen to nightingales in the coppices, to gather primroses and pussy willows and talk about spending their lives together. Wryly he acknowledged that May evenings were best for that, or hanging over a gate on a July night with a ripening cornfield a pace away and scented summer woods beyond. He was going to do it in cold September rain and a drear end to a wet, unhappy summer. Well, then, he would have the ghosts of all those men and maids walking with him, who had come to understandings. It did not matter that they had in after years been miserable or violent, or sunk into indifference and petty squabbling. Youth and hope were all. They would be walking with him and willing a right outcome.

They set off into a meadow not far from Tom's cottage that had not yet been desecrated by the tractors and bulldozers. Immediately Tom found a snare in a hare run. It was a work of art, the stick a piece of young ash, carefully cut and tapered, rubbed over with successive layers of earth, with a well contrived copper wire loop with a running slip knot. It was set at precisely the right height to take a hare round the neck as it ran along its 'road'.

"A poacher closes all the other hare roads in a meadow. He runs a hand along a few feet of it or spits on it," said Tom. "It's as if he's put an impenetrable obstruction in the way. The hare will turn back and take another road, and another, until it goes down the only road which is still open and unimpeded."

Tom removed the snare.

"No gang does this," he continued. "It's an individual, a solitary." He was struck by the similarities of his own position. "Like me. Obstructions everywhere," he said lightly. "Only one road to go. But I don't think the snare is quite so lethal."

"Is it Benjie's work?" Hilary did not respond to the analogy.

"I expect so. He told me once that he would poach until he died."

"You sound ready to put up with his poaching."

Tom took a deep breath. "Much has happened to me. I shall stay here and see the season through. Give my notice to quit on February 1."

"What will you do?" Hilary was trudging beside him down a hedge. She sounded only marginally interested, and Tom felt his resolve jolted.

"Do what you've been suggesting and use my languages. Get a job." He did not mention the astronomical sum that he hoped eventually to find for a good house and enough land to farm, to begin another dynasty, but to his own liking. He was already realising the enormity of the task, and questioning whether he could change his character and his inclinations enough to accomplish it.

"Why not leave now?" Hilary said, laying her hand on his arm, stopping him, turning to look at him straight for the first time for weeks.

"I have obligations to see the season through."

"Gailsford couldn't care less for you. He's a disaster as a country landowner. Cut your losses. You won't need a reference from him where you are going. Let him flounder in the mud he and the rains have created."

"You would expect your employees to honour their commitments."

Hilary shook her head. "It's not as simple and straightforward as that. Don't you see? By all means work hard. That's good as a basis. But you have to play politics, too."

"Do you?"

"All the time, my poor ingenuous Tom."

"Are you playing politics with me? Playing hard to keep?"

"I wouldn't admit to anything."

Tom began at last to understand. "I'm going to do what you want me to do. I'll need more money to give you and our children what they should have materially, and spiritually, too." He was running ahead of himself, knew that he was babbling. "I expect we'll have big problems to contend with. You in your high managerial position, me trying to emulate you. I've no idea what I shall do. But I do know that we'll manage well enough." He stopped. The rain was sheeting down, rivulets forming at their feet. Schiller stood motionless, staring at them, shivering a little as the water droplets bounced off his well oiled coat.

Hilary laughed. Tom grabbed her round the waist. "Well, will you marry me, then? And help me with this professional metamorphosis?" he asked crisply.

"I expect so."

In October not only did Tom's relationships with the people who mattered to him improve dramatically. The weather changed. The rain gone, high pressure brought sun and warm southerly winds. The pheasant responded immediately, putting on weight and consequence. Clear sharp light bathed the woods and fields. Doddington-Smith had tractors out ploughing in the stubble of his miserable wheat and barley crops. He seeded autumn corn. The oilseed rape sown earlier on newly prepared land grew apace.

The police rang all the gamekeepers in the county. The poaching gangs were active. They were well informed and well organised. The high price of a brace and the fine weather also brought out the shoot-from-the-car brigade. They had caught two or three, but there were others. In the west country clear skies and colder weather sweeping down from the north Atlantic brought some fog and caused a concertina pile-up on the M5 not far from Tom Gibson's erstwhile native place.

Tom's gamekeeper friend caught a local man from Glanby with a folding .410 fitted with a silencer. He turned out to be Ernie Crawshaw, and this time he was up before the magistrates. Tom told his friend about his theory and his action in letting him go last year. He now reckoned it had been a selfish way of handling the situation, leaving him free to raid a neighbour. He apologised. It seemed that gamekeepering was becoming more problematic, and there was a need for greater cooperation across the district and coordination of efforts. Gone were the days when estates had two, three and four gamekeepers. Despite the money made by well organised and well stocked estates from the wealthy city people, the men to do the work and preserve the game from predators were few in number. Tom still held to the first shoot of the season in November. He fed wild and reared birds with grain and saw them plumping up in the weeks of fine weather. He spent part of every night patrolling, walking up to 20 miles in every 24 hours. He and Schiller fined down to the point of thinness, perpetually hungry, always on the move, ready to erupt into action.

Then Gailsford telephoned. He wanted a shoot in October. He did not care that the pheasant would not have filled out. He had important guests and could not resist telling his gamekeeper the names of the illustrious in the world of finance who had agreed to come. The names meant nothing to Tom, and the episode prompted him to order the Financial Times. If he was going to make his fortune in his new environment he had better start familiarising himself with it.

On a fine, misty morning, still mild, with lapwings and gulls following the ploughs of Doddington-Smith's workforce, Tom worked out the drives on the ground. They could just have six without beating the same territory. Two were likely to have more wild birds than the others, the terrain least disturbed by the farming operations. He called in at Shepherd's Pightle to tell Benjie about the youngsters from town out in cars shooting the roadside pheasant.

"They're not important," said Benjie.

Tom nodded. "It's the professional we need to worry about. The gangs are becoming stronger and bolder."

"There's your real enemy," said Benjie.

"And yours, too?" asked Tom.

Benjie grunted. "You know so."

"With motorways, poachers take the birds up into Yorkshire, down to Hertfordshire, for forward delivery to London. They're well organised and have their outlets. Demand is heavy."

"Are you asking me something?" Benjie sat across the kitchen table from him. Heilke busied herself at the stove.

"One day they'll hit the Gailsford estate. I know it. They've already visited similar operations in the county. Even at £6 a brace there must be an element of –" He stopped. "I nearly said 'sport'. But it's more 'adventure'. A night adventure with mates you can almost trust, out in the woods and fields, making some money but also taking risks, living. The excitement."

"Never," Benjie exploded. "You're talking rubbish. They're despoilers of the countryside, of our heritage. For lucre, for gain." Tom listened as Benjie held forth.

Heilke left her stove. *"Sei ruhig, ruhig."*

"I believe they'll come," said Tom. He knew at last why he was here, looking at Benjie, massive and angry, with his Heilke leaning over him. He saw his mother in her still, despite the differences in temperament and spirit. He saw Benjie now as the only father figure that he had ever had. He repeated himself. "They'll come, one night or another. I mean to be ready for them."

Benjie stood up, and Tom had an inkling of what he must have looked like in battle. Capable, calm in action, able to consider all the foreshortened, immediate requirements of his men and weapons, and the enemy's dispositions. And he would be cunning and agile, and implacable. And now there was that older countrywise Benjie peeping out – adventure-loving, enjoying pitting himself against others, and wanting to be younger.

"If it's a gang of professionals, call me."

"We'll need to go over the terrain, make plans. The moon's full and they won't come now. We've time to prepare," said Tom, relieved and grateful.

The first shoot of the season was over. Tom had done everything in his power to give his employer good sport. His beaters had been trained to something approaching perfection by the retired schoolmaster. The pickers-up included the neighbouring gamekeeper and others with trained dogs. The drives had been ever more carefully worked out. There had been sewelling to persuade the still immature birds up into the air, to have them 'exploding' over the guns. And the day had been sunny and just crisp enough to set the blood tingling. All the servants of the shoot had been in good spirits. Good walking weather, and good to be working together in a fundamental country enterprise. The money was nothing, the comradeship everything. Tom was part of it, perhaps a pivotal influence. The mood of bonhomie was not matched on the other side, save for the Northamptonshire knight who greeted Tom and the neighbouring gamekeeper by name. Charles Gailsford's other guns were all City men, two of them practised shots, three novices. Tom recognised one novice from last year. He contrived to be between Gailsford and this man, with the gamekeeper covering the other two novices.

The drives had shown up the difference between the wild birds and the reared. They had been mixed in the waves sent over by the beaters. With the reared flying low and falteringly and the wild birds higher and faster, the novices, including Gailsford, had been confused. Of the experienced guns, Sir Norman Crook had picked off high birds with deliberate coolness while the other two had taken their fill of the reared birds.

Nothing had pleased Gailsford. "I'll see you later, Gibson," he said. "You've a lot to account for. Bloody awful birds. Letting poachers catch you napping. And don't give me overwork and weather as an excuse."

"Very good. I'll wait for your call."

137

The call did not come that weekend. Gailsford went back to London. Tom saw Hilary on the Sunday evening and for the first time told her in full about the Devon acres, the house, the traditions, and the inheritor of the estate, and why. She said little but kissed him warmly, and he almost confided in her his dream of another estate.

"When can we visit my parents? You ought to speak to my father. He won't eat you. It's my mother you'll have to be wary of. What about Christmas?"

Tom shook his head, sitting beside her on her chintzy sofa, with a glass of white wine. "Unless I'm sacked before then, which is on the cards, I'll be here at Christmas, protecting my charges from the poaching festive spirit."

"A waste of time. Putting yourself at risk." Tom had noticed that since their reconciliation Hilary had become proprietorial of him. One part of him loved it, the greater part. The smaller, the renegade part of him, wanted to head for the furthest marl pit, to hunker down and listen to the life of the woods and fields. It might just include a certain elderly poacher of his acquaintance.

"The poaching gangs are out. Prices are high for pheasant. They'll visit me one night when the moon has waned. Quite soon, I think. I'm out every night, and I'm doing it not for Gailsford but for myself. Perhaps I did renege on the Gibson tradition, perhaps I could have compromised, got myself a staff job. A few more years – three to be exact, as I've just found out – and I could have resigned my commission and taken over in Devon." He saw that Hilary was listening closely. "Can you understand that in a way I'm seeking to make amends? I'll be a better businessman, better husband for you, a better father to our children, if I work it out for myself on Gailsford's estate."

Hilary squeezed his hand. "I do see that. But I still hope he sacks you."

Benjie and Tom were in the Red Lion. Roger Hoggett was behind the bar, disconsolate at a poor turnout on a clear October Saturday night. He looked hard at the two of them knocking back their first pints of bitter, sitting not in the centre of the barroom nor by the coal fire but away by the door leading to the pub's lavatories. Although it was still early in the evening they were both yawning. Benjie came up for refills.

In a suspiciously short time Tom was back for two more pints. He seemed to want to be certain that Hoggett had noticed him, as a barmaid served him. A few more customers came in. Within half an hour Benjie was back for their fourth pints, telling Hoggett how he had been up since four in the morning, picking, pulling, washing and trimming, and packing vegetables.

Tom and Benjie seemed inordinately addicted to going through the door beside their table, out to the whitewashed Gents in a lean-to in the yard. With their fifth pints they bought two bags of potato crisps. Hoggett served them and soon after went through to where his sitting room lay, and where Tom had no doubt was a telephone. He was playing a hunch, and he and Benjie had enjoyed the game. They had done their best not to seem more drunk than they should be. Their only regret was that so much quite passable beer had been poured down the urinal.

There was drifting light cloud and a sliver of new moon, and gentle wind from the north-west. Tom and Benjie were close to the northern end of the green lane, by a chain of small fields of rough grass and fallow not yet touched by Doddington-Smith. Spinneys, a small wood, a stretch of Scots pine windbreak with hazel and thorn understorey and several marl and sand pits gave warmth, shelter and food to the best of the wild birds and a concentration of reared birds from a release pen in a spinney. Tom reckoned the poachers would have made a reconnaissance.

"A poacher's night," said Benjie with irony. "Light enough to see your way. Dark enough to move from shade to shade without being seen. Only a little wind." He had his lurcher with him, the silent impassive Khan, kept on a short lead, using him as a hypersensitive extension – eyes, nose and ears – of himself. By contrast Schiller was free, listening to the night, making small forays into the darkness, always coming back quickly to Tom. The two men carried no guns but had sticks and rubber torches.

"Tell me again what the police said," Benjie asked.

"There's an alert out for a raid on a big estate in the south of the county. The police have to cover it but think it may be a blind. They'll take our hunch seriously, and will 'come by', as they said, later in the evening."

"A third time would be no coincidence. Hoggett, I mean," said

Benjie.

"The police said we weren't to tangle with a gang but to get a message through to them." Tom knew that in neither of their heads was the idea that they should act only as scouts.

The lurcher growled very softly, more a faint trilling in the back of the throat. After a moment Schiller moved closer to Tom so that his flank rested against his leg. He too growled, imitating the older dog. Tom rested his hand on the labrador's head for a moment. One day Schiller would be a multi-skilled gamekeeper's dog – retriever, beater, pointer, watcher and companion, and in the last resort a fighting dog. Tom hoped the last quality would not be needed tonight, suddenly apprehensive for the young dog.

Now they saw the headlights of cars and heard their engines.

"They're backing into the green lane," said Tom, watching the headlights lighting up trees and a gate.

It was here that Benjie Kerr took over. "We'll nobble the man they leave with the vehicles. Let's move."

Tom was on the instant content. No, more. At ease in company he loved and trusted, questioned maybe occasionally, but knew in the end that thoughts and reactions were close. They reached the green lane and crept along until they could see the cars. The green lane went before them up an incline, so that cars, men and dogs were silhouetted against the night sky. There were five men and three dogs. Labradors, they thought. Guns, too. They saw the outline of three.

Schiller was restive, close to Tom. The lurcher's calm was unbroken. As one of the poacher's dogs let out a short bark and a following whine, Schiller opened his mouth, and Tom quickly laid a hand on his nose. At the moment before action Tom had seldom felt happier. He saw Benjie's bulk out of the corner of his eye, remembered Sergeant Penfold from his platoon in Northern Ireland and the gamekeepers Turner and Brown who had known these fields so well. He derived support, gained courage from the thought that these men were in a sense with him now. And greatest of all – support from Benjamin Kerr, alive, alert and vigorous, beside him.

Without too much noise, but evidently not worried if they made any, four men and the dogs went off into the pasture, heading, so Tom surmised, towards the first spinney. They saw the outline of the fifth man with his gun stand for minutes, then walk towards the hedgeline.

"He's in the hedge. There's a biggish ash," Tom breathed into

Benjie's ear. "He'll be leaning against the trunk."

They backed down the green lane for some yards, crossed it, went through the hedge into a field and began advancing towards the cars. This was a clay field ploughed up and sown to autumn barley. The furrow by the hedge contained troughs of standing water. The dogs had to be kept under tight control, and Tom put Schiller on his lead. When they were about 30 yards from the man, Benjie put his hand on Tom's arm.

"Stay here with the dogs," he said softly. "Be ready to come up the lane fast."

Benjie went forward. Tom quickly found a gap in the hedge and moved himself and the dogs into the lane. Crouching by the hedge he heard noises from the spinney, the strangulated sound of silenced .410s. A fraction of a second before Tom heard it himself, the lurcher suddenly strained at his leash. A single chopping sound. Tom launched himself on to the dark track of the lane, running, feet high, with no intention of being tripped. The dogs ran with him restrained by their leads, miraculously keeping out of his way.

Benjie was already tying the man's hands. "Gag him, Tom," he said. "There's rag in my left-hand pocket."

Tom did as he was told. They propped the man against the ash. While Benjie broke the shotgun and took out the cartridge, Tom removed the cartridge belt from the man's waist. A crackling voice from the ground at their feet startled them. Tom located the radio by torchlight.

"Stan, come in. Everything OK? OK? Over." It was a simple shortrange radio. Tom depressed the 'send' switch. He spoke through his handkerchief.

"Stan here. Everything's OK, over."

The receiver popped and snapped. "The birds are falling into the bag. Roger'll be along with a load. He stays there. You come back here, Stan, with your gun. You read me? Over."

"I read you. Over and out."

Benjie grinned his approval. "Hoggett?" he queried.

"That would be too good to be true. My turn, I think," said Tom.

They crossed to the other side of the lane and pressed through the hedge into the ditch. They lay waiting some 20 feet apart, their dogs with them, now both off their leads. The lurcher was calm, Schiller excited and having difficulty in staying still. Tom had to hold him by the collar and caress his head gently. Once again the lurcher alerted them with a faint trill in his throat. They saw the torch flash as someone came out of the spinney ahead, trudging across the pasture as if heavily laden. Tom thought of his father in the library telling him he was a coward. He wished he had thought it all out before the interview and could then have told him of the apprehension and uncertainty before action, but how when the moment came to fling himself into the fight there was nothing but coolness and a clear understanding eye. Training, long years of training, assert themselves, and perhaps even the blood told. The blood of Gibsons who had experienced almost every war on land, big and small, for over 300 years. But then he thought wryly of his German grandfather, a doctor and musician, from a long line of Bamberg musicians and medical men. The man in the pasture was making for a spot almost equidistant from Benjie and himself. Tom moved in the ditch, edging on his side along it, watching the man's occasional torch flashes, seeing his shadowy figure looming larger and larger. Schiller was an embarrassment. None of his training had included such a movement. He objected to being pulled by the collar. Yet he kept his mouth shut, pulled back only now and then as Tom came closer to Benjie.

"Stan, where are you? They're bloody heavy. Stan?"

"Here I am, Roger," said Tom, springing to his feet, letting go Schiller's collar, throwing himself forward in a waist-high tackle to bring Roger hard to the ground. Even winded the man fought hard and yelled, until Benjie came to help. It was the landlord of the Red Lion. They gagged him and tied him up with pleasure and dragged him into the ditch.

Taking the radio, they moved rapidly across the meadow to the spinney. Tom stuffed the shotgun and cartridge belt under a thorn bush. The poachers were going south down a thick windbreak. Torches flashed, the silenced .410s snorted. They were making noise, not caring, their blood lust up, intent on killing pheasant, convinced of their invincibility. Beyond the windbreak on a gentle rise was the last of the big untouched fallows with a large pit in its centre. This one had not been marl but sand, and it had not been landscaped. The natural colonisers had clothed it. A few birches, some gorse and thickets of thorn which in the years had thrown up small trees. The pit was warm and dry, quite deep and well sheltered. There were tangled refuges on the slopes and it was a favoured nightground for wild birds. The bottom of the pit where the diggers had removed the sand down to subsoil, was free of tall growth, covered in matted grass. The gang would inevitably go to it when they had finished with the windbreak.

The radio came alive. 'Roger, come in, Roger.' The two men looked at each other. They waited. 'Bloody hell, Stan? Did you take the radio?' Slowly Tom raised the instrument and spoke into it. "Sorry, I didn't think. Over." There was a pause, then the radio crackled angrily. "Where are you, bloody Stan? Meet us at the pit, then. Over." Tom answered with feeling. "I will. Over and out." He remembered to switch off the radio.

Silence settled in the pit where Benjie and Tom and their dogs waited. Their arrival had disturbed the birds, some had gone but most had settled again when Tom had whistled. Both dogs were kept under tight control. Three men with silenced shotguns would probably push through the thorn and gorse bushes at different points, their torches off until they and their dogs were into the pit. Benjie would take the nearest man, go for a knockout, and Tom would try for the same with his man. They would then converge on the middle man. The dogs might give the game away, their own and the poachers'. There was an element of uncertainty and risk. Weighing up the possibilities Tom felt calm and steady. Whatever the outcome he was happy, elated, with Benjie as a fighting companion.

Suddenly the poachers were at the pit edge and Tom could see them outlined against the sky in a gap between the gorse bushes. One of them was markedly smaller than the other two. Tom pictured the mean small features and the wispy beard, remembered the nasal Birmingham accent.

"Where's that bloody Stan? He should be here," said the same voice. They stood waiting for several moments, then the small man spoke again. "Let's get to it."

The dogs came first, the three poachers seconds after. The labradors set up a flurry of startled barks and whines. With precision Tom hit out with his stick at his poacher. The man dropped, cursing, and Tom landed on top of him, shouting now, trying to tell Benjie he had muffed it. This one was big, young and strong. As they fought, rolling over and over on the pit floor, Tom was aware that Schiller was snarling just beyond them, aware also that the poacher was losing strength. He loosed his grip of the man for seconds and hit him hard on the chin. He

143

went limp. Old trick, old trick, Tom told himself, and hit him again.

Not four paces away Benjie was fighting with his man. The lurcher was attacking a labrador. The other dogs had disappeared. Tom could not tell the outcome but he feared immediately for Benjie, big as he was, up against a man half his age. He came to his feet to go to Benjie and was recalled by Schiller's growl. Up the slope was the small man, a gun in his hands, aimed at Tom. The light came on and blinded him. He could not remember where his own torch was. His brain told him he was 10 paces from the gun's muzzle. He threw himself sideways hoping to lose the light but it followed him, and he knew the small man was summoning up the will to fire. He saw a black shadow launch itself at the poacher, and the gun fired, a desultory plop. The thud as the shot hit came with no whimper, but in his brain was a scream of anguish as he flung himself up the slope in a direct frontal attack. The man seemed to wait for him, do nothing to defend himself. Tom seized the gun and broke it over his head, watching him fall down into the pit. Schiller lay stretched full length. His master found his torch in his pocket. The dog had taken the full charge in his chest and had died instantly. Tom threw the gun away, turned, with his bare hands extended. The small man was coming round, swearing foully.

"You shot my dog."

"Pity it weren't you, gamekeeper."

Tom put his hands round the man's neck, his knee on his chest. Schiller was dead. Schiller who had been set in that close working companionship that only gamekeepers and shepherds fully experience. His dog, the odd one of the litter, with such promise. His dog.

A hand was laid on his shoulder. He reared up and turned to face Benjie.

"Let the man be, son," said Benjie quietly. "No need to add to mayhem."

The poacher wriggled away and started to get to his feet. Tom knocked him to the ground. Benjie produced more cord from his pockets and they tied all three men, leaving them ungagged.

"They can shout their heads off," said Benjie. But it was the police who shouted as they crossed the fallow to the pit.

Tom took off his waterproof jacket and laid Schiller's body on it. Together he and Benjie carried him to the gamekeeper's cottage in the wood.

14. Fog

At dawn the next morning Tom Gibson dug Schiller's grave out on the edge of the cottage vegetable garden, long gone to the wild. It was a fitting resting place for the dog, whose short life had been lived close to this habitation, close to the life of his gamekeeper. Spading up the chalky subsoil, Tom felt the welcome sweat of effort on his body. He recalled incidents of their lives together, of Schiller as gundog, companion – and defender and perhaps saviour. Now he believed he was guilty of his companion dog's death. He should never have had him out there. He laid Schiller gently in his grave and quickly shovelled back the soil, leaving no mark above ground to tell that the dog lay below.

The police interrogated not only the poachers but their captors. It looked as if the brains of the gang might be revealed. Hoggett's pub was temporarily closed. November came in with fog. Everywhere that the sky was clear of cloud there was brilliant sun with sudden dense fogs. There was a pile-up of lorries on the M4 and another, lesser, accident on the M6 in Lancashire, both in daylight. At night it seemed the traffic moved with more caution.

The fog did not deter Gailsford from coming to his country house. He had time to spare for sorting out what he believed was the shambles of the farming on his estate. Doddington-Smith needed all his small experience to placate, to explain, to promise that the following year would be better. The gamekeeper was evidently going to be next.

Tom was with the Kerrs when the telephone call came. Heilke's brother-in-law, the air marshal, spoke to Benjie. Irma was gravely ill, a sudden turn for the worse. Could they come? She was at home in Bedfordshire, having refused to go to hospital to die. She was asking for Heilke. The air marshal was tight-lipped, controlled. He was sorry to bring them out in such weather, would meet them at the station if they came by train. Although of course using the motorway they could be with Irma in half the time. Heilke took the news calmly. She must go immediately, Irma was her only relation. They were busy making preparations so that they could leave. Kenny would come in at once and would feed the livestock, live in the house and look after the two dogs. They would start as soon as Kenny arrived.

Benjie proposed to go in his Morris Traveller. Heilke, pale-faced, did not berate him for not having bought the new van that she and Tom had been urging on him. Tom intervened. He would take them in the Land Rover. He would fetch it while they finished their preparations. He must tell Doddington-Smith he was going. Give him half an hour.

Tom ran through the night, a cloudy sky, a light night with occasional glimpses of a half moon, when the track, the trees and the land were bathed with silver light. No sign of fog here. He 'phoned Doddington-Smith and found that Gailsford was with him. Gailsford wanted to see him immediately, urgently. Tom explained to his friend Richard that he had to leave for 24 hours – a matter of death. Richard was cowed yet persuasive. It would only take a few minutes, but Gailsford had to leave and needed to see his gamekeeper.

Reluctantly Tom agreed. He telephoned and spoke to Benjie, told him that he would come on immediately, to wait for him, and said that they needed the reliability of the Land Rover. He was already split between loyalties. All his upbringing had been with duty as the enveloping driving force. Duty to school, to regiment, to brother officers, his men, to the Devon land and its servants. Duty came before self in the Gibson family tradition. He understood, had done so for many years, had been true to the principles, neither slavishly nor unintelligently. Now he had a duty to answer 'the colonel's' call. And a duty to aid friends in need of him. Only friends?

He drove quickly to the big house. Gailsford was not with Doddington-Smith, but had returned to his library. Tom told Richard he would be away for two days. It was a family matter which took him away again. Richard did not question him, and came with him to the library. The land agent knocked and entered, only to be sent out of the room. The tycoon was on the telephone and remained on it as the minutes sped by. Tom walked up and down the elegant Georgian hallway. He closed his mind to Heilke waiting impatiently for him to come. Deliberately he willed the slow movement of Mozart's Symphony No. 29 to come to him, soothing nerves. The composer had written it when he was 18. Eighteen years old and able to write music that brought solace and love to the sorely oppressed hearts of men and women. Fifteen minutes had passed. No one should spend 15 minutes on the 'phone. Nothing warranted that, neither business nor love.

"Try him again," he said to Richard. Now he was the senior officer, not to be denied. Richard knocked again, loudly, opened the door.

"Mr Gailsford. Gibson is here to see you."

"I'm on the telephone, blast you."

"Gibson has to go on to the estate. I told you about the poachers –"

Gailsford put his hand over the mouthpiece. "Get out, will you."

Tom was already in the room. He stood cap in hand as if a respectful estate servant of yesteryear, then came forward ahead of the land agent.

"You wanted to see me urgently, Sir," he said quietly, almost eagerly. He saw that Gailsford was pleased with his humble stance, then became wary. Tom Gibson was a big man physically, and something of his background had filtered through. Now he stood pacifically, the county class fallen on hard times. He kept his eyes on Gailsford until the man dropped his own.

"Come in, then," he said. He lifted his hand from the mouthpiece. "We'll talk tomorrow. Have those papers at the heliport."

He turned to his gamekeeper and a sarcastic note crept into his voice. "Now you've bulldozed your way in, let me tell you that I think your efforts at raising good birds are about as successful as this government's efforts at keeping down inflation." He paused. "Your first shoot was a disaster. You promised me eight shoots this season with good birds."

"I didn't specify the quality of the birds. That was not entirely in my hands."

"Like Doddington-Smith here. Excuses. The weather, the rain, the predators, the poachers. Nothing about Gibson being a lousy gamekeeper, not up to his job, lazy, inefficient –" He was searching Tom's face for a reaction, disappointed that the steady gaze continued without visible change.

"Mr Gailsford. Gibson captured five poachers –"

"You keep out of it. You're two of a kind." He paused, turned to face Tom once more. "I want six more shoots, good ones." He handed Tom a piece of paper. "On these dates."

Tom glanced at the paper. "The reared stock is poorly grown. The wild birds are better but too few to give that number of shoots. Three more at the most, and the third will be poor if the guns are half-way successful on the first two."

Gailsford leant back in his chair. "Listen, Gibson. I will have those shoots. You'll find the birds from elsewhere, from outside. I don't even mind if they come from your poaching friends."

For a moment Tom did not understand. Richard was quicker. He gasped.

"You mean –" began Tom.

"I mean you will buy them. Crate them in. Your beaters will release them."

"It's inconceivable," said Tom, shocked. No countryman worthy of the name, no shooter, no one who cared passionately about country sport would ever countenance such a confidence trick.

"Inconceivable?"

"I mean no disrespect –" Tom was thrown off centre, gathering his wits to answer. "There are patterns of behaviour in the countryside, in this county, in all deep rural places –" He stopped. It was hopeless to try and explain.

"Don't mess me around, Gibson. Will you crate in pheasant for me, or will you not?"

Tom sighed. He felt released. Hilary would be pleased. He would spend Christmas with her family.

"I will not," he said slowly. "It's against a normal honest shooting life in the English countryside, and it's dead against my code of ethics and practice." He smiled at Gailsford, and became aware of Richard, close to him and tensed up.

Unexpectedly Gailsford returned the smile. "There is someone who will," he said. "So you, my failed public school friend, are sacked."

"In the best of good causes." Tom succeeded in sounding jocular, for Gailsford frowned.

"Be out of your cottage in a week. You've a Land Rover. I'll take the keys now."

Tom stiffened. "I need it –" he began and corrected himself. "I'll need to feed the birds, to do my work until you've a new man –"

"Don't worry about the work. It'll be done." Gailsford held out his hand. "I'll take the keys now."

Tom pictured Heilke and Benjie waiting for him. Kenny would have arrived. They would be anxious, listening for the sound of the Land Rover.

"It's unreasonable to deprive me of transport," he said. "Let me keep it for the week, please."

"You're sacked, Gibson. You can walk."

Tom contemplated telling Gailsford at last what he thought of him, but with the Kerrs waiting, this was not the moment. Slowly he produced the keys and laid them in Gailsford's hand. His mind was already darting to Hilary's cars. He would ask for the Volkswagen.

"I'll be leaving, then," he said, turning and laying his hand on Richard's arm as he made for the door, and taking a stricken, easily read message on the young man's face. He went through the door, hearing Richard telling Gailsford that he, too, was leaving, and to hell with landowners who had no feel for rural niceties.

Richard caught up with him in the hall.

"You didn't have to join the ranks of unemployed," Tom said.

"I can't work for the man. This was the last straw."

"I don't think the real countryside will hold it against you."

Tom used the telephone in Richard's office. There was no reply from Hilary. He knew she was due back. It was now 7 o'clock. He dialled the Kerrs' number, and while he waited began to think over the alternatives. He had a spare set of the Land Rover's keys in his cottage. He could therefore take the vehicle. He rejected the idea. Even if Richard drove him to the cottage and back, it would take too long. Besides, he had no wish to add car thieving to his accomplishments, and make Richard an accessory. He would be in enough trouble with his land agency. The telephone rang and rang. Where were they? Out with Kenny giving him last-minute instructions? Surely not both of them. He tried Hilary's number and she replied. He would be round immediately.

They drove to Shepherd's Pightle in the VW. Tom had told Hilary in his clipped sentences about his sacking and she had reacted with relief and happiness. And she had insisted on coming to Bedfordshire and had wanted to be part of the rescue operation. She drove the car, going cautiously as there were wreaths of fog. They found Kenny alone in the living room, wonderfully glad to see Tom as he thought his responsibilities were about to be shared but disappointed and worried when Tom gently explained that they must follow the old Morris Traveller. When had they left? Kenny did not know and became flustered when he saw the crestfallen look on Tom's face.

"When you arrived, what did you do, Kenny?" asked Hilary.

"They'd fed all the animals," he replied at once.

"Did they tell you they were waiting for Tom?"

The boy nodded at once and brightened up, staring at Tom.

Tom let Hilary talk. She was quiet-voiced, earnest and sweet. He wondered whether anyone in her business life had seen her like this. He thought not, and marvelled at his good luck.

"They had their suitcases ready to put into Tom's Land Rover?"

Again Kenny nodded, but his face was clouding.

"And Tom didn't come."

He shook his head, troubled now.

"Tom wanted to, but he was in difficulties," Hilary said. "Did they say they would have to go in Benjie's old car?"

Kenny closed his eyes for a moment, opened them.

"Yes, yes, she did. Mrs Kerr. She was sad. Benjie wanted to wait, but she said to go."

Hilary spoke nonchalantly, as if the next question followed on naturally from those that had been asked before.

"What time was that? Did you see a clock?"

For a moment Kenny stayed with his mouth open, dismayed. Then he grinned, jumped to his feet and went through into the kitchen.

"We were in here," he said. "The clock said 7.25 when they left."

They had missed them by 15 minutes.

There was only one sensible way to the motorway, across 20 miles of B roads. The road went through Glanby and the southern part of the county's hilly land, then on to the flat silt lands and to higher ground through limestone villages. Otherwise a driver could take the main road to the town, go round on the ring road and out on the old coaching highway across the limestone hills, all double white lines and sharp twists, slow if there were lorries on it, and almost always there were lorries. Benjie would know this, and he would most probably take the country route. And in 20 miles they had a good chance of catching them up before the motorway. The Traveller was old and Benjie drove slowly. The VW handled well and Hilary drove it like a sports car, using the gears. Now there was little fog and the sky was largely overcast. Tom watched the road, not worried that he was not driving. His girl drove well, relaxed in the seat, knowing the car's power and potential. They would find the Kerrs before the motorway. Then they would be cramped in the car, but nothing mattered. He and Benjie would curl up in the back and leave Hilary to take them all to Irma's deathbed. And they would arrive in time for the sisters to talk about people and places they had loved, and say goodbye.

150

Quite suddenly, in a village on the edge of the higher country before the siltlands, they came up behind a Morris Traveller going at less than the 40 mph control. But it had no roofrack, and two large dogs looked out of the rear window. They passed it and were soon out in the country again. Tom realised that he did not know the registration number of Benjie's car. The moon appeared, bathing the empty road ahead with light. Tom could see drystone walling, an oak or two, the edges of big fields, a copse, and a hare quite close. The road fell away round two sharp bends and they were on the flat land.

When the fog appeared it was as suddenly round them as the newscaster had described the fog in the M4 pile-up. A wall of fog, visibility cut to next to nothing. Hilary came down through the gears, crawled, flipped on her fog light. The faint light from her one small instrument panel lit up her face imperfectly. She was aware, every sense stretched. She was also more beautiful than Tom had ever seen her. She had come without hesitation, brought her own car, understanding his need to find the Kerrs. He remembered her, close to him, the night of the poachers after partridge, walking back along field edges when the Gailsfords had left them to find their own way back. He remembered her in the sanctuary of her bedroom that first time, and later in his own spartan upstairs room in the gamekeeper's cottage. He remembered her cooking with him, and the night she burnt the sauces. His mother, poor Siegrid Gibson, had never had the chance to be a close comrade, so very close and loved, and loving.

The fog cleared. They were in another village. Red fog lights showed ahead and cars passed them. Now the road was clear again, and Hilary increased speed.

"You can move in with me," she said "I won't have to share you with pheasant and poachers."

"Any ideas about jobs?" he asked, fighting hard not to regret the solitary life of a gamekeeper.

"Yes. I'll make some telephone calls. What grade of degree did you get?"

"A 2:1."

"That's impressive. How many years were you in the army?"

He told her, and for the first time mentioned his tours in Northern Ireland and his part in the Falklands war. Then he changed the subject. "I've been left some money by my father. Enough for a modest house, I think." When he had said that he was uncertain what else to say.

Hilary was concentrating again. The moon had reappeared. They were still in the siltlands, making good time, travelling at about 60 mph. Benjie would only manage a maximum of 45 mph even with Heilke urging him on. Tom imagined the noise in the old Morris – engine, suspension, transmission and tyres – and his heart went out to them. If there was no fog ahead all would be well. Tom looked at Hilary, and decided it was as good a moment as any.

"When I've found myself a job that pays £20,000 a year, will you marry me?"

Hilary laughed. "That'll be a little while."

"Would you consider £14,000 a year?"

Hilary had to brake suddenly for a lorry ahead. There were roadworks and a queue of vehicles on a bend and a line of red brake lights showed. Some still had their rear fog lights ablaze. They could see the traffic lights in the distance. There were upwards of 20 vehicles waiting.

"Do you think the Kerrs are in the queue?" she asked.

"I'll check." Tom was out and running up the side of the vehicle line. He was soon close to the traffic lights ahead and he could see that there was no Morris Traveller. He walked back to find Hilary and her VW. They were through the roadworks and out with a straight road in front of them before Tom spoke.

"Would you?" he asked.

Hilary laughed. "Persistence is a good trait. The answer is yes. I'll marry you. I'll want to continue to work, perhaps even when the first baby comes. I've built a career I wouldn't want to give up until – well, there are too many domestic responsibilities, I suppose."

"When?"

"When you're settled in a new career. The amount of money you earn won't be immediately important if I'm still working. That's if you don't mind a wife who's earning more than you – initially."

"Initially," Tom agreed. "Why don't you pull over here. I'll drive. You've done very well."

A few miles short of the motorway the fog closed in. One moment they were in the clear with moon and stars in the sky, the next visibility was down to 20 yards.

"I read somewhere about simple radar sets for vehicles which would tell the driver what was ahead in fog, and act on the brakes semi-automatically," Tom said. He was tense with the discomfort and the sudden sense-deadening quality of the wall of yellowish-white fog. He brought the car to a crawl until, as suddenly, the fog disappeared and the moonlight and orange lights showed the motorway junction ahead.

"They've gone faster than we thought," Hilary said.

"If they took this route. If not, they may be further north. We have to take that chance."

"How will we find them on the motorway? And what can we do?"

Tom thought for a moment. "Probably just make our presence known and then keep with them. They know the car – we went to dinner in it."

The motorway junction was clear of fog and brightly lit. As they came in to join it two things happened. In the same instant they both saw Benjie's Morris Traveller, cruising in the slow lane, as if its occupants were on a Sunday outing. There was no mistaking the battered car with its roofrack. And the VW's off-front tyre blew out.

With military precision Tom changed the wheel, every movement controlled, calm and quick. He let some air out of the spare, but not enough, and the car ran unevenly. Tom soon pulled into a service area, checked the tyre pressures and filled up with petrol. He was greatly relieved that the Kerrs had reached this far. There was no sign of fog, and they could soon catch them up. And if not, well – at this point he realised that he did not know the air marshal's address in Bedfordshire. But he knew the name. Urquhart. Sir Iain Urquhart. Heilke had been at pains to tell him that they had both married Scots. He pulled out into the motorway going up through the gears, listening to the noisy air-cooled engine in the rear, pushing the little car. The moon rode high in the sky. All was clear, and Bedfordshire still 40 miles away. Time enough to catch up with them.

Here was another junction. Tom slowed involuntarily as a line of vehicles with flashing blue lights raced down the slip road. Two, three, six. They were ambulances. He and others on the motorway let them swing into the middle lane ahead of them. His heart sank. He glanced at Hilary who turned an apprehensive face towards him and put her hand briefly on his at the wheel. They said nothing. Now there was a fog-prone area of the motorway, well lit with orange fluorescent lights. And no fog. The road led up a long incline. They could see the ambulance lights ahead. Wisps of fog appeared and thickened. Now it was dense and Tom reduced speed rapidly until they were moving at 15 mph. Cars passed him in the fast lane. A long-sided lorry – it seemed to go on for minutes – slid ahead of the VW on the left.

"This is awful," Hilary said, her voice unsteady. "I can take most things except heights and fog. I think of those multiple crashes. A hundred vehicles. Cars crushed between lorries. Lorry drivers killed by loads breaking loose and ripping into the cabs –"

"Gently, love. Think instead of our life together, stretching ahead through the years."

The fog lifted for 200 yards, then fell like a winding sheet over the motorway once more, with visibility only a few paces. They both tensed, expecting the fearsome jolt of a vehicle running into them. Both thought of the nightmare holocaust of twisted metal, of lorries with their heavier bones tearing into frailer motor cars, of screams and flames, of crushed and burnt dying people. But no cars or lorries ran into them, none forced their way past. Tom could see the dim circles of a vehicle's lights behind him. There was nothing ahead except a dense wall of whiteness, nothing to guide him or keep him in a lane. He was in first gear.

The winding sheet was suddenly lifted. The road ahead was clear, with little traffic. The moon and its silver light was a welcoming illumination, chasing away the dark thoughts of the ambulances. The motorway swept them up a long, gently curving slope, and then they topped the rise. There before them on the down slope were three lines of halted traffic. And beyond, a bare 400 yards ahead, was a confused mass of lights, with the flashing blue lamps of police, ambulances and fire tenders. Then he was down the hill and his view was cut off. He coasted towards the traffic jam and halted. Once stationary they both heard a car radio blaring out a pop song. It shocked them. Tom had an urge to find the car and smash his fist into the uncaring idiot who allowed the inane raucous shouting to pollute the air when people ahead were wounded and perhaps dying. He directed his anger towards the pop fiend. His thoughts rushed round the timing. They had seen the Morris Traveller pass on the motorway. Then the blowout, then checking tyre pressures and buying petrol. Half an hour at least. The Kerrs would be trundling off into the Bedfordshire countryside at this moment, unaware of what had happened so soon behind them. They would – they could be.

"I'm going to see," Tom said.

Hilary put her arms round his neck, kissed him hard, pulled back and touched his cheek with her fingers.

There was no Morris Traveller in the lines of waiting vehicles. Then a police cadet stopped him, asked him to return to his car. The boy was shaking with emotion. Tom gripped his arm and squeezed it, turned back and disappeared from his sight. He slipped across the central barrier, moving more cautiously, and found himself soon enough in the midst of the crash. Here was a lorry carrying drums of molasses. Some had rolled on to the tarmac and a few had split and spilt their contents. Cars lay spreadeagled across the lanes, bonnets crumpled, boots stove in. All were quite recent, nothing like an old Traveller. Three more lorries, one a tall-sided furniture van on its side, were as deserted as the cars. He went on, dodging from lane to lane, from vehicle pile to pile. Cars, lorries and vans in 200 yards of destruction and death. His fieldcraft kept him free of the rescue services. He saw them in action and marvelled anew, as he had done during his army career, at their sadness and calm, hiding such love and care, as they tended the injured, brought out the dead. There was no Morris Traveller. He was near the front, where some vehicle had braked hard as the fog fell across the motorway and those behind had been too little alarmed, too careless, too complacent. And the whole terrible multiple crash had rolled out its awful music of smashing metal and rending bodies behind them.

Now he was approaching the front. An elderly Mercedes and a supermarket lorry had begun it. Flooding him with relief, Tom felt as if the silver light of the empty motorway ahead was leading him to the two people who had brought him back into the world, shocked him out of his introspection and self-pity, made a man of him again. He thought of Heilke, soon if not already with her sister. He thought of Benjie out fighting alongside him the night of the poachers. He wished he had not hit Benjie so hard the night of the table game. But it had been then that he had finally realised. Benjie. Heilke. He turned to go back to Hilary, and saw, tucked in underneath the back of the supermarket lorry, a Morris Traveller with a twisted roofrack. The doors were open, half off their hinges. The chassis and bodywork concertina'd, the bonnet smashed, the engine moved into the front seats. And Benjie's suitcase, and Heilke's, still in the back among the vegetable crates.

"Hey, you. What are you doing?"

This policeman was older and experienced, coldly angry.

"Where are they? Are they injured? Dead?"

"Who are you? Where have you come from?"

"This is my parents' car. I was following them. The name's Kerr." It seemed to Tom entirely natural that he should have said that.

The policeman looked away. He knew genuine tears and grief when he saw them.

"I'm very sorry. They've both gone. They wouldn't have known much, wouldn't have suffered." He took Tom's arm at the elbow and began telling him the procedures to follow.

15. INHERITANCE

Tom Gibson examined his new domain minutely. The dogs followed him everywhere, the springer bitch running a little to fat with lack of exercise and the normally expressionless lurcher watching him with careful eyes. Kenny helped, had transferred his loyalty and his affection complete to Tom. Together they scoured the six acres, saw geese, chickens and guineafowl, and the quail houses and runs. There were five long greenhouses, grass leys, small arable patches, the vegetable land all built up into beds four feet wide, and huge compost heaps. Tom found out what there was for winter and Christmas sale, and discovered a forward planning book. There was a carefully indexed client book. All the account books were in Heilke's round, neat hand with crossed sevens. Tom could and did pick up the seven-days-a-week work, building up to Christmas.

November had begun in fog and finished with snow. Early snow, said those Devon men, meant none for Christmas and a mild January. But Devon had to be expunged from memory. Heart, head and hand had come to another countryside. Every stick and stone of these six acres now belonged to him. He was continually amazed at his fortune. Heilke had said mysteriously that something must be done about Tom's disinheritance. And now this. He ached with sadness for Benjie and Heilke, imagined working with Benjie about the steading, dreamed up wonderful evenings with good food and the crisp chatter of colloquial German. He ached, too, at first from the hours of work, and perpetually because of Hilary's misery.

"Sell the place, Tom. You asked me to marry you when you were earning £14,000 a year. I want to marry you. I've put out the word for you. Your languages are ever more important in an economic bloc like Europe." She had continued. "I want children, Tom. Two at least. I'll need a husband who can earn commensurately." He knew what she left unsaid – the private education, the comfortable middle-class home, good holidays, friends from the same professional and business background. Tom had only a vague idea of what he could squeeze out of Shepherd's Pightle annually. He had capital from his father to put into the place. He could probably rent more land about the village.

"There's an increasing market for organically grown food," he said.

"Nothing to the growing market for your potential talents in

European business."

Tom was unable to answer.

"You've reneged on your word," Hilary said sadly, and did not cry or bluster.

"Circumstances have changed. I've a good house to offer you. Together we can make a go of this place."

"I'm not a Heilke, bred to the soil, to labouring in the fields." Hilary spoke with feeling.

"I don't ask you to be. Just as Benjie didn't buy a new car – he could have afforded it quite easily – so he didn't mechanise much. We can. And buy or rent more land."

Hilary was silent. "I shall continue to have to travel," she said after a few moments.

That came as a jolt to him. He had pictured Hilary always at home of an evening. Of course he would help with the cooking and washing up, and give a hand with the children. But she would always be there. He began at last to see the size of the problem. The incompatibility of careers, the absolute requirement to strive hard to make a marriage like theirs work.

Hilary left on a week's visit to the north and Scotland. For Tom there were winter salads and vegetables to pick for the market. Geese were fattening, there were quail, guineafowl and cockerels to be slaughtered and prepared. He and Kenny worked the long hours together. The boy was happy to be with Tom, deferring to him yet offering him small kernels of sound advice. But when the work was done Kenny went back to his parents' warm house and a plate piled steaming high with food. Some evenings Tom could not face cooking for himself, but went out to the Red Lion, reopened under new management, but with the same micro-oven-heated deep-frozen meals. He played music all evening at home. His hi-fi equipment poured out from tapes and records, and from Radio Three, huge quantities of balm to a troubled soul. He listened to Gerald Finzi's 'cello concerto, the fresh English countryside vigour and ethereal other-worldliness blending with his feelings. Mozart, Haydn, Schubert, Schumann and Brahms. Each night he rolled into bed physically tired and could not sleep for worrying how he could keep faith with all the people he loved.

He received a letter from a company in the town with a head office in

Birmingham. Miss Aston had talked to them about him. There might be a post that would interest him. Could he come to Birmingham for an interview? Could he telephone immediately since two Continental directors were over and it would be advantageous for all concerned to meet. Totally unsure that he wanted such a job, Tom promised Hilary when she rang from Glasgow that he would go. He drove to Birmingham in his new VW pick-up.

The interview went well from the first moment. Besides a sharp-eyed Englishman there were German and French directors, each anxious to test his competency in their languages. He was entirely frank about his lack of business experience, emphasised his man-management attributes. They took him to lunch and he spoke German and French throughout the meal.

"Your German is extremely good, Herr Gibson," said the one director. "But hardly explained by a good university degree. Perhaps the odd phrase from Bavaria makes me wonder?"

"You are perceptive, Herr Hartmann. Perhaps you are from Bayern yourself? And, yes, my mother was from Bamberg."

The Frenchman questioned him closely about his sojourn in France. Tom was amazed at how well the whole affair went. He appeared to lead all the time, asking pertinent questions himself about the training he would need, about the amount of travelling – he would be married soon and must think of that. Only towards the end did they tell him the salary. The money was much more than he had expected, even a little more than he had suggested to Hilary as a minimum for marriage. The job was based at the office in the town, where the main manufacturing took place. They would let him know early in the new year. The Frenchman smiled encouragingly, the German hoped to see Herr Gibson again, and yes, he was from Munich himself.

Only on his way home through the darkening countryside, watching night fall over winter lands that he saw with observant, clear eyes, did he realise that he had done so well at the interview because he had not really cared whether they offered him the job or not.

Tom had a call from the ex-schoolmaster who had held his beaters' line together. There was a new gamekeeper in his cottage, a man from nowhere identifiable, who knew little about gamekeeping. He had London friends. Was it true what young Doddington-Smith had said about crating? Tom told him everything he knew. On that Saturday there was a shoot on Gailsford's estate. No local man came to beat or pick-up. Living surrounded by the estate, Tom had been acutely aware of the woods and fields that were no longer for him to wander over. On the Saturday he did what others had done – he took to the green lane with the springer and the lurcher, surprised at how roles were reversing. There was a truck parked near the 50-acre wood, and Tom reckoned the crates were already in place. He could work out without difficulty where they were, ready to be opened and give a large quantity of ill-presented birds to Gailsford's guests.

That evening his gamekeeper friend telephoned to invite him to a shoot as a picker-up, and to talk. The country people were closing ranks on Charles Gailsford. Perhaps his days as lord of this particular manor were numbered.

Hilary came to Shepherd's Pightle for supper. Tom asked about her trip, told her about the crating and the village cold shoulder. He reckoned Gailsford would put the place up for sale within two or three years.

"Not quite long enough for me to earn enough to buy it," he concluded, joking. "You know – put our two estates together, make a more rounded holding."

At mention of earning enough, Hilary began to glow. She took it as a strong pointer that Tom was meeting her on her own ground. "You should set your sights higher," she replied airily. "The house wouldn't find itself in Country Life. We'll need ceilings with fine plasterwork, a chapel, and numbers of gazebos dotted about a park. No park here, not to speak of with pride, that is."

They talked about Christmas. Yet again Tom was tied to livestock. He could not leave it all to Kenny. No matter. Hilary's parents had indicated that they would come north, her brother too. Her father was mobile again after his hip operation.

"I've a question to ask him," said Tom.

Hilary nodded. "He'll like that, and ask a few himself." She paused. "Are you any nearer being able to keep me?"

"Not immediately, I fear. There'll be a good deal of hard work, climbing the ladder, pushing people off it."

"You mean – ?" Hilary came into his arms.

"Only that I've seen them already." Tom gave her an account of the interviews, and as he did so two parallel pictures came into his mind.

160

An office with fluorescent lighting, centrally heated, air conditioned, making a nonsense of the changing weather, and work with high stress, tension factors and timid, unnatural sweat. And the six acres of Shepherd's Pightle where there was rain, sun and snow, gentle westerly breezes, howling north-easters, sweat that was free and warranted, soil under the fingernails, and a pair of crows that flew over towards Gailsford's 50-acre wood. The pictures cut out abruptly and a loving, happy girl was still in his arms, anticipating not only the weekend before them but a successful outcome to this interview or another quite soon.

In the run-up to Christmas Tom brought in four village women to help with the huge amount of vegetables to be pulled, picked and prepared, and the birds to be made ready for the oven. He took the produce round to Benjie's clients and marvelled how the goodwill that Benjie had built up was, after a few minutes of regret for Benjie and his wife, transferred to himself. On a whim he called in at the French restaurant and renewed acquaintance with the chef and his sister. They would like his produce and wanted to come and see the smallholding.

The snow kept to Scotland. England's weather was crisp and dry, with blue skies and the sun veiled from time to time by light cloud. Tom was delivering orders until late on Christmas Eve, and met Hilary's family for the first time at a festive lunch on Christmas Day, and for the present-giving session afterwards. Hilary had bought gifts on behalf of Tom for herself and her family. Conventional things – books, soap, perfume. She was so evidently in love and happy. Her parents were charmed by Tom. Her father enjoyed the 'hand-in-marriage' interview that Tom sought on Boxing Day. Only afterwards did Tom wonder whether he had been honest with Jack Aston. While not saying outright that he was changing direction in his career, he had indicated the probabilities and said he was applying for jobs. He had talked with Hilary's mother and found her much less fearsome than he had been led to believe. The brother who collected stamps and was a long-distance walker came to Shepherd's Pightle on foot on the day after Boxing Day when Tom was hard at work, and unconsciously sowed doubt in Tom's mind as he looked round with astonishment at the smallholding and envied any man who had such a life. He quoted

Alexander Pope's poem at Tom – 'Happy the man whose wish and care a few paternal acres bound . . .', written when the poet was 12 years old, as he pointed out. The Astons left with Hilary for home again to welcome their American family over for the New Year. Tom had regretfully declined an invitation to go with them. He had genuinely enjoyed the 'ordinary family Christmas'.

Tom's resolve to change direction was bolstered every evening by a 'phone call from Hilary. She had plans to enlarge the house at Shepherd's Pightle, turn the six acres into paddocks for ponies. They would probably pull down some of the outbuildings – tidy it up. Lay out a proper garden, have a tennis court, maybe a swimming pool. She was confident he would get the job.

One night before the turn of the year the snow came back in earnest, giving the lie to the old country saying. Tom woke to a white, crisp world. He fed the livestock. Kenny struggled in from the village an hour late and was sent home after downing a mug of tea. No cars came down the lane. Tom beat the bounds of his estate, followed by Benjie's dogs who were now his shadows. The snow revealed the wildlife movements. He saw where pheasant had sheltered in his hedges and found the track of weasel and stoat. At the outermost bound furthest from the house a fox had crossed the edge of the paddock. He saw where the animal, most likely a big dog fox, had paused. He could imagine it sniffing the geese, the fowl. The springer was immediately on to its scent, looking at Tom, waiting for permission to follow it. Tom called her off. On the other side of the hedge lay Gailsford land.

All morning as he worked he kept his mind on the decisions he would have to make. If they lived here he would have to let the smallholding go. He went into the barn to sharpen a knife at the grindstone. He looked about him at the result of Benjie's hard Fife upbringing. It was Benjie's true insurance against bad times. Money from insurance companies, national savings, unit trusts and gilts were all very well. But this was the real wealth. The tractor and its implements, feed for stock, organic fertilisers. Apple crates, seed trays, pots, beehives, a pump for the underground cistern which took water from the barn and house roofs. The workshop. And above all the land in good heart. If bad times came a family could eat and sell enough produce for the real necessities of life. Tom had a vision of Hilary turning her expressive eyes to heaven at all this 'back-to-the-simple-life'. She believed in economic growth, sell more in bad times at lower prices, squeeze ever more productivity out of people and machines. Yes, economic cycles were always with the business world, but efficiency, thoughtful provision, belief in oneself and one's products were what counted. He had not shown her Benjie Kerr's barn of treasures, had not talked to her of his modest near-genius as a smallholder.

At lunch he tried to recreate Heilke Kerr's near-genius with a swiftly produced meal. He sat in the kitchen listening to a lunchtime concert. He had heated soup from Heilke's deep-freeze. Heilke. He recalled his first sight of her when he had been reconnoitring Shepherd's Pightle, and his instant belief that she was German. He and Hilary would spend their honeymoon in Germany. In the spring. They would go to Bamberg. See Munich, and the great rococo and baroque *Schlösser*. In the spring. Maybe he would try and trace his cousins.

Tom went out to do make-and-mend work. Weak winter sun shone on the snow. The lane was still closed. The dogs followed him everywhere, but were restless. As in his vision when recounting the Birmingham interviews to Hilary, a pair of crows flew over the smallholding heading for Gailsford territory. He thought about what they would see. The fields, the pastures, the new plough would all be covered deep in snow. They would see the long windbreaks, and the 50-acre wood where he had caught Benjie unawares, where Benjie had exacted his revenge. And the green lane, the ribbon of public way, a curse to the gamekeeper, a boon to the poacher. Quickly he finished his work. There were still two hours of daylight. He would walk the green lane again. It would just be a recce. He might meet his successor. He took both dogs. For the hours of daylight and afterwards when night had fallen and the snow and a moon lit up the woods and fields, Tom Gibson and his dogs roamed the Gailsford estate.

All the familiar sounds were there for him. Tawny owls, pigeon, roosting pheasant, coveys of partridge snug in the snow. There were hare in the meadows. Tom moved through the wood surrounding the gamekeeper's cottage, keeping the silhouette of the great holm oak against the sky. Lights shone in every room. There was rock music and the sound of women's raucous laughter. The watchers went home across the fields. Tom hoped the crisp snow would last long enough for the gamekeeper who was no gamekeeper to see their tracks and be angry at the trespassers.

"Have you heard from them?"

Tom enjoyed pulling the letter from his pocket, unfolding it slowly. He rejected the fresh air of Shepherd's Pightle. This would be a swift but calculated change in direction. After all he was only 33. Half a lifetime to come, and with Hilary. Well, perhaps more than half to run. He hoped so. The job had to be a means to an end. Riches enough to attain the fresh air under bigger and better terms.

He handed her the letter. She kissed him then and there. Before supper they celebrated with champagne that he had had the foresight to buy. After the meal they left the washing up, although both agreed that Heilke would not approve, but would understand and condone with a little persuasion.

Next morning Hilary had a big breakfast of bacon and scrambled eggs ready for him when he came in from feeding the livestock. She also had a plan.

"Do you really want a farm? Hundreds of acres, a big house?"

"I'm bred to it. In the end it's what I would be best at," he said. "And happiest."

"Then you could be sitting on the means of acquiring it." Hilary was triumphant . "Of course there's the little matter of planning permission. But retirement villages are becoming popular and local authorities look favourably on good schemes, well designed and planned, with good landscaping. On six acres you'd get maybe 40 or so. The barn could be turned into a restaurant and clubhouse. The wardens could live in this house." She was carried away with the idea. "After all, the village with its shops is only a mile away. It's not as if they'd be immobile old people. They'd be living in their own community, be able to have the best of both worlds – their own houses, a clubhouse with meals and care when needed. And miniature golf, bowls, a swimming pool –"

Tom choked on his scrambled eggs, thinking of Benjie's barn no longer with its treasures, and the silence and refuge of it from snow and wind, tempest and rain, all destroyed.

"Or the barn could be turned into a couple of houses. As for this house, perhaps the downstairs could be the clubhouse, with wardens' accommodation upstairs."

Heilke's kitchen would disappear. Tom looked round it now, at the kitchen range, the beech table, the pots and pans on their racks. And the big north German dresser. Since 1730 this had been a family's home on a smallholding. Maybe they had supplemented their income with a trade. Weaving, glovemaking, straw plaiting, skilled tree surgery.

"What do you think?" asked Hilary, watching his eyes, seeing him begin to eat again. "You wouldn't have to do the work, just cooperate with a developer. It would make enough money to buy an estate on the turn. Here or further north certainly. Even in the south-west."

"Not Hampshire?" he queried foolishly, frightened by the ghosts of Benjie and Heilke and all the men and women who had toiled on these acres, eaten their soup in this kitchen, mended tools by the light of tallow candles and the hearth fire.

Hilary brushed aside the question as being from someone in shock. Joyous shock. "Someone has to be entrepreneurial. You'll have to make a great deal of money to found a dynasty."

She went off to her cottage. She had another American trip to prepare for. Only 12 days this time. For the rest of that Sunday Tom worked outside making up his orders for Monday morning. As he pulled and washed parsnips he pictured Benjie working alongside him, and imagined the talk they might have had about the wild and secret ways of hare. He thought often of Benjie's big capable hands, ingrained with soil. A man who seldom wore gloves for love of contact with the earth. Benjie would say, and Heilke would agree with him, that hard times were bound to come again. The world's economies were cyclical, right down to villages. Land, productive land was the real wealth. And a productive wife as Heilke had been productive. The men were lucky who managed to choose wives who would complement their strengths, lacks and needs. All done at an age when lack of experience was evident and when foolhardiness was uppermost of their traits. He dared not think of his father and his mistake. Hilary was productive, surely. A great worker and earner. But in whose vineyard? Not his at Shepherd's Pightle it seemed. And he was due at her cottage for supper. He packed up his deliveries ready for an early start. While he was changing his clothes he took out the firm's letter and read it again carefully. He would, so the letter said, travel often, especially to France and Germany. He longed to see both again. Would Hilary and he be travelling to different countries at the same time? Children, horses, dogs, cats – who would look after them?

It was pitch dark outside on a chill January evening. He would walk into the village. He stood outside his house, close to his barn and his kennels where his dogs moved restlessly, knowing that he was there. His geese, his quail, his chickens, his fruit trees and bushes. His, his, his. But not his in verity, his only to cherish, enjoy and use for the span of a life. The night was silent save for the small sounds of the animals. He heard in his inner ear the auctioneering of lock, stock and barrel, the buildings torn apart, all Benjie's treasures revealed and scattered, the trees uprooted, the pastures and the productive arable and market garden land dug into for sewage and water lines, overlaid with houses and roads.

Sitting beside Hilary on the sofa in her living room, Tom took a deep breath.

"I've thought about our future method of earning a living, and where. I should like to carry on at Shepherd's Pightle," he said gently. He mentioned the annual income that the Kerrs had managed, and what he thought he could get with more mechanisation, more concentration of product lines, more marketing, and probably more land. He explained, holding her hand, touching his ring on her finger, how he had arrived at his decision to upgrade a mini-estate. They would have money to enlarge the house, add another bathroom and bedroom, a bigger living room. He did not say that he believed any other decision would be breaking faith with the Kerrs. He stopped talking, his voice trailing away, and she withdrew her hand.

Hilary was near to tears. "You're such an old-fashioned man, like my father."

"And like your mother you've been foolish enough to fall in love with one," Tom said hurriedly, hoping.

"I need time to think," she said. Tom saw the practical business brain swinging into action, assessing all the possibilities, as if he and she and their close loving were only some of the aspects to be considered.

"You are the wife I want," said Tom, divining her thoughts. "We'll dovetail in our lives together. What's between us is plenty strong enough."

"I'm not sure I am right for you, if you're going to be a smallholder." He could see her mind fleeing to her glossy, high-powered executive life.

They talked over supper, round and round.

"I need time to think quietly by myself," she said at last, touching his

166

face with her hand. "I think you should go home."

She played with the engagement ring on her finger, pulling it halfway off and then pushing it back on her finger. Tom watched her fingers, then saw tears begin to well in her eyes.

"I love you, Hilary," Tom said earnestly. "If it doesn't work at Shepherd's Pightle, we'll reassess."

She brushed away the tears. "I love you, too, you know that. But I just don't know," she continued unhappily. "Everything was so right, and now it's wrong." She looked down at her hands. "Your ring will help me to think straight while I'm away."

16. WENN DU ES WÜSSTEST . . .

Tom Gibson marked up the 12 days of her absence on a large calendar in the kitchen. He worked from long before dawn until late at night. He did every job he could find that was physically stretching so that he went to bed tired out. The snow had gone and mild dry weather came across the country from the south. At night as he cooked and ate his meal he listened to the happiest music he possessed – music that was grand, triumphal, funny, and spoke of overcoming the miseries of life in the freeing of the spirit. Nothing introspective, sad or mournful. No opera, for opera too often spoke of love and misunderstanding between lovers. The music buoyed him up.

One morning when there were five days to go he received a postcard from Hilary, reminding him exactly of her US postcards in the summer. That morning, too, searching for posts in the barn, Tom found a padlocked door in one corner almost obscured by a pile of apple crates. He checked outside that it led to a lean-to building that must have been a cowbyre but now had its doorway to the outside closed up. There was no key so he fetched a hacksaw. Inside, the stalls were still in place and here were more of Benjie's hard-times necessities. In the last stall were empty ferret hutches and, hanging by the manger, were nets. He handled them, opened them out as best he could. A long net, several gate nets, and rabbiting nets. In the manger was a stock of ready-made snares, for hare, for rabbit, maybe for pheasant, too, if he was right about Benjie's poaching heyday, watching pheasant using a hedge and snaring their little walkways through.

He came out, found the posts, and worked with Kenny to strengthen the long quail cages. He thought of the estate that surrounded him, where a gate net could be placed and how many pairs of hands would be needed to manage a long net. He thought about rabbiting with ferrets and nets. He had done this often in Devon when his father had been away. And he thought about Benjie Kerr, a countryman of his own persuasion in so many ways.

Next day he picked and prepared vegetables for his town outlets. He arrived at the French restaurant when the chef and his helpers were sitting down to their meal and was invited to join them. The dark girl from Moulins, sister of the chef, served him his food, sat next to him, and seemed to regard him with special interest. They all paid him the compliment of talking rapid French among themselves and to him. Monique asked him again about his farm and said once more that she would like to visit it. She was a strongly built, efficient girl, used to working long hours, perhaps 28 years old, independent-minded, sensible and attractive, too.

In the evening doubts redoubled in his mind. He could not think of anything or anyone but Hilary, and half-believed he had made the greatest error of his life in not accepting the job. He prowled round the house, listening to the same grand, happy German music. Nothing cheered him. He caught a whiff of her scent in the bedroom they had used together, and plunged away to explore some of the rooms that he had hardly seen. In one small bedroom there was a chest of drawers and a wardrobe which explained why he had found few clothes of Benjie's elsewhere. Hanging there were clothes which marked Benjie's progress from the Fife coalfields to becoming an officer of the Cameronians, and then an independent small farmer. There was a uniform. Tom stared at the ribbons on the left breast. In the chest of drawers he found a box with the decorations and medals themselves. A Military Cross, and a Military Medal. He had served in North Africa, Italy and the North-West Europe campaign. Tom remembered the drawing room in Devon and the polished mahogany display cases. Why not here at Shepherd's Pightle? The start of an unmilitary dynasty that nevertheless had managed to do its duty when wars had been disruptions in the lives of ordinary people. Hilary would be unsympathetic to the idea. She came from a very civilian family. Hilary. He pictured her in New York, enjoying the business entertainment – dinners, cocktail parties, all those avaricious, libertine high-flyers. Of course it was not all like that. Have faith in her. He did have faith. Remember Hilary so often, as close as two human beings can be to each other. So close and loving. He wished he had not refused the job. He would have adapted. But then there was the smallholding. His land handed down in trust to him from Benjie and Heilke. They must have loved him, as he had loved them, still did as he walked their acres, lived in their house, ate at their table. Was he making this mystical passing on of responsibility for land an excuse for being selfish, for denying Hilary the middle-class life she wanted?

He needed to bring his mind to another, quieter activity. He found himself dressing for the outside, taking a torch and an ash plant. He went to the kennels, brought Khan out. Sally, the springer, displayed her upset in a series of whining barks and he gentled her, telling her that her day but not her night would come.

Soon he and the lurcher were in the green lane. There was no question of the dog being to heel. He paced beside Tom, very close to him without a leash, and Tom soon learned to stop when he did, probe the darkness in the direction Khan was facing and move on when he did. Drizzle turned to sleet. The pair crossed a pasture, skirting the 50-acre wood and went on quietly towards the north. Tom thought about gate nets and positioning them. He knew from his own experience the lighter land where hare were likely to be, knew from Khan's information, relayed to him so simply, where hare were.

In time he found himself back in the field where he had first thought he had contacted his poacher. He slipped into the marl pit. Tonight there was no steady icy wind. The trees above him were still, the only sound was of dripping water. He crouched where he had crouched on that night, amused that the black shadow he had perceived all those months earlier was now beside him, silent and watchful, standing so close that he smelled the wet hair. He rubbed Khan's head, realising that in his undemonstrative way the dog showed affection and reliance by standing so close, and that he brought to the pairing no mean intelligence and experience. Tom caught his breath, thinking of Schiller who had met his unjust end in another pit not far away. That had been his master's fault. And now he was risking Khan. Well, no other fool would be out on such a night. No other fool. Chastened and apprehensive, Tom led Khan back into the safety of the green lane. Anyway he knew precisely where, if ever he had a mind to, he could place a gate net and send the lurcher bowling round a meadow to bring hare into the trap.

Tom was working in the barn when the postman's van came to the door of the house. There were still letters, bills, circulars and charity demands addressed to the Kerrs. He had dealt with them all punctiliously. This day there was little except a letter for him from the United States. Postmarked Denver, Colorado, it had taken five days to arrive.

He took the letter to be a good omen, but sensed immediately he opened it that it was a fair copy of a draft that had been worked over. She was not coming back for another three days. She was going to Canada. Meanwhile she wanted them both to use the extra days to think

170

very carefully about a life together, whether in town or country, and whether it would work. For her part, especially when she was travelling, she believed business was her life. A husband and children were entirely possible if they could be worked in sensibly. If and when babies came she would want to go back to work immediately. That meant a full-time, live-in nanny, and implied living in the town. She was a career woman first and foremost, and extensive travel was part of the job. She could only see their lives jangling at every turn. There would be jealousies, recriminations, all the prime ingredients for a foundered marriage.

With the reading of the letter still unfinished, Tom went inside the house to sit at the kitchen table. The words of a reply were already forming themselves in his brain. At least give it a go. If necessary he would sell Shepherd's Pightle. They would live in the town. He would find a job. They would compromise, both of them. Only give it a go.

He turned over a page and read on. Hilary now told him that despite so much that was right between them, especially the physical side, the wrong things were stacked up. Were they possible to shift? She doubted that they were. He was a countryman and he should never try to be anything else. Business, especially as a travelling salesman, no matter how high-flying, was emphatically not for him. She finished on a pragmatic note. Life was a business to be successfully managed. The head must always rule the heart. She urged him to think very carefully and objectively – the last word underlined. If they decided to part, a clean break was probably best. She assured him that she, too, was thinking deeply. She did not mention love.

Tom joined Kenny and worked for the rest of the day. He was sombre and withdrawn until he saw the effect he was having on the boy. So he told him about plans he had for the steading, bouncing ideas off him. Darkness fell and Kenny went home. Tom wandered round his six acres. On the face of it the marriage ingredients were a recipe for disaster. He could see that, and he supposed that Hilary must be right and had had the courage to be honest. But what about commitment? His and hers. He had to be prepared to change in order to hold her. He saw that clearly. If she would not give Shepherd's Pightle a chance, then he would give it up. Maybe the job was still open. The Kerrs would have to forgive him. It was a matter of the greater need. But Hilary had once said that they could be an unbeatable team. At Shepherd's Pightle, too. Surely? So he seesawed between hope and despair.

As he entered the house the telephone was ringing. It was Monique from the French restaurant. When could she come and see the farm? He invited her and her brother over for lunch on the Monday, when the restaurant would be closed.

By Thursday Tom was in a ferment of indecision but working and planning as if Shepherd's Pightle would continue. He laboured without Kenny, who had wanted the day off to go to an uncle's funeral with his parents. The clouds were low, dark grey, letting down from time to time a shower of cold rain. He worked outside. There was plenty to do. Much to read at night, too. He had to be able with his father's money to raise the income from his land substantially. He needed two or three good ideas. For once in his life, the solitary was unattracted by his own company. When lunchtime arrived he could not bring himself to enter the house. Heilke's solid, gentle presence was there, not entirely approving of Hilary but trying hard. 'Yes, we'll love her, too, Tom. Both of us. If you love, then we do.' She would approve of Monique no doubt. They came from the same stock, give or take a frontier and a thousand kilometres. He sat in the barn, wrapping sacks round himself to keep warm, then threw them aside to take the dogs out into the small pasture at the far side of his land. Tom romped with the dogs, even Khan becoming playful in a dignified, surprised way. He admitted then that he would never be a great money maker, he had no entrepreneurial spirit, no abilities for commerce. He was a country chap, used to having the sky over him, used to observing the minutiae of country life. He would never make a business man even to France and Germany. The realisation depressed him further. He went back to work, hungry, until dark came. Then he walked into the village with the dogs and went and looked at Hilary's darkened cottage. She would come tomorrow evening and he would know his fate.

That evening Tom Gibson cooked bacon and eggs and the smell of the food cheered him up, just as the completion of the meal cast him down again. He had the evening to get through. And he would drink nothing. Music would be his numbing alcohol. The sprightly, joyous music that he had played had ceased to work its magic. He searched his records and tapes and decided on some songs by Richard Strauss. There was one that teased his memory, but he listened first to the Four Last Songs. They were suitably heart-shaking but not the one he wanted. Here it was – *Cäcilie*, the words by Heinrich Hart. Before he played the song he found a copy of Hart's poems among his books and read the poem with sadness. He was indecisive. Every way he looked a black, sad present and a lonely, unfulfilled future presented themselves to him. If Hilary did not decide to throw in her lot with him, he was lost. And why should she? She had her own ideas of how life should be conducted, and her own needs. He understood that well. There seemed no room for compromise if he stayed at Shepherd's Pightle. And, if she came, how would he ever compensate her for her loss of career? And if he left the countryside? He pushed the thought away. She had said he would never make it in business.

He put on the tape, went to sit beside the dead fireplace, then in a frenzy fetched paper and kindling as Strauss's song filled the room. *'Wenn du es wüsstest, was Träumen heisst von brennenden Küssen ...* If you knew what it is to dream of burning kisses, of walking and resting with the one you love ... *von Wandern und Ruhen mit der Geliebten ...* if you knew you would soften your heart ... *du neigtest dein Herz'*.

He lit the paper, laid some of Benjie's dry birch logs against the kindling. In a few moments the fire was drawing and roaring up the chimney. Thursday night. He had the night and all tomorrow to get through, and then, if fog, ice, contrary winds, congested skies and airports did not hinder her 'plane, she would be home in time for him to see her on Friday evening. She had said she would 'phone from Heathrow, somewhere between noon and one o'clock. The soprano who sang Strauss's song with such yearning, sang on. *'Wenn du es wüsstest, was bangen heisst in einsamen Nächten ... du kämest zu mir ...* If you knew what it is to be afraid on lonely nights ... you would come to me'*. He imagined a thunderous knocking on the door, but knew that it was he who must push forward, be confident, definite, convincing, if he was to have her. He must go into her territory. He must be waiting for her at her cottage – no, would meet her at Heathrow. He sat up straight in Benjie's fireside chair, wanting to believe that it was Benjie who had put that idea into his head. After all, he had always felt influenced by those who had gone before. How much more so by those who were still so close to his heart. *'Wenn du es wüsstest ... du lebtest* *mit mir* ... If you knew ... you would live with me'. The music ended. Tom listened for minutes to the sound of the fire, then fetched the fireguard. Hilary had said that life was a business to be successfully managed. Well, just this once more his heart would rule his head.

Tom put on his outdoor clothes and boots, fetched a torch, a game bag and one of Benjie's short heavy sticks. Outside, the night was low-ceiling'd and he could see the lights of the village reflected on the under-bellies of the clouds. He went through the barn to the old cowbyre, sorted out a gate net and stakes, took a 2lb hammer from Benjie's tool rack, and regretted that he had no freshly peeled hazel twigs. Rounding the house on his way to fetch Khan, his thoughts were already on a certain pasture and a hedge gap when he stopped to listen to the familiar night sounds. Between the ululations of tawny owls calling each other he heard a car coming fast down the lane from the village. It took him several moments to recognise the throaty air-cooled sound of a VW beetle engine. He was angry with himself. Even that set his heart racing. She was in Canada, doing the business she was good at and loved. He shouldered the stakes and the net, stuck the hammer in his game bag. The car lights showed. Tom could hear the engine change its note as the driver changed down to use it as a brake, driving the car like a sports car. It was turning into the track leading to his house. He flung the stakes and the net down beside the barn, threw the game bag after them. He began running towards the approaching car, shouting her name.

Hilary was a day early. She had finished her business in Toronto and advanced her flight by 24 hours. She had tried to 'phone from Heathrow but had had no reply. She told him this between kisses, told him she had come without strings attached, just as he said that he would get a job, go anywhere, do anything. They agreed that they had to be together.

She had come with suitcases and, as if they were an earnest of her commitment and resolve, the pictures, the small pieces of furniture from her bedroom, her sanctuary. Tom carried them in, pausing to look at the Victorian painting of the girl with the untrammelled, expectant, happy look on her face. He saw the look mirrored on Hilary's face and knew that his own expressed the joy that rocked him.

"We'll put her in our bedroom. We'll put them all there," he said. The words tumbled out again. "I will get a job in the town. We can live here meanwhile. Kenny can carry on during the day. We'll have to cut down the operations. It'd be another source of income." That way, too, he would keep faith with the Kerrs. Benjie's barn would stay intact.

Hilary came into his arms. "You'd never make it in an office, my love. I shall do a horticultural course, and book-keeping. I should like to keep bees on a considerable scale, put hives out in orchards and up on the commons."

Tom looked at her with love and astonishment. "You did say once that we could be an unbeatable team."

"Let's try here," she said. "We shall need to add value to our produce. Something like cheesemaking. What about goats?"

Tom made a face. "Where did you get such an idea – I know, I know – someone has to be entrepreneurial."

After a while Hilary broke away. "I'm ravenous," she said.

"So am I" he lied. "I'll cook. Only bacon and eggs, I'm afraid. Too late for the deepfreeze."

"I expect you've depleted it. We must build it up again. But not with poached game."

Tom saw Benjie out on the Gailsford estate, carrying a game net and stakes, his lurcher beside him. He saw Heilke turning a practical peasant's blind eye to the provenance of the hare, the pheasant, the partridge that he brought her.

"How did you know I'd been peeling hazel sticks?" he asked.

He would keep the rabbiting nets and destroy the others, and the snares. It was the smallest of sacrifices to begin the larger ones that he would make to match her own. He swore to himself that he would keep faith with Benjie and Heilke, and make it up to the living Hilary.

In time he sat down happily to a second supper.